Kate O'Riordan is an award-winning novelist, playwright and television screen writer and was a recipient of the Tribune/ Hennessy Prize for 'Best Emerging Writer'.

LOVING HIM is her fifth novel after THE MEMORY STONES. She grew up in the West of Ireland and lives in London with her husband and two children.

LOVING HIM

Connie and Matt Wilson, once childhood sweethearts, have worked hard to achieve their dreams — their lovely London home, their three beloved sons and a stable marriage. When they go to Rome for a romantic weekend, they enjoy exploring, eating, drinking and making love. But a random encounter sets off a chain of events that turns Connie's existence from predictable, but blissful, domesticity to dangerous obsession, when Matt announces that he is not coming back with her and she returns to London — and their three boys — alone.

Books by Kate O'Riordan
Published by The House of Ulverscroft:

THE MEMORY STONES

KATE O'RIORDAN

LOVING HIM

Complete and Unabridged

ULVERSCROFT
Leicester

First published in Great Britain in 2005 by
Pocket Books, London

First Large Print Edition
published 2006
by arrangement with
Pocket Books, an imprint of
Simon & Schuster UK Ltd, London

British Library CIP Data

O'Riordan, Kate
    Loving him.—Large print ed.—
    Ulverscroft large print series: romance
    1. Life change events—Fiction 2. Spouses—Fiction
    3. Large type books
    I. Title
    823.9'14 [F]

    ISBN 1–84617–140–7

Published by
F. A. Thorpe (Publishing)
Anstey, Leicestershire

Set by Words & Graphics Ltd.
Anstey, Leicestershire
Printed and bound in Great Britain by
T. J. International Ltd., Padstow, Cornwall

This book is printed on acid-free paper

For Donal

20130905

I would like to thank the following for their help and guidance: Ian Pearson, Liz Mair, Dr Paul Starrs, Paschale McCarthy, Phyl McCarthy. My painstaking editor, Melissa Weatherill, and my agent and friend Maggie Phillips.

1

Connie dragged her wheelie weekender case through the Arrivals concourse at Heathrow. She headed straight for the taxi exit. It might have been an idea to phone her friend Mary to ask for a lift; the prospect of the queue, the taxi itself, was daunting, given what had happened. But then she would have to say it and the words weren't in yet. Her sons she had to think about too. What would she say? Should she overplay or underplay, there really was no way of knowing what the best approach might be. After all, she wasn't entirely sure herself where to place the events of last night and this morning on the Richter scale.

Outside, it was unseasonably humid for June. What sky could be seen above the multistorey car park sagged miserably. Air felt thick and powdery like packet mushroom soup. A step into the monochromes of a black-and-white photograph after the high blue-yellow skies and ochre chalkiness of Rome. A twisting tendril of smoke from a woman's cigarette drifted into her nostrils. She joined the long queue for a taxi.

Two torpid, evilly bored children jostled just ahead. One kicked her shin by accident and their sweating father apologized, shunting them on. Connie waved a hand to show it was nothing but he'd turned already. With their hot, gleaming faces and glowering expressions, the children looked back at her like a pair of hot cross buns.

Smoke peppered her nostrils again; she longed for a cigarette though it was fifteen years since she'd had one. Perhaps she'd take it up again once she got home. The thought of home made her gulp. At airports you were neither here nor there. You could be anyone, living someone else's life. For a brief while you could even manage to lose your own. But of course it was waiting for you — at home.

Her mobile trilled deep within her shoulder bag. The eldest, Fred, no doubt, checking their plane had landed on time. He was orderly that way. She cleared her throat to get rid of any telltale quavers but in any case the phone stopped by the time she'd rooted it from the pit of the bag. R u home? He'd left a text instead. Yes, she thought, yes yes. She smiled at one of the hot cross buns, practising her cheery face, the one she would attempt shortly with her sons before she would tell them the news. The boy turned away disdainfully.

The second she clapped eyes on her round smiley taxi driver, she knew he was a serial talker. Ordinarily, she would have been quite pleased to while away the half hour or so to Twickenham. More often than not, they were grumpy and monosyllabic once she'd given the address, it being too close a fare for the wait they'd already put in. But his smile didn't fade and he closed her door with a flourish. A sense of panic welled up in Connie. Inside the cab she fiddled ostentatiously with the zip of the weekend wheelie but that distraction was exhausted in no time. His mouth was opening. Connie narrowed her eyes and stared out of the back window in deep meditation. She added a little frown for better effect. Here was a troubled woman, late thirties, no make-up, unbrushed copper curls, thinking deeply troubled thoughts. A deep sigh blew from her mouth, eyelids batted up and down rapidly. Surely that would do it — she darted him a glance from the corner of her eye. No, he was going to be maliciously boring.

'Someplace nice?'

'Sorry? Oh yes. Rome.'

'Rome was it? Lovely city. Lovely. I went with the wife five years back. Or was it six? No, five I think it was. Lovely. All them steps.'

'What? Yeah, lots.'

'Nearly done her knee in going up that Vatican. 'Linda,' I goes, 'you ain't going up them steps not with your knee. Remember the Eiffel Tower what happened?' Halfway up her knee goes, mind you, she was in trouble before that what with the weight she was packing in them days. There we was, stuck in the middle of the city of light, not up, not down, until I reckon the only way this lady's coming down is on her backside if you'll pardon. That's how we done it. Plonk plonk, stop for a breather, plonk plonk, the whole way down. Hours it took. So no way was she going up that Vatican I'm telling you. Would that lady listen?'

'No?'

'My love you are correct. Round and round, up and up. I'm going, they'll have to helicopter us out of this one. No way would you get a stretcher in this joint. You never seen a more determined woman. Halfway up there's a chance to change your mind and go back down again. You been?'

'Sorry?'

'Up the Vatican? No? You should, view's worth it. We made it all the way to the top. Could've filled buckets with the sweat pouring off of our faces. Her knee lasted the whole weekend though. I mean, that was the morning and in the afternoon we was up

4

them Spanish Steps. Steps again. Eh?'

Connie raised her eyebrows and gave a slight shake to her head. She'd long ago realized that there was something about her face that invited confidences from strangers, especially in shops. She could talk with her face, Matt once said. He thought it amusing the way people continually spoke to his wife. Not being a man of surplus words himself.

This particular day, though, Connie would have given anything, a limb no less, certainly a kidney, to be driven silently home. Matt, she thought, what have you done?

'Been another hammer attack near Twickenham,' he cut across her thoughts.

'Not another girl dead, I hope?'

'Badly injured. Badly. But they think she'll live. What a world eh? You'd think *somebody* could figure they was living next to a loony with a hammer. Just like the other five — came up from behind and whacked her. Left her for dead, poor child. Daylight hours. Same route as my own daughter — No way would I let her walk on her own until they've got this bastard, if you'll pardon.'

The girls tended to be youthful and blonde. The attacks went back over a couple of years. There didn't appear to be any motivation other than sheer brutal insanity. Two girls had died. The randomness of that.

Parents who had weathered childhood illnesses, the school tour worries, dreads of muggings and rapes, cancer scares. The same panoply of terrorized anticipation that coursed through Connie's head from day to day about her own sons. They couldn't possibly have factored in the odds of their beloved child standing in the wrong place at the wrong time in close proximity to a creature bearing a simple weapon, intent on death. She was uneasy feeling relieved that she only had sons. But there was no guarantee that the attacker wouldn't change his choice of target. She wanted to give her thoughts over to the parents of this most recent victim but the taxi driver was blathering on about his wife again.

He had moved on to the Forum. Linda had been hugely taken with that. He liked going places with her because she put her own slant on things. Brought them to life so to speak. For instance, when they stood in the orchard or whatever it was at the Forum, Linda had gazed across at the Colosseum and he knew from the way her mouth was open that she was thinking something. What is it gel? he asked her. Imagine if we was gardeners, she said, imagine if there was a big brouhaha going on over there at the Colosseum. We'd be leaning on our shovels saying I wonder

6

who's on now. Who's got the crowd giving it large? We'd be familiar with all them household names, same ways we'd know all about Chelsea today.

'Brought it fresh to life in that second, she did. Funny knack some people got. You packed the Forum in, yeah?'

'Yes. The first day we went there.'

She could see that he was mulling over the 'we' but thankfully as they inched through Feltham, he was back to Linda in Rome again. This time in a restaurant, nothing special, eating the best pizza she'd ever had in her life. Why couldn't they get pizza like that back in London? That Pizza Hut stuff was no way the same.

'Our anniversary today.'

'Sorry? Oh you and Linda. Congratulations. Shame you have to work.'

'Always work the anniversaries.'

Linda didn't think the leather goods in Rome were as cheap as she'd expected. Things like coffees and meals out were good value though. She loved the mopeds but didn't think they'd work back home. The weather. She cooked Italian for weeks after they came home, same as she'd cooked French for weeks after Paris but that time she did all the chopping and preparing at the kitchen table with her leg out on another

7

chair because of the dodgy knee. She'd have a go at anything, his Linda, cooking-wise. But never could get a handle on perfect pastry. It was, she said, a mystery.

By the time they got to the last big roundabout, Connie was just managing to drown him out. He was talking directly to her by then, insisting on eye contact through the rear-view mirror. She watched his eyebrows shoot up and down. Once he threw his head back and bellowed a laugh at some foible or other of Linda's. She sounded pretty ordinary to Connie's ears.

A rush of spiteful glee coloured her cheeks for a second. But when he deliberately slowed down on the approach to the first turn off so that he could get to the end of Linda in New York (the sky was like long narrow ribbons cut up by the tall buildings and the pretzels were too big even for her mouth) Connie thought there was nothing for it — he would have to die.

Just as she was contemplating which method, the gush of talk came to an abrupt stop. They actually drove in silence for maybe a whole minute. He seemed lost in some private reverie and Connie closed her eyes with relief.

'Left here!' She managed to call just before he overshot the turning.

'Sorry love. Million miles away.' He smiled to himself. 'I was just remembering . . . driving, you know, your mind goes over . . . ' His voice trailed off.

Connie scrabbled about in her bag for pound coins. A twenty pound note folded and balanced on her knee in readiness. She hardly dared look at the house, somehow expecting to see a momentous change there, too. Curtains were still drawn on the first floor windows. No one but her ever bothered to pull them back to let daylight in. Her three sons seemed to like gloomy corridors, lights on in their bedrooms in the middle of the day. It gave her an uneasy feeling, reminding her of dressing in the murky igloo of her room for school. The long trudge with the streetlamps still on, red dust from the Consett Iron Works giving what light there was, an eerie orange glow. Only a bleary wash in the sky by the time she'd lined up her pencil case and exercise books.

'Well, I'm glad you enjoyed your visit to the Eternal City,' the taxi driver said, though Connie hadn't really indicated one way or another what she'd thought of Rome. 'Never been back myself. Maybe next year eh?'

'You'll keep Linda away from the Vatican though, won't you?' Now that she was leaving him, Connie felt she should say something just in case he thought he'd bored her, which he had, but she wouldn't like him to think so.

'Passed on, my Linda. Three years now. You're all right, these things happen. Love of my life she was. That'll be twenty-two pounds my love.'

He drove away before Connie could think of anything to say.

'I'm very sorry,' she called after the cab. She managed to get the weekend wheelie up the narrow tessellated tile path to the front door. On the step, she parked the wheelie upright and slumped on to it leaning forward with her head in her hands. 'So sorry,' she repeated until tears burbled up and suddenly her shoulders were heaving.

The door opened and Fred stepped out, eyes widening. He looked around then put a hand on his mother's bobbing head.

'Mum?'

'Fred pet. You'll have to help me inside. I've come undone a bit.'

'What's going on? Where's Dad?'

Connie took a deep gulp, clasping her hands on her lap tightly.

'He's still in Rome.'

'Is he all right? Mum — was there an accident?'

She shook her head, still concentrating on the hands, drawing her feet together now too, anything to help do herself up again. She was a pair of scissors that had fallen open and could not be forced to close.

'When's he coming back then?'

'I don't know.'

'What d'you — '

'Truth is, I don't know if he's ever coming back.'

No no. That was all wrong. Far too dramatic, she was just being indiscriminate with her misery. The black pupils swelled in Fred's eyes taking in almost all the brown iris. It wasn't fair to lunge a blow like that at him. She put several fingers to her forehead, rubbing.

'Sorry. I'm just . . . Well, I don't know what I'm just. Let's go inside. Don't say anything to your brothers. I'll talk to you properly later.'

She tried a reassuring smile, felt her lower lip wobble and thought better of it. A hand on his shoulder was about as much as she could manage for now. He flinched and that made her want to cry all over again.

'Later, okay?' She nodded, waiting for a reciprocal nod; he seemed dazed but inclined his head slightly. Her whole body yearned for the click of the door shut behind them. And when they were in, the door clicked, she let out a gush of pent-up breath. This is you

— the house sang to her — it's still waiting for you that intricate cobweb at the top of the stairs, so perfect she couldn't bring herself to swipe with a brush. Waiting for you dead slugs in a beer trap in the first flower bed in the garden, waiting, too, rubber scuffs on the wooden kitchen floor and a tiny triangle of peeling wallpaper on the first-floor landing. Small imperfections she allowed to make the house more homely, these things existed within her knowledge so that even the not quite perfect was within her control.

There was a lot of scuffling and thumping about going on upstairs. Joe and Benny attempting a last minute clear up. If she didn't keep on top of their room for more than a day it turned into a pigsty, four days and three nights meant a sewer. The hall was covered in muddy football boots, slung hoodies, trainers with the odour eaters hanging out, kitbags, heaped school ruck-sacks, chewing gum wrappers. There was the fusty sweaty smell of young male under-pinned by the scent of something sweet. Usually the pile up sent her into a frenzy of barked orders and stiff index finger pointing — 'You you and you, that that and that, upstairs, in the wash basket. Nowww.' But today there was something immensely com-forting in the detritus of normal home life.

She picked her way over the mounds which made Fred's pupils swell again. She should be marshalling.

He pushed open the living-room door. The carpet showed fresh drag marks from the Hoover. She could smell polish. Three orange gerberas hung limply from a much too big vase. Her favourite flowers.

'Thank you Fred,' she said. 'You've done a great job. And the flowers . . . '

He shrugged and pulled his mouth down. But she could see that his eyes were eating her face.

'Boys!' she called upstairs. 'You're out of time. The mess will have to wait.'

There was a last furious scuffle, Joe tumbled down first, jumping two steps at a time. He nudged against her by way of greeting and went straight to the kitchen. Benny, the youngest at nine, came down slowly, almost shyly. He was slightly built with copper hair like hers and green eyes that belonged to neither family. He shuffled across to her until the tips of his socks touched the top of her shoes. If she reached for him too suddenly he would withdraw. It had taken her all of his nine years to figure out just which way to play him but she was getting better at it.

'Hello Bunny boy. Have you been good?'

She kissed the top of his head breathing his hair in but remembering not to linger.

'Excellent,' Fred said proudly.

'And *him*?' She nodded towards the kitchen.

Fred made a so so gesture with his hand.

'Not bad. Mary gave him a right bollocking the second night and he settled down after that.'

Connie smiled. It was a genuine smile which stayed on her lips for a while without a trace of wobble. A surge of relief washed through her. Things would work out fine. She'd make some soup though the day was ridiculously sultry; Joe could skateboard down to the corner shop for some crusty bread. While the soup was simmering, she'd tackle the hall, then the kitchen, leaving upstairs for later that night. The various tasks would be apportioned equally and fairly though her sons would moan and quibble anyway until she would have to raise her voice, not hugely, just enough to find their motivation for them. She was the only woman in a house of four males after all, which meant that she was rarely less than three loud shouts away from anarchy.

She hoped that in the future three deserving wives would give her merit for the part she played in the domestication of their husbands. But it was unlikely. Doubtless, they would find their own flaws in her sons, petty things that Connie had overlooked in the grander scheme of things, and often she would find herself staring out of the kitchen window, playing out imaginary arguments with imaginary daughters-in-law in defence of their husbands. In defence of their upbringing. She was going to make a hopeless mother-in-law. The best she could wish for was that at least one of these women would have a sense of humour, that alone Connie considered the greatest virtue in a would-be daughter-in-law. A sense of humour got you through anything.

These thoughts flickered across her brain like background noise. A remote persistent version of them was always there once she'd stepped through her front door. They were soothing, something to run with or drop as her fancy dictated, much like the constant drone of Radio 4 in the kitchen. She was ordinary like the taxi driver's wife, Linda, really — it took someone else's perspective to make you extraordinary. She wished she'd been kinder, he'd lost the love of his life after all.

Warming to her renewed sense of direction she plotted the rest of the evening out in chunks. She'd call Mary after the soup and thank her for watching the boys for the weekend; she would yawn ostentatiously in a bid to dissuade her friend from the almost nightly visit. Tomorrow once she'd got a handle on things, she'd ring her mother. Hopefully by then in any case, Matt would have called to say that he was on the first available flight home, he'd temporarily lost his mind, found it again and let's never mention this episode, ever, if it was all the same to her and if she might find it in her heart to forgive and forget. She would, indeed, find it in her heart to forgive and forget but not until maximum pulp had been extracted from his bone marrow, which she reckoned might take say, a month, maybe slightly longer depending on how well and how arduously he grovelled. It would all be something to laugh about in years to come while meanwhile they could sink back into the steady, reassuring level of mild unhappiness or was it happiness — they'd come to depend upon. Yes. Soup.

'Everything's going to be all right,' she said to Fred to get his pupils back to normal. They obliged beautifully because her 15-year-old eldest trusted her in a way she never felt she deserved.

'Joe!' she hollered. 'We need crusty bread and check the fridge for milk.'

'Where's Dad?' Benny asked.

'He'll be along later,' Connie said, parking the weekend wheelie by the bottom step.

'He went straight to work?'

'Something like that. Benny, have you been wearing those socks since I left?'

★   ★   ★

It was no easy feat avoiding Fred's watchful stare throughout the evening. Every time the phone rang she jumped and started cleaning something. The calls were for Joe everytime. Girls with wheedling, pleading voices as if they could mentally exhort her to put in a good word for them just by taking the call. The voomping music from the bedroom he shared with Benny meant that someone had to trudge up each time to tell him Tasha or Sophie or Emma wanted him on the phone. Their names always seemed to end in vowels.

Down he would jump, landing with a slap of bare feet on the tiled hall floor. A casual riffle through thick sandy hair with one hand while the other reached for the phone, reminding her with a charge of his father. She didn't ever mean to listen but it was difficult to ignore the series of grunts which would ensue. 'Uh-huh. Uh. No *way*. You serious? Uh. Uh. Yeah bye.'

Joe's mobile had been taken off him when she discovered he'd been using her credit card for porn lines. Then when he appropriated one of the house hand sets for his exclusive use, she cut back the phones to just one in the hall with a cord attached. Still, he used her mobile if she forgot for a moment to take it out of her bag to hide in her room somewhere. He couldn't use his father's because Matt loathed all phones, especially mobiles, because they forced him to speak. He used Fred's if only to piss Fred off. Sometimes she disliked her middle son with an intensity that made her head swell.

She constantly bickered with Joe in a way she would have found deeply distressing with the other two. There was never cause to doubt for a second that when he was emitting shards of charm with the glittering ease of light refracting from a diamond that he was after something. He was the son she felt she had the least hand in and the one she worried about the least.

Fred got to the phone before her for the fifth call. This would be the one, she felt certain. It was impossible to hear what Fred was mumbling but there was nothing to indicate that it wasn't the usual mumbling tone he used with his father. Matt would be wondering how much his son knew, how

18

much she'd told. She felt a spear of self-satisfaction that she'd managed to hold tough. She began to hum while scooping crumbs of crusty bread into the waiting cup of her other hand. What would she say? How many degrees of Arctic drift could she possibly inveigle into her everyday queries. Tomorrow you say? Yes, I'll come and collect you. Yes, the boys are fine, wondering where you are is all. Well, of course they *noticed*. Pardon? I haven't said *anything*, what would I say? I think it's up to you to find your own explanations, don't you? I am perfectly calm thank you. Don't I? How do you expect me to sound, Matt?

By the time Fred came back into the kitchen she was already in mid-argument, her face working silently doing his expressions, then hers. In fact, she was feeling quite elated. It was pleasant to be so gloriously and incontrovertibly in the right. Her eyebrows gave a cool lift in Fred's direction.

'Mary,' he said in a flat voice. 'She's on her way.'

'Now?'

'I didn't think there was any reason to say not to.'

'Well, no.'

'So what are you going to tell her?'

'Shh Fred, Benny might hear.'

'He's in the living room. The door is closed.'

'Even so.'

'Even so what? *What?*' He was growing exasperated now and she couldn't blame him.

'Sit down pet,' she moved to the kettle. 'D'you want a cuppa?'

'Not right now.'

'No, me neither.' She took an opened bottle of wine from the fridge and poured the contents into a glass.

Fred followed her movements, keeping his spotty face impassive, chin resting on the bridge of his hands. Only the pulsing tobacco-coloured eyes gave any hint of his consternation. Even as she was commanding herself to tell him the truth, as much as she knew at any rate, she was also seeing the lawyer in him.

'I don't really know what to say to you,' she began, pulling up a chair to face him across the table. Her voice sounded like it was being aerated through a sieve, there was too much oxygen; what she needed was a poisonous draught of carbon dioxide. She cleared her throat and pressed down hard on the wooden surface. She was depending on his unflappable nature, if he flapped she was done for.

'Right. Well, we went to Rome. Mary told me about this little place she stays, close to

20

everything with a roof terrace from where you could see — '

'Yeah yeah?'

'We were having a nice time. No arguing, I swear. The first day we just walked and walked. We spent hours in the Forum and Dad was in his element. He said he didn't need to see anything else that was enough for him. You know what he's like about history and stuff. He followed a book with all the names of the buildings and who was who and what was what. Very interesting if you like that kind of thing. Then we spent the rest of the evening at the Colosseum. Fascinating. You should see all the underground passages where the wild animals and gladiators were kept. I was more than ready for an ice cream myself but I plugged on because your father looked like he'd died and gone to heaven.'

Fred's eyes had pinged at the ice cream; she knew exactly how to rope him into a story.

'That night we ate at a small family-run trattoria. Wonderful food but I won't go into that now.' She used food to relate a story to Fred as she would use clothes, fashion, to relate the same story to Joe later, if necessary. 'We were like two stuffed pigs laughing and joking our way back to the hotel. The next day we couldn't decide where to go next, Dad

21

wanted to start at the Vatican and work our way back across the river and I wanted the Spanish Steps because I could see from the guide book that there was good shopping around that area and I was a bit afraid that I wouldn't get to — Anyway, we tossed a coin in the end. Very democratic, don't you think? There was the teensiest argument after that and your father went to the Vatican and I went shopping.'

'Did he come back? How teensy was the argument?'

'Don't be ridiculous, of course he came back. We had a splendid evening walking the Villa Borghese gardens, watching the sun go down over Rome. I can't tell you how lovely that city is.'

'If everything was so lovely and wonderful, where's Dad?'

Connie splayed her fingers on the table, studying them with deep intent. She wanted to convey that what would follow would be painful for her. Not least because she was going to have to extemporize somewhat from now on and she would have to remember it word for word later in the unlikely event that Matt didn't turn up tomorrow. She let out a gusty sigh.

Benny strolled in and she made to change the subject to buy some time but Fred was having none of it.

'Out Benny.'

Without a word Benny withdrew like a reel of film played backwards. The kitchen door was shut again.

'Go on.'

She could see Rome now as it appeared that evening. The flesh tones accentuated by golden grainy light dipping in and out between the swollen breasts of innumerable domes and cupolas. She had to clear her throat again.

'Well, it's hard to say but I think it really started as we were looking at that sunset. Yes yes, it's coming to me now. We were standing on this lookout area with all of Rome spread out beneath us looking as if the sun had just melted over it. I felt very happy. I reached out to squeeze Matt's hand, maybe even give it a kiss, to mark the moment. But he'd moved a little and he'd turned his head away. And I think he was crying.'

'Crying? Dad?'

'I think he was.'

'Why?'

'I don't know. He wouldn't say. Said I was imagining it. But for the rest of the evening and all through the night he was very, very quiet and withdrawn. I woke several times and he was standing by the hotel room window just looking out. In the morning he'd left a note saying he'd gone for a long walk and for me to have breakfast as usual and he'd catch up later. I waited all day around the hotel and he didn't turn up until early evening.'

'So there was a blazing row in the lobby and he walked off?'

It niggled her that he looked so relieved. Yes, she had embarrassed her husband and sons from time to time by raising her voice in public but, really, that wasn't to blame for *everything*. They didn't seem to understand that women were different. They couldn't sit on a pending argument like Matt, brooding over his egg like a jealous hen. There were four males bumping into one another in their efforts at skulking. Dropping suitcases, passports, boarding cards, tumbling each over the other dominostyle in public places just so that no one might notice them. The odd well-appointed bark from her was essential if they were ever to actually get anywhere.

'As it happens there wasn't a row. I thought he looked ill. He said — He said that he didn't feel he could go home just yet. He needed time to think.'

'About *what*?'

'I don't know. He wouldn't say.'

'So you just said, 'yeah okay, take your

time, see you when you get home.' I don't think so.'

There it was again, that cross-examining lawyerish streak. He was good, thinking ahead of her while she was having to think on the trot. It was quite reassuring in its way that she was still drafting her customary bar charts of her sons' careers. That's what your four walls, solidity, gave to you — perhaps travelling was a bad idea. Her voice settled on a more even keel.

'I stayed very calm, Fred. Very very calm. You can imagine the panic I felt. I thought he was off his chump. I said, 'Right, let's just think about this. Let's just calmly go and have a bite to eat and talk through what you're feeling. I'll give you some of my herbal rescue remedy, we'll get through this evening then we'll get you home in the morning and straight to a psychiatrist.' '

A smile danced on the corners of Fred's lips.

'You didn't.'

'I did. Well, something like that. Wouldn't you?'

'This is crazy. I mean *Dad*. No way. What else happened? What's the thing you're not telling me?'

'Fred, I'm as bewildered as you. All night we talked. I should say *I* talked. I said all the things you'd expect me to say. What'll the boys think? What kind of behaviour is this? You're their role model for God's sake. And what about the dental surgery? What am I supposed to say to everybody?'

'What did he answer?'

'He just looked blank.'

Fred's eyes were pulsing again as he assimilated the information, such as it was. He looked at her quickly then looked away when she didn't add anything. It was important that she didn't add extra little embellishments now that she might forget later. It was also important that she manage to keep up the vacant, confused look so that he couldn't see the flashes of terror that had nearly overcome her when she was describing Matt's face. This whole ridiculous incident would be over by this time tomorrow evening if she could just keep a steady rein on things.

'What d'you think?' Fred said at length.

'No idea. What do *you* think?'

'He just let you go to the airport? Where did he go?'

'Stayed on at the hotel, I suppose.'

Fred scraped back his chair. Twin livid spots spread across his cheeks.

'Fine then. Let's call him straight away and tell him to get his arse back here.'

'Leave it for tonight, pet.'

'We can't leave him wandering around Rome off his chump.'

There never was a less likely person commended to the universe to go wandering around Rome off his chump than Matt. The prospect made her chuckle. At first she thought it was a hiccup but that was quickly followed by another gurgle and another. Fred scratched his head.

'What? Is this a wind-up then?'

'I'm afraid not. It's just the idea of your father — '

'Am I hearing all this right? I mean, I mean — *Dad*?'

He sat again. She felt a pang of pity for him. Fifteen going on eighty-three. No girlfriend. He wasn't just being let down by his father, he was being let down by his best friend for Christ's sake. A purple spot throbbed on his chin.

'Okay, we'll leave him for tonight but we're calling tomorrow if we don't hear anything.'

'Okay.'

'It's going to be fine, Mum. Just a temporary midlife crisis or some shit like that.'

That made them both smile.

'What should we tell your brothers?'

'We'll tell them Dad decided to stay on for what — a conference or something. Yeah, a big dentists' conference. You don't know how long he's going to be.'

'What a good idea. I wish I'd thought of that.'

He was raiding the top shelf of a cupboard for her secret stash of chocolate which evidently wasn't all that secret.

'You knew you'd have to tell me the truth, didn't you?'

He was pleased that she'd treated him as an adult, which she'd pretty much been doing since his legal career was decided when he was five, maybe six at a push. People said that kids came with their own clear-set personalities, treat them all the same and still they'd all turn out differently. Then there were genetic factors, position in the family factors, state of play of the marriage during infancy and a whole slew of factors you couldn't even begin to regret in hindsight, all contriving to assemble the future person into someone other than you might wish.

Secretly, however, she had a sneaky suspicion that you played the touch of a hand in the mixing bowl yourself. With the lawyer in the bank, hadn't she given Joe an easier run? Just to see what he might do with the freedom? He could be the rock star — the movies maybe, he had the looks. Something creative at any rate, though any signals had yet to emerge. He'd be fine once he'd gotten over the drink and drugs stage. And Benny — well, Benny she would just have to mind for ever.

'Mary's on her way.' Fred looked worried. 'What're you going to tell her?'

It occurred to Connie that already she and Fred were in cahoots to redeem Matt's honour. She remembered a play she'd seen once, *Six Characters in Search of an Author*; for how long was she going to have to be the author of Matt, making up a version of him that would tally with whoever was listening? She could simply say to Joe — 'Your dad wanted a longer holiday — without me,' and Joe would shrug. 'Dad's still working', to Benny — a shrug. There could be a thousand Matts out there; if he stayed away long enough she might have to cover for every one of them. She thought if he walked through the door right this minute, she could easily stab him if only to get the numbers down. One Matt, one version — dead.

'I might tell Mary about the conference.' She considered again, Mary was so astute. 'Or I might tell her the truth, same as you.'

And mostly she had told the truth. She was certain that Matt had been quietly crying when they were looking at the melting sunset. He had looked ill and strangely gaunt when he'd told her he couldn't come home. She had remained unfeasibly calm.

She'd just neglected to mention Greta.

2

Mary would have made a splendid horse. The sort of big-boned, reliable animal a farmer would have wanted for his fields once upon a time. She had a long expressive face with a jawline deeper than her forehead. Soft hazel eyes with hoods that recessed far into her skull and high, appley cheekbones heightened the equine effect. In her bare feet she reached nearly six feet with broad, angular shoulders above sinewy forearms and plate-like hands which were traced in knotty veins that stood out like fat worms. There was nothing she could do about those hands even if she cared, which she didn't. The clusters of veins were usually accentuated by daubs of paint in any case.

This evening there was a long streak of yellow along her greying shoulder-length curls, too. When she ran both sets of fingers through her hair, the yellow broke up like light on water. The streak would last until it eventually washed out but by then there would be several fresh replacements.

As Connie had talked her through her first impressions of Rome, Mary's eyes had glazed over, remembering her own first visit over twenty years ago now. They sat in the late evening gloom of the kitchen sipping red wine. The occasional creak of floorboards overhead signalled the boys upstairs. Perhaps Mary had just assumed that Matt was up there with them, she hadn't asked after him yet and Connie was busily staving. It was one thing dealing with Fred (not to mention the other two yet to come) but Mary was brutally intrusive if she suspected fobbing.

While she prattled on about the Forum, taking pains to adequately convey Matt's ecstasy, she was doing arithmetic on another level. She worked with Mary four days a week. Tomorrow, in the studio they were starting on a new card. They had set up the Alternative Card Company together over five years ago. More as a private joke than anything, but it had taken off to their surprise. Most evenings Mary popped by if only for five minutes. She was so often there, the rare occasion when she wasn't prompted one of the boys to casually enquire, 'Where's Mary?' the way you might the family dog.

Connie was adding and subtracting quickly; if Matt didn't show in three, at an extreme push, four days *tops*, she would have to tell Mary about meeting Greta in Rome and by then anyway, there would be an entirely different complexion to the episode. By then he would be a missing person officially. For now, his absence in her head remained *this* episode until it could become *that* episode.

'You had to give Joe a bollocking I heard.' Connie refilled their glasses.

'He loved it. I loved it,' Mary said with relish. 'I wish I owned that boy. You could bawl him out for ever without the slightest fear of damage to his psyche. His ego is inviolable. I adore him.'

Connie smiled. Many times she'd witnessed Joe and Mary launch at one another's throats with the gleam of rabid dogs in their eyes. It would start with their brand of familiar nettling banter that no one else seemed to understand. They made their own rules up, trading insults one day, punches to their forearms the next. Nobody in the family took a blind bit of notice of them any more but Connie was certain that some day, a passer-by would look in the living-room window and call the NSPCC. How could they not? There was a horsey, six-foot woman, streaked in paint, towering over a willowy teenager bellowing in a pungently aristocratic tone: 'Come on boy — you call that a punch? I'll show you a punch.'

Joe had managed to deck Mary one

evening with a jumping headbutt and when she came round she could barely speak with admiration. He was tops, he was abso-bloody-lutely magnificent.

It was an unlikely friendship which had endured since Connie first came up to London. She was a secretary in an advertising agency doing her best to modulate her strong Geordie accent. She felt gauche about practically everything, her working-class background, the way she dressed, the colloquialisms she still used, even her old-fashioned gold neckchains; no one seemed to wear gold any more. The other secretaries or personal assistants as they were now called, seemed languid and emaciated, forever draped in clingfilm black. Bent over their desks they looked like a row of commas.

She was eighteen, still in her Princess Diana ruffs and satin bows stage herself, with her copper curls tortured into the worst similitude of the most famous haircut on the planet. Matt was twenty-one, working in a pub some nights, tending suburban gardens at weekends to augment his meagre college grant. Often, he only began his night's study at midnight. They barely bumped into one another in their cramped digs off the Holloway Road. In the years that followed, Connie made a brave stab at trying to

34

reinvent those Spartan times in the usual 'we was poor but happy' pigeonhole but they defied even her optimistic reportage. They were mean, caustic years little lightened by their youthful sexual appetite.

Post-Falkland war London was a hungry place full of contradictions. While the black-clad lower echelon staff at the agency were in the main girls with Crufts' pedigrees, the blokes that owned the agency (they always referred to themselves as blokes) were rough Eastenders with glottal speech containing no consonants. 'Awwigh ma'e?' By turn, along the open-plan plebs floor all she could hear from the commas was, 'oh rahht, oh rahht'. You could say your mother had just dropped dead and they would nod, 'oh rahht'. If they didn't wear black in totality, they wore navy sailing sweaters with pin-striped shirts peeping over the round necklines, collars pulled up full at the back so that two wings brushed their jawlines at all times. They weren't going on any boats later that evening for pity's sake. She couldn't for the life of her make sense of any of it.

At first she'd lumped Mary in with the posh birds. Her braying Shires voice ululated from one wall of the open-plan all the way to the other. Back then Connie honestly believed that you couldn't be a normal decent human being if you talked posh. The two were simply incompatible. Though what constituted normal, it was certainly not Mary, but she turned out to be the most decent, honourable person Connie had ever met aside from Matt.

Mary was a junior graphics artist with the firm. Only somebody forgot to tell her that she was junior. There was hardly a day went by when she didn't cause an uproar. She breezed into the conference room, portfolio under one arm, a half-eaten apple in the other hand, trailing clouds of musky perfume in her wake.

One day she would arrive for the weekly brainstorming session draped in a jewel-coloured sari, plain brown-leather thong sandals barely containing toes that seemed to sprout in odd directions. Above the double straps each with a buckle on the side, solid ankles and calves sported thick leg hair the like of which Connie didn't believe any woman could grow let alone advertise. Another day, Mary would turn up in slashed jeans daubed in paint and a white singlet which barely contained her long, flat breasts. There being no question of a bra, ever. She was so exotic to Connie's mind that she had to be a lesbian.

She wasn't a lesbian as it turned out but

she was very talented which made the blokes put up with her tantrums and perfectionism for as long as they could. Connie found her in the toilets one day, sobbing her eyes out because she had such a crystal-clear idea how a certain project should be executed and the bosses were making her compromise. She was genuinely pained and her simple honesty struck a chord with Connie who was at the time engaged in a Herculean effort to remake herself as someone entirely new.

She started hanging out with Mary, visiting clubs and bars at all hours. They went to the theatre, to art exhibitions where Mary painstakingly opened up a whole new world to Connie. She began to see the point of London after all. Matt was happy that she wasn't stuck in their grim room every night having nothing to do but watch him pore over his books. If he ever felt a trace of envy or jealousy, it certainly didn't show; he said he was glad she was having a good time. For her part, she was a bit ambivalent about his magnanimity. She'd have liked him to be just a little jealous.

She wanted him to like Mary but she also wanted him to see her as a possible threat to their cosy twosome. In any event he just took to Mary in much the same way she had. Despite the social, cultural, pretty much every type of difference in their backgrounds, Matt appeared to experience the same ease in Mary's company. In a city that seemed hostile if not belligerent to their lack of social graces and excruciating self-consciousness, their newfound friend was true and uncomplicated like the friends they'd left behind in Consett, County Durham.

'I can't believe I've finally got you both to Rome,' Mary was saying. 'Didn't I tell you Matt would be dazzled?'

'Umm.'

'So where — '

'Thanks for minding the boys. D'you know they hardly crossed my mind the entire few days? We should go away together more often.'

'Of course you should!' Mary pulled a face. 'The place wasn't too messy, was it?'

Only like a grenade had gone off, except for the living room which Fred had restored. Mary didn't see mess or rather she didn't view the natural accretion of items dropped and left as anything other than the natural way of things. It was the upper-middle-class way Connie decided, no doubt used to space, to servants. That was another thing that had surprised her when she first went south. In her terraced street in Consett the women would vie for neatest house; they scrubbed the front door step, even the pavement outside, some of them.

Their windows gleamed and smelled of vinegar. It was the only thing that could cut through the perfidious rust powder that rained down on the town each night from the belching stacks at the Works, a place of heat and molten metal, smoke and fumes. The red dust which poured out of the chimneys covered everything, houses, lines of washing, cars, anything vulnerable to the open air. Over the years the successive layers of dirt and dust had built up into a permanent film of red grime which stained the whole town. Women scrubbed the bricks of their houses, etched not just by the corrosive dust but by the acids and sulphur fumes permanently broiling in the atmosphere. But indoors, tiny rooms were laid out with doll's house precision.

Down south, very often the larger the house the greater the mess. She tried hard over the years to lose a little of her own compulsion to have everything just so. It was just as, with Mary; just as you left it.

Mary's own higgledy-piggledy mews house near Kingston was a shrine to her lack of interest in material things. Why not sit on an upturned wooden crate if that's what came to hand? Why bother with matching plates? It was such a relief to sit amidst the confusion sipping tea from a grimy mug and not have to worry about plumping cushions or if you should put something under your mug on the scarred table top. But a relief Connie simply could not bring herself to extend to her own home. It simply wasn't in her blood.

'You know what I'm like.' Connie tried a little fake laugh. 'You could've had cleaners in and I'd still have to tackle it myself.' She said this in case Mary had noticed the item-swept hall or the scrubbed kitchen floor. Which, of course, she hadn't but now she was looking.

'Where's Matt?' she asked idly.

'He's still in Rome.' Connie kept her voice as casual as possible; she took a long gulp of wine polishing the base of the glass with one finger, for all the world as though Matt were frequently 'still in Rome'.

'Come again?'

Connie got up and began to tidy things from the table. Over her shoulder she said:

'There was a conference at the hotel. You know, the one you recommended? Would you believe dentists. From all over the UK. Before I knew it he was talking to people and it seemed interesting so he uh decided to stay on for a while. He didn't say how long exactly. I forgot to check,' she added in a rush. With her back to Mary she squeezed her eyes shut and waited.

'That's odd.'

'How so?' Now her buttocks were also clenched.

'I don't remember a conference suite at that hotel.'

'No? Well, there is. Very small. You'd hardly notice it. We were quite surprised.'

There was a silence as Mary digested this. Connie began to hum and wipe the counter top. Her face was atomic, she didn't dare turn around just yet.

'He's made a mug of you! Oh the crafty boy,' Mary exclaimed.

'What d'you mean?' Connie forgot her face and turned.

'He knew about that conference all along. I recommended several hotels, no wonder he chose that particular one. Dentists from this country, you say? You've been had.' She snorted a laugh.

Actually it was Connie who had chosen but she wasn't about to work against her own favour.

'I thought it was a bit of a coincidence.'

'Subterfuge. Never thought he had it in him. Hah!'

Connie felt giddy with relief. There. A few days bought.

'I'd better make a move.' Mary rose, still

quietly snorting. Though if Connie had evinced anger she, too, would grow indignant. Whenever Matt and Connie were going through a frosty patch, Matt would find himself on the receiving end of two cold shoulders in his kitchen at night. Mary instinctively picked up on Connie's vibes and mimicked them without thought. Thus Matt might say, 'What's up, Mary?' just for conversation and receive a noncommittal grunt for his pains, coupled with a put-upon look. It was that look that both amused and irritated Connie in equal measure. She knew she was observing her own face, reflected. And it did look pretty silly. The observation interfered with the exquisite pleasure of being put upon so that she wanted to clap Matt and Mary's heads together for making her appear childish to herself.

Joe barged in just as she was about to leave.

'Did you snitch?' he immediately asked Mary.

'Naturally.'

'What did she say?' he demanded of his mother. 'I didn't do nothing.'

'Anything. What's the anything you didn't do?'

'Nothing.' A huge scowl, it made him look even more handsome. Not a blemish on the taut, sallow skin while Fred was getting through two troughs of anti-bacterial cleanser a month, it wasn't fair.

He wasn't sure now if Mary had snitched or not. She stood shunting a tapestry bag on to her shoulder staring blandly ahead, tongue poking through a cheek.

'So you didn't say something.' It was a statement. Mary continued her bland stare.

'Joe, if there wasn't anything or nothing or something to snitch about, why did you ask Mary?'

'Because she made my life hell while you were away.'

'Joe. Your mother insisted I do.' Mary feigned hurt.

'It was just meant for a joke,' Joe protested sensing a trap.

'Your jokes aren't funny to other people.' Connie had unknowingly adopted the same bland façade as her friend. She hadn't a clue what he was talking about but they were just about to corral him with the slick efficiency of two sheepdogs working in seamless calibration.

'It was just the tiniest bit of bacon.' His voice had taken on a familiar self-justifying wheedle.

'Even the tiniest bit,' Connie responded, poker-faced.

'I just wanted to see if he'd notice. So he

did. So what? I don't think he'd even eaten any before all the bloody song and dance. Over what? I mean, you couldn't hardly see the speck I flicked in his omelette. I mean, I'm not sure I even did it on purpose. It just flicked. Off of my fork. For Christ's sake. Why's everyone always having a go at me in this family?'

Mary sucked her ample teeth, her eyes rolled heavenwards.

'I get it.' Connie flushed with temper. 'You had to try it on, didn't you Joe? You just couldn't leave Benny to make his own choices. If he wants to be vegetarian, what's it to you? D'you know, you make me so mad. Poor Benny.'

'Oh poor Benny. He's a freak. Everyone thinks so. You should hear what they call him on the street outside — '

'Don't! Just don't you say another word,' Connie hissed through gritted teeth. She glared at him, he glared back but she sensed that this time he would retreat. Probably because he wanted something and the one sure way not to get it was to rip out the tangle of deepest fears reposited in her guts. His gaze flickered to Mary and Connie knew she had won this round. A brief stay of execution because one day he would come right out and say all the things she never wanted to hear.

Mary thumped him roundly on the shoulder. 'That's for thinking I'd snitch.' She left, whinnying with delight at his sour expression.

A sudden, acute weariness settled upon Connie. The kind of instant irresistible weariness she'd experienced in the early months of all three pregnancies. She slumped on to a chair and held her head, her eyes were almost closing. She would rather stick electrodes under her fingernails than deal with Joe just now.

There he stood, glowering, awash in his ever-heightened sense of indignation. The inadequacies of her own children sometimes made her want to choke.

'Joe,' she said calmly, 'you mustn't tamper with Benny's food again. It's not fair.'

'So I'm to be fair but nobody else has to be fair to me. Right. Got it. Next!'

'I'm not in the mood for an argument.'

'Where's Dad?'

That threw her slightly. Her head came up more suddenly than she intended and she felt giddy again.

'He stayed on in Rome for a couple of days. Well, maybe a few days. Then again he might be home tomorrow. It's a conference.'

'Oh right.' He shrugged, chose a green apple from the fruit bowl and walked out of the kitchen tossing the apple from hand to hand. The door clicked shut after him.

'Oh rahht.' She stuck her tongue out as far as it would go.

★ ★ ★

The house was quiet. The flick of a light switch upstairs signalled Fred turning in for the night. They were all on half-term so there shouldn't be a stir until midday again except for Benny who always rose early. She'd had to put Joe in the guest room because he wouldn't let Benny go to sleep. He was angling for the spare bedroom in any case so it was probably a deliberate ploy. Really, he was overdue his own space but she loved keeping one bedroom preserved in the house and it had been decorated in creams and beige tints quite unsuitable for a teenage boy. She had been hoping to do the loft quite soon when she would put Fred up there and Joe could take his room. There was a bunch of magazines on the coffee table with features on loft conversions.

They'd sold their souls to the devil ten years back to buy this house. A wide red-bricked Edwardian with large sash bay windows framed in white. It was a gutting job at the beginning. They lived in two rooms with a makeshift kitchen, then she realized she was pregnant with Benny and they had to borrow even more to hasten the project along. She did room by room from magazines not trusting herself to have any innate taste. Matt said she did a terrific job but then he cared even less than Mary about such things. She was always the one looking for more and more security and what could be more secure than a red-bricked, large house on a corner plot on a sought after street with original features and a state of the art interior? Plus a nuclear family to go with it?

Now you're sucking diesel, her mother had said when she saw the completed picture. At first she'd thought they were daft to take on such a wreck. Throwing fine brass away. Funny what a log fire, a sink-into sofa, suede footstool for aching corns and your knitting resting cosily on your lap could do to reverse your opinions.

And what was it all for? Connie felt a touch woozy from the wine earlier as she glanced around her living room with original corniced coving and marble feature fireplace. Subtle honey and cream candy-stripe curtains draped in extravagant swathes of silk no less. There were matching twin glass pendants with crystal tinkling bits over the dining area (closed off now by the original panelled doors restored to former glory) and her ivory sink-into sofa on which she was sitting echoed the one exactly opposite, coffee table in between. I'm a fraud, she thought miserably. A complete and utter fraud. The luxuries she'd craved satisfied only the wants she herself had created.

Still the phone didn't ring.

★ ★ ★

Fred grunted goodnight when she looked in. He was lost in a cocoon of duvet, a few dark spikes of gelled hair peeping from the funnel. She went next to Joe looking resplendent in the centre of the king-size guest bed.

'Night Joe.'

'I've got football camp tomorrow, remember?'

'Okay, I'll call you.'

'It's not that. Can you make my sandwich ple-ease? It just means I get longer in bed. I'll cycle, you don't have to take me. And sub me a tenner just until Friday? I need to get something. Maybe you should leave it out now on the kitchen table in case I forget to remind you.'

'Joe, do you have to make demands just because you see me. Is it some sort of misguided affection? Couldn't you just once, simply say g'night Mum?'

'G'night Mum. Are we on for that tenner though?'

'Whatever.'

She stepped across and turned off the bedside light. Once she'd pulled the duvet up under his chin she bent forward to kiss his forehead.

'I'm fourteen,' he said, though not aggressively.

'I know.'

'You're all right,' he said, 'like yeah.'

'That might be the nicest thing you've ever said to me.'

Her eyes were stinging as she pulled the door shut. Though she knew in her heart and soul the tenner had more than a share to do with it. Still.

In the bathroom she tidied away tubes of hair gel, anti-dandruff shampoo and phallic-shaped body sprays. The room was a nightly testament to expectation and the edges of yearning. Three whiskery toothbrushes in various stages of disintegration stood upright in a mug. They always took on the personalities of her sons. The three appeared engaged in a tripartite conversation from which she was excluded. A runnel of sweat rolled down the back of her neck. She moved on, filling the night with ordinary things.

Benny was outside the covers, thrown diagonally across the bottom bunk. She straightened him and left the covering halfway up; it was hot and airless and he suffered from the heat. He moaned in his sleep. She leaned over and breathed in his milky scent. His cheeks were flushed and hot to the touch. She trailed her knuckles against one side of his face for a moment. Spidery eyelashes fluttered but he remained in a deep slumber. Bunny boy. What names do they call you Benny? What little torments do you suffer every day in silence? He was different, of course he was. There was that fazed, uncomprehending patina in his green gaze as if he viewed the world through premature eyes that weren't quite ready for it.

Close to God that one, her mother said once. At the time Connie had felt a sour spurt of irritation. It was well intentioned but her mother was implying that his lack of worldliness made him a little, well, simple. The real trouble was that he was far too complex. You love all your children the same, Connie thought, trailing knuckles down the other side of his face. But there's one you love so, it hurts your heart.

★   ★   ★

50

She'd insisted on a brass bed. They had to make love saying shh shh. I am shished, it's the damn bed. Under his pillow, Matt's sleeping boxers lay crumpled and somehow accusative. She sat up with her hands clasped across her chest, mobile phone plonked close by. It was late, Italy was an hour ahead, he was hardly going to call now. She thought about calling the hotel but then thought if he didn't answer. Or if they said he wasn't in. Would that make her feel better or worse? Of all the times she'd wished he'd carry a mobile phone like every other normal person on the planet.

Most probably he'd just show up tomorrow with a sheepish expression and a bag of swag for the boys. Mad gadgety stuff which would require batteries they'd never get until in one of her tidying jags she'd throw the whole lot straight into the nearest bin (which was never that far).

For now she was putting Greta clean out of her mind because if he did show up tomorrow that's where she would stay, consigned to waste disposal. There would be words, of course, angry words at first perhaps, but Greta's name was the one word that would not be spoken. 'She's here.' That's all Matt had said. Not, 'Look who's here' or even 'She *is* here', to indicate any foreknowledge. Simply that, 'She's here' as if for all the world he'd been expecting her to turn up just about anytime in any place. Almost to align her thoughts elsewhere, Connie waved an impatient hand in front of her face.

'We're going to Rome to work on our marriage,' she'd said for a laugh to Mary. She imagined two people locked in a room poring over some blueprint. Yes, well, I think we could do with some work here and possibly here. The foundations are still in reasonable condition but the brickwork pointing needs seeing to and the roof is ooh dodgy. Heating system needs an overhaul, there's a leak in the downstairs loo and the outside guttering is shot to shit. Though on the whole she thought they'd pass the building survey because their increase in equity over so many years far outweighed what little work still needed to be done.

In truth, their building was in pretty good shape. Their lives were almost placid. The fears and worries they'd harboured when the children were little were mostly faded now. Except for Benny, she still worried about him every day but she felt that Matt was more in tune with those worries and he listened more sympathetically when she had to voice them from time to time.

She felt that there was an increased

tolerance between them, the things that would have made them angry once no longer had the same potency. Perhaps it was the not-too-distant approach of middle age or perhaps so many years together had worn them down but not hopelessly, simply to a gentler place. It was the unspoken complicities in a long marriage that kept the building's foundations firm. Still, she had to make light of their weekend away to Mary.

Why did she have to make a joke of everything? Why was that necessary? She knew it bugged Matt sometimes, yet when things had become pretty rancid between them, for a generally serious man, he used humour to get them back on track. He knew just how to ridicule both her and himself in such a way she simply had to laugh. He knew how to puncture the clouds forming over her head to let the rain spill out. And often he used himself as the butt of the joke, which, was in a way, his gift to her.

There was the morning some years back when she'd been grieting on about something or other, she knew it herself but she hadn't slept well and he just happened to be in the firing line. So what? Take it like a man. She was extolling what he called magazine stuff, almost revelling in the tired uselessness of it all. The being taken for granted, the lack of observation on his part, why did everything have to be pointed out? Why couldn't he be more *pro*-active and not simply reactive when she was pushed to give him a bollocking? Yes, *pushed*.

Then she would be overcome with remorse. He looked so tired some nights after an arduous twelve-hour day doing a job he did well but cared little for. It both irritated her and filled her with sympathy when, despite his best efforts to stay awake to chat after dinner, his head would inevitably tilt forward and he was gone in a matter of seconds. Sometimes she would reach for his hand and kiss the long, lean fingers. Even asleep he was still so handsome he could make her blood boil. Long, feathery eyelashes made a boy of him again.

What had happened to that boy with sandy, floppy hair turning in a field on the farm where he grew up, to give her a shy grin? Embarrassed by his own pleasure at the tilled, inside-outed earth, the anorak of polluted smoky sky above, two long evening shadows moving forward as he walked on with his brother, Stanley. Everybody in those days wanted a Wilson lad, they were uncomplicatedly big.

There were times they argued (we are *not* fighting boys, we're having a *conversation*) when she was sure they could both leave the room, attend to some minor chores and just press play and record. When they were finished whatever tasks had beckoned, they could simply return and pick up at any point because there was rarely any maverick note of surprise. You said . . . excuse me — you certainly did, I was sat there on that sofa and you quite clearly said . . .

There was the day he scratched his head right in front of the fridge and asked: 'Any beers in the house?' They had company but she simply couldn't resist, she simply couldn't. She got up from the table with a benign smile on her face. 'Move aside and let me check for you, pet.'

There was the morning he couldn't find some patient's file. But he'd *left it right there* by her loft conversion magazines. A double whammy, she was always throwing out *important stuff* and costing him a fortune to boot. She'd told him he was an egotistical shit just like their middle son (which was both untrue and unfair and she was immediately sorry but not sufficiently sorry to retract). That stung, she felt rather than heard his whoost intake of breath. He removed himself to the bathroom to regroup. Her bath was already run and she hoped he wasn't going to take all day. He came out zipping up with a smile on his face. 'I've just pissed in your bath. Have a nice day.'

All day she couldn't stop laughing. It was only passing the time, wasn't it? It was normal, everyday, moderately unhappy stuff. There were good days and bad days — on the good days they believed that bad days would never come again and on bad days they couldn't remember anything good. Were they so different from every other couple they knew? It was the battles as much as the making up that kept them alive, kept them interested.

And there were times when the secret to success came with knowing when to concede. Like the evening on the way home from a crowded barbeque at Mary's when Matt pulled the car into the kerb and turned to her. She knew that expression and winced in anticipation; he was tight-lipped, running fingers through his hair as he chose his words carefully. Matt always chose his words carefully, she envied him that restraint. He said: 'I don't wish to be one of your funny stories any more, Connie. D'you think we could move the record on a bit?' His sober tone was disconcerting, she hated when he disapproved and so fell on him in a frenzy of kisses and apologies, rewarded with a smile that split his cheeks but with that hint of shy perplexity in his conker eyes that came when she was being tabloid emotional.

The next time they were in company she refrained all evening from telling even one joke about teeth or his patients, she bit her lip when a couple of the women went on in that forced sisterhood — you know what men are like — way about their own husbands. She had been buying into that because it had seemed the smart thing to do, the ironical, helium tone of the south. The chatter ran smooth as chocolate, subjects segueing with practised ease and without a funny story to hide behind, Connie's hands shook with inadequacy. Looking across the table at Matt, the way the other men deferred to him, his height, his silence (something she'd not noticed before, the quiet table manner to her mind, gauche, unsophisticated, betraying their roots), she realized that while her northern lad had remained steadfast in his skin, she had bought the entire package all the way down to a basement-bargain, vague, discontented middle-class malaise. She sent him a smile and a let's get out of here soon look. He grinned back then lifted his eyebrows to whatever the man next to him was saying, never impolite, if unengaged. Dour, robust integrity setting him apart from the man who was starting on the male retaliation with a witty story about his wife which made her look superior to his own knowing simplicity. Too clever by half the bloated self-deprecation while everyone laughed, clinked glasses, and knew he didn't mean a word of it. And there he sat, her big honest farm boy, comfortable and resolute in his silence — if he had nothing to say then he would say nothing, such a simple equation, so self-evident, it passed most people by. She darted a glance towards the door and they left shortly afterwards. She could hardly wait to get those big ingenuous hands on her.

A scuffling sound downstairs interrupted her thoughts. Benny, most probably, rambling aimlessly around in a state of semi-sleep which meant that something was bothering him. So he had detected her anxiety after all. Not in a conscious way, it didn't work like that with Benny, but she understood that on a sensory level what he was doing was checking the temperature of the house. She waited until a creak on the stairs, followed by another, signalled his return to bed.

'Matt,' she said to the empty pillow. 'Where are you? This is your home.'

Really, when she considered, the only serious arguments had been about their youngest and even those had fizzled out over the years. But when Benny was a toddler, sufficiently quiet and withdrawn enough to form jagged rocks in Connie's throat, Matt couldn't or pretended not to see there was anything strange about the child's reclusive behaviour. He didn't like to be touched. It had been so different with Fred and Joe.

He rarely cried. Rarer still to hear him laugh. He was complete unto himself from his first day and his self-possession terrified her. She wasn't working in those days and she thought she would be taken by the men in white coats. With the older boys in school, it should have been a breeze at home all day with Benny. The trouble was more time with her youngest, and alone at that, was all the more time to worry herself senseless at his peculiarities. Then there was the strain of hiding that worry from Benny himself. Everything about the child sparked a dozen contradictory reactions in Connie. To be fair to Matt, he simply couldn't win. On the one hand, she wanted him to admit there was a problem, while on the other, she wanted his calm acceptance of his son to go on. Oh, she could be so unreasonable in those days, picking fights about silly things so she didn't have to confront what was really bothering her.

One particular evening a row erupted out of nowhere and Matt's seemingly endless patience finally snapped.

'Connie,' he'd interrupted her in mid-flow, 'we both know what this is really about. All right, let's take him to a psychiatrist if that's what you want.'

'Did I say anything about a psychiatrist?'

'So *what* is it you want? What is it you don't have? What don't I provide?'

That last really got to her. The assumption that it was within his remit to provide her happiness or not. The assumption that he was the provider and she the provided. How dare he?

'Provide?'

'Yes,' he nodded his head but she could see that he was already rueing his choice of word. 'I mean the term loosely.'

'As in?'

'You're not working. I am. I provide the cheque. That's all I mean. Don't make more of — '

'No, please. I think you should expand.'

'Let's not. Aren't you bored with it? I am. I said a stupid thing, I'm sorry.'

'You're just tired now and you want your bed. Well tough. Explain *provide*.'

'I put the food in the fridge. You cook it. Drop it now.'

'How can I? You came out with that one word. You came out of the closet. You provide and the rest of us are simply provided for.'

'You just want a fight.'

'Do I? Do I really?'

She had no idea that she was going to strike him until the palm of her hand connected with his cheek. His head snapped back, he looked at her from that angle through slitted eyes damp with fury, mouth compressed into a thin white line. 'You shouldn't have done that,' he said quietly.

'I know.' Her hands flew to her own cheeks. 'I'm so sorry. He worries you too. It's just you're better at dealing with it. I am sorry.'

On the telly Newsnight was reporting on the AIDS epidemic in Africa. The infected orphans were heart-rending. Earlier, there had been a feature on a major earthquake in the Philippines, over three thousand people dead. It wasn't even the first item on the evening news. That had been the crash of a jumbo closer to home, three hundred and fifty-seven dead passengers. Three hundred and fifty-seven devastated families. It was an easier number to imagine than three thousand.

She looked at her sheer silk drapes over the window. The brown suede footstool at her feet. The crystal lights they'd argued the cost. The not-to-mention sink-into sofas. The tawny pure wool carpet with inch-thick pile.

61

The gleaming blonde solid wood furniture. In the hall, rows of relatively new trainers with whatever was the current logo most desired. Upstairs her children were tucked up in their beds, safe for the night. It was all here. Everything she loved and needed.

'Connie, what could we possibly *want?*' he said. She looked at him through a blur of tears. If they wished their son to be different, he wouldn't be the son they knew and loved. And if they didn't wish precisely that, he was never going to fit in.

She touched the red spot on his cheek, an imprint of her own hand, branding him, soiling his simple goodness with the mark of her own nameless wants. A deep burning shame shuddered up from her belly. Indeed, what could they possibly want?

'More.' It came out in a whisper, her shoulders lifted in a shrug.

She expected revulsion to creep across his face. But he slanted her a glance, shoulders rising in a corresponding shrug. Hands moved out from his sides, palms facing her in a helpless gesture.

'I know,' he said. She realized he was momentarily stunned that he could so comprehensively understand what she meant. 'Aye, I know.'

She was crying then and he held her. They

rocked together back and forth, holding on so tightly they were forcing breaths out, each the other. She kept reaching up to kiss the cheek she'd slapped.

'It's okay,' he murmured. 'We're here. We'll be fine. Benny'll be fine. It's just a rough patch.'

Later, they made love and it was gentle and tender between them, gracefully fluent as though it were like that every day. They used their bodies to make their silent apologies. She lay back afterwards while he slept and thought: this is it, this is all more should be.

They'd come through all of that. Through Fred's pneumonia and Joe's near expulsion from primary school. And now there was Greta.

3

Greta's apartment was on the sixth floor in a modern block. The living room faced on to a balcony which curved around the corner of the building. He could see a little of the Vatican dome to the southwest in a chink between the blocks, there was precious little else to remind him that he was, in fact, still in Rome. For whatever reason, she had chosen a bland, modern suburb which could have belonged to any European city. Perhaps it was to do with finances. She called him inside.

'What are you doing out there?'

'Admiring the view.'

'What view?'

'Yes, I was wondering about that.'

'It's anonymous.'

'And you like that?'

She smiled, the crooked way he remembered, one corner of her mouth curling up as though she were constantly mocking someone, perhaps herself. He noticed her left eyebrow lifted when she was asking a silent question; that, he had forgotten. She was still beautiful. Older of course, there were grey hairs mixed in with auburn now which she wore in a sharp bob halfway down her neck. The long fringe slanted across her face, obscuring her eyes at times, but he was certain it was her own colour. Around her grey eyes rimmed with ludicrously long, spiky lashes, there was a fretwork of tiny lines which creased concertina fashion when she smiled. Above, the solid black eyebrows retained their perfect winged shape; he noticed the hairs still looked as if they'd been oiled, each one individually.

She had a tiny brown mole by her mouth. It was the mouth which really told the passing years. It looked tighter, less willing to laugh. There were two dark scoops of shadow under her eyes. The darkness deepened to an almost navy blue metallic sheen in the recesses by the bridge of her nose, as though an inky thumb and forefinger constantly pressed in there.

Slimmer than he remembered, too, having lost the soft roundness of teenage years, though she'd never carried excess weight. Her tensile elasticity saw to that. Even in repose Greta was never entirely still, some part of her anatomy moved, usually her fingers, flexing and unflexing as they played an imaginary piano.

As he watched her quick movements around the living room, checking ugly modern window blinds, bending to retrieve what appeared to be endless mounds of clutter, it came back to him. The way Greta took over a room. The way you had to watch.

'I don't know why you felt you had to do this,' she said, palming discarded clothes from a buried sofa to slap a seat. 'Sit!'

'I don't know either.' He sat as directed. Somewhere in the back of his mind he felt he must know, he simply hadn't had the time to examine that knowledge yet. For possibly the first time in his life he was entirely responding to instinct. How ironic then that something she had long advocated should cause Connie pain.

Even the brief image he allowed his mind to flash of her face as she left the hotel earlier this morning made him want to gag. Her eyes were raw, she was electrified with a rage that had finally rendered her speechless after a night of talking, but it was the confused almost childlike resignation in her gaze as she looked back at him from the moving taxi that was etched on his memory. He shifted uncomfortably, craning around to see what Greta was up to. She was pouring water into two large whiskies though she hadn't asked if he still drank the stuff. A stolen bottle from her mother's house was the last time they'd drunk whisky together. The day he'd cut her ponytail off in a drunken stupor. He brought it up now and she narrowed her eyes, trying to remember.

'Oh yes. What were you thinking of?'

'Clearly I wasn't thinking. You weren't even cross, you just laughed and whipped my face with the braid. Your lovely long hair. Your mother took a broom to me though.'

'Hair,' Greta said, handing him a glass. 'So what.'

She curled up on the opposite side of the sofa, tucking bare feet under her buttocks. The mound of crumpled clothes she sat upon raised her slightly higher than him so that he had to look up to meet her gaze. She lit a cigarette and clicked pills from a dispenser with the same hand, swallowing them down with a gulp of whisky. Her nails were long and scarlet. They always were.

'So.' She blew a stream of smoke towards the ceiling. 'What did you tell your wife?'

Your wife. It was strange how those words somehow diminished Connie. As though the 20-year-old marriage was an incidental event which had merely interrupted the original pairing of Greta and Matt.

'I told her the truth. That I was worried about you.'

'There's no need to. Worry, I mean. I told you that yesterday.'

Matt drew his hands down his face. He might have told the truth, much as he'd understood it himself, as to why he was staying on in Rome for an indeterminate while but he hadn't told Connie that he had arranged to meet Greta yesterday. He'd left a note saying he was going for a walk, then stayed out all day. Little wonder Connie had looked frantic with worry when he finally returned.

No, this new dishonest version of himself had begun before that. For over a year he'd mulled over a nugget of information about Greta's whereabouts. Hardly even a nugget, an old mate from Consett had met an old mate, who *thought* he'd seen Greta Parker tending bar in an American joint in Rome. The man had retraced his steps on the pavement for a closer look but there was no sign of her behind the counter. Had to be his imagination. Still, it stayed in his mind and as the hotel was close by, he made a point of looking in the window of the American Bar each time he passed just in case. He never saw her or whoever looked like her again.

Matt had wanted to know which hotel or what area his mate's mate had stayed in. It was just that he had been planning a trip with Connie to Rome for the longest time. No lie there, their friend Mary was always urging them to go. He buried the information in a lode containing similar trivia in the untrammelled prairies of his mind. It might well have been coincidence that led to his walking down that particular avenue with Connie two days before. An unconnected memory spark that compelled them towards the American Bar in the middle of the afternoon, when there was still so much to see. A more dishonest man could try telling himself these things but Matt had always worn his honesty with the sober, presbyterian pleasure of his father before him. At least I'm *that*.

There was a wooden circular bar counter with a central section for bottles, shelved to the ceiling. They'd ordered two beers from a waitress and sat poring over a menu offering American fare for lunch. Both of them expressing the simultaneous thought that it was a shame really, not to mention a waste of valuable time, to be sat there in Rome on a glorious afternoon, mulling over a choice of burgers. Not at all what they'd come for. But they were tired and contented after their morning's excursions, he to the Vatican, she to the shops. It would be good to take stock and plan out the remainder of the day. Connie glided her hand over his on the tabletop and he leaned over her shoulder to scrutinize the laminated menu. His breath left a bloom of moisture on her cheek. She was ready for him, he could tell, there was just a way of knowing after so many years together. They were warm and close after an earlier argument about where to spend the morning and he felt his groin stir at the prospect of making love later, before a long, lazy dinner.

When he glanced up, Greta stood behind the counter. She must have been at the farthest side all along. Maybe he froze or made a little involuntary sound because Connie also lifted her head. 'She's here,' Matt said. Connie looked but still didn't get it, not immediately, then her mouth formed an O shape. She didn't say anything.

He made his way over from their table. Greta's expression remained bland and impersonal for a second, just another customer, until one corner of her mouth tweaked up in a knowing fashion. *Oh you.* The smile seemed to glide up her face gradually until it reached the pallid grey eyes. They kissed formally, both cheeks, it was stupid banal conversation — My God! — How many years? — So how've you *been?* — Well, of all the bars in all the world.

Connie was on her way over, a watery, preparatory smile on her lips. Matt quickly said to Greta: 'Are you here tomorrow? I'll come and see you. Around this time.' How dishonest was *that?* There was every possibility that far from the rather dull and unadventurous man he had been steadily growing into, with little resistance it had to be said, he was, in fact, conniving, unstraightforward and a bit of a mystery. And dear Christ almighty, what were those tears about later in the Borghese gardens with Connie? What was that? Crying in public and there was nobody dead.

'You okay?' Greta cut across his thoughts.

Matt realized he'd been staring at the floor, a perplexed frown standing out on his forehead.

'I'm really not sure what I am. Or how I am.'

'Welcome to my world.' She rose up suddenly. 'Look, I'll fix us supper, just whatever's in the fridge, then we'll get you out to the airport. Bound to be flights to Heathrow all evening.'

'Aye. That's the best thing.'

He could see her from the corner of his eye flitting about in the small kitchenette off the living room. There was a lot of clanging and banging from pots and pans for just whatever was in the fridge. She reached up on tiptoe at one point, revealing a sideways triangle of white flesh between her skirt and top. His lips compressed, he'd licked that very spot a lifetime ago. He knew that just above lay a mole similar to the one by her mouth. When she lay naked in his arms, his finger would circle that mole over and over, tracing patterns on her back but always returning to that one spot. Her head tucked under his chin with her hair splaying across his chest would smell of lemon. She used it in her final rinse, for shine she said.

Yesterday, when he went to meet her at the appointed time at the bar, having spent all night and all morning telling himself he wouldn't, she'd simply finished serving a customer and walked out into the hot air with him. He hoped he wouldn't get her into trouble. She said she was the manager and she could do what she liked. Matt smiled to himself; whatever she was she'd have done what she liked. They walked for at least an hour in complete silence. Occasionally he put his hand to the small of her back when they were crossing at lights. When they finally stopped to sit under an awning at a café, he automatically ordered black coffee for him and tea with milk for her.

He had the impression that if he asked her what had happened way back then, so long ago, she would smile crookedly, drain her cup and disappear into the ether once more. He wanted to ask though, desperately. It was making him sweat despite the cooling breeze that blew off the river to flap around under the canopy.

'So, you married little Constance Bradley,' she said halfway down her tea. It wasn't meant as a putdown to his wife, he felt sure. It was just that Greta had left Connie back in time when she was the young girl hanging around the Wilson farm, sometimes catching Matt and Greta posted to a tree in mid-snog. They'd found her amusing but often shooed her away. There was only a few years between the three of them, nothing that would count now, but back then, the three-year Greta and Connie gap meant the difference between climbing up a tree and kissing up against it.

If they ever considered Connie at all, aside from shooing her, it was to chuckle at the blatant crush she had on Matt's younger brother, Stanley. She was forever making offers of help around the farmyard and generally getting in Stanley's way. Matt's mother welcomed her though, she made the hens lay eggs, she said.

'How has it been?' Greta asked. He assumed she meant the marriage.

'Good. No, better than that. We've had our ups and downs, you know how it is.' A pause. 'Do you?'

'Yeah.' She drained her teacup.

'Kids?' he asked.

She nodded. It was the first time he really noticed the depth of shadow under her eyes. She gazed across the Tiber to the other bank, oblivious to him. He wouldn't have been surprised if she'd suddenly opened her mouth to deliver some heart-stopping opera aria. Tragedy, and he had absolutely no doubt there was that, had lent her beauty a luminous, violet quality. You could taste it in the air around her, like lavender. Like so much else about Greta, he wondered what had happened. She frowned and pulled herself into the present.

'Any photos?' she asked.

He pulled from his wallet an old shot of the boys together. Actually, now that he looked at it through a stranger's eyes, it didn't do justice to any of them: their smiles were too plastic, too put on, you couldn't help but think they were faking another version of themselves for the camera, which, of course, they were. Kids trying to look cute, rarely did. He shuffled along rapidly.

There were faded baby photographs too, some with Connie in a variety of hair-dos holding them. He sifted through those until he found the individual school shots taken last year. He told her about Fred, how adult and caring and guile-free he was, how he

74

acted as referee when his parents were at loggerheads and how he patiently forced them each to listen to the viewpoint of the other when all they wanted to do was draw blood.

'You know how it is,' he added, hoping to draw her out.

'When I want to let rip, I let rip.' She smiled. 'I'm not sure I'd like somebody restraining me.'

Matt felt a little slighted on Fred's behalf at that. Nevertheless, he had to concede that there had been times when he'd wished that his eldest wasn't quite so even-handed, when he'd wished for Fred a spark of Connie's spontaneity, so lacking in himself. Feeling he had to compensate lest they sound deadly dull, he played up Joe's wild side, how he didn't seem to give a damn about anything much except listening to music if you could call it that. Mean, seriously violent stuff about killing this motherfo' and that motherfo'.

He found himself flushing at how quaint and outdated he must be sounding and by the time he got to the end of Joe, Matt wasn't entirely certain whom he disliked more, himself, for so easily dismissing a slightly wild though good-hearted boy in search of a cheap laugh, or his son, for his transparent simplicity and general all-round lack of achievement which made dismissal so easy.

She was nodding, thumbing the photographs, turning them over to look at dates. Of course, they meant nothing to her, why should he have thought they would? And yet, he was disappointed, he'd stupidly expected a stronger reaction, jealousy or envy perhaps — covetousness. He felt he'd given a very poor account of them. She held out a serious Benny, grimacing like a miniature gargoyle for the school photographer.

'Who's this?'

'That's Benny, the youngest.' Matt didn't want to say any more, he'd done such a bad job of the other two that anything about Benny would be like clubbing a baby seal over the head.

'He's got Constan — sorry *Connie's* hair.'

'Aye. He does.'

'So,' she said. 'I'd better head back to work.'

'I'll walk you.' Matt raised a hand for the waiter to bring the bill but found himself ordering more tea and coffee instead.

There didn't seem to be any sense to any of this; what was he doing here with Greta when Connie was waiting for him back at the hotel, doubtless half out of her mind with worry? Of course, she'd seen the tears yesterday evening, coursing down his cheeks like a bloody baby. She'd asked him naturally enough, but her eyes were darting from side to side along the ground like someone whose favourite auntie had just exposed herself full frontal, cackling, on the kitchen table, before the family Christmas gathering. Was this it then? The infamous male mid-life crisis — you met an old girlfriend and suddenly the life you never lived blows up in your face? How ridiculous. In just another minute he would get a grip on himself, shake Greta's hand, perhaps kiss her cheek and everything would go back to normal. Perhaps they might even exchange phone numbers each knowing full well that they would never ring.

'How old is he?' Greta asked of Benny.

'Nine. Well, eight when that was taken.'

'You haven't said anything about *him*.'

'He's — different to the other two. There's nothing *wrong* with him, you understand. It's just that if I — if I tried to explain, it might sound as if there was. What I'm trying to say is, I wouldn't explain him very well.'

'That's okay. I had a seven-year-old. He wasn't very — explainable.'

Her face had settled into a rictus-like mask. She clenched her lips. Matt reached across the table and grabbed her hand. It was clear her son was no longer alive.

'I'm very sorry, Greta.'

'Of course you are.' She began to cry, very quietly at first but a couple of uncontrollable, spurting sobs made people turn to look. When he moved to pull his chair closer to her side, she raised one palm towards him. Don't come near her, it would only make things worse. He waited until she grew calmer then held the cup to her mouth.

'Here. Take a sip.'

She swallowed with a shudder. The dark bruised circles under her eyes stood out in relief from the chalk face; the effect was strange and almost sepulchral like the head of a skeleton. He realized fully how thin she was, she must never eat. She tucked her long fringe behind one ear. He passed her a paper napkin and she blew her nose.

'Sorry.'

'How long ago?'

'Two years. He'd be nine. Like your Benny. No more questions Matt, please.'

So much had happened since they'd last sat together and yet they'd just lived two ordinary lives with their quota of tragedies that would, after time, only remain extraordinary to them. Nothing like the lives they planned when he lay on top of her in the long hay, waiting to enter her once more. That was how he'd seen the future then, always somewhere inside Greta.

They walked along the lower bank of the Tiber, in silence again. The water was soupy and a peculiar shade of green that made Matt think of Benny. To lose a child, he couldn't begin to imagine. If he had to choose, if there was a Sophie's Choice moment like in the book, which son would he surrender? He didn't know. None most probably, they'd all have to die, alongside their father.

A hot, intense sun was making towards the west. Rome wasn't entirely baking yet but there was a sense of expectancy in the stolid air, of the blanket heat to come, of wide tree leaves drooping in pitiless, yellow haze. He'd never been before yet he felt certain he was picking up on Greta's sensory familiarity. It had been that way once.

Cars honked endlessly up on the thoroughfares above the river, mopeds revved, waiting at lights. Sightseeing pleasure boats glided by cutting through opaque water, emitting sounds of chattering tourists. They climbed steps and stood on the Ponte Sant'Angelo looking down at a row of barge-like houseboats, at least Matt assumed people actually lived in them. Greta pointed to a series of statues on tall plinths lining the bridge either side.

'They're copies of Bernini's animated statues, we call them the 'Breezy Maniacs'.'

'We,' he thought. The Romans and Greta? It was next to impossible for him to extricate her, his memories of her, from Consett. He didn't say anything, just listened politely while she pointed out various landmarks in a dull, lifeless drone as if by rote. She was talking to a tourist.

The vast rounded bulwarks of Castel Sant'Angelo stood at the end of the bridge to their right. Originally a mausoleum for the Emperor Hadrian, it had subsequently served as a papal fortress, barracks, prison and now, a museum. It was worth a morning to tour the four levels inside, Greta advised, if he ever returned to Rome. She glanced at him briefly. Hair blew across her face, he pushed it back behind her ear.

Further along, the dome of San Pietro, which to Matt seemed like a polar magnet in this city, was washed in each indent of the circular pelmet by subtle gradations of orange. He had the impression of a huge cut-glass goblet upended. Greta followed his line of vision.

'You'd need to allow a day really, if you want a proper viewing. Don't go in the summer — the queues.'

'Whatever you say.'

'Am I boring you?'

'No. Not in the least.'

80

In truth, everywhere looked just as beautiful as yesterday. There was nothing boring about Rome. If anything the city was almost sluttish in her wanton exhibitionism. Down every alleyway, around every corner, there was another exquisite monument not even listed in the standard guidebook. The city spewed out art and history and culture like the fresh water geysering up from her hundreds of fountains. Enough already, was clearly never in the Roman lexicon. And the perverse thing, he realized with a spasm of shock, was that what had intoxicated him as recently as yesterday morning meant nothing at all to him now. She might just as well have been introducing him to the delights of Birmingham. It wasn't Rome or culture or statues making his loins ache or his breaths come in staccato-like bursts. All he could see was auburn hair and pebble-grey eyes.

Greta sighed and slipped her arm through the curve of his own. It was an entirely unconscious gesture which didn't require a response but he couldn't help pressing the locked arm towards his ribs. She didn't pull away and he couldn't quite remember when he'd last experienced such complete and unquestionable happiness, only tempered by a profound certainty that if he walked away from her at the end of this weekend, he would never see her again.

They crossed the bridge, heading nowhere in particular, while Greta shooed away Africans selling fake designer handbags. He realized, with some surprise, that she was speaking in a foreign language he couldn't understand.

★ ★ ★

While she cooked, he took the opportunity for a wander around. The large, square living room was standard fare for a modern block, white walls, tiled floor with a couple of rugs, the bare minimum of furniture. He suspected the few chairs and sofa were rented, too, it didn't look the kind of stuff a woman would lovingly decorate her shelter with — too, yes, anonymous. She hadn't bothered with pictures on the walls, either. Everything bespoke temporariness and he figured she hadn't been living there all that long. A couple of years at most. There were no photographs on display.

The room gave on to a narrow hallway, three doors led to a main bedroom, a tiny boxroom, with a foldout bed against one wall, and a bathroom. If he'd thought the living room was cluttered with clothes, her bedroom was a war zone. There were puddles of garments littered across every surface, as if she simply stepped out of whatever she was wearing and left it there. She probably only did a tidy when she ran out of things to wear. Odd bits of jewellery were scattered on the ground and over a single chest of drawers. An earring by his feet, matching partner over by the farthest wall where she'd presumably flung them and one had ricocheted back.

He had the feeling that the clothes and jewellery predated the apartment, they looked too expensive for this place. Even he recognized some of the labels on a few jackets and there was little doubt in his mind that the diamonds studding a casually thrown bracelet were the real thing. What then? Divorce, and she just got to keep the clothes on her back?

He was about to leave when a tiny silver frame caught his eye. It was on a cabinet by her unmade bed. A small, dark-haired boy's face stared solemnly at the lens. Her dead son, he assumed. The face had been cut from a larger picture, a man's hand grazed the top of his head. Matt opened the top drawer of the bedside cabinet and there were dozens more photographs within, all of the boy, all similarly culled from presumably larger family portraits.

The only other contents were small phials of pills. As much as a dozen though some were empty. The pharmaceuticals read the same in any language, antidepressants, sleeping tablets, she had uppers, downers, knocker outers, something to regulate every part of the day and night. Greta was a walking pharmacy which accounted for the glazed look in her eyes moments ago which he'd mistakenly attributed to tiredness and the whisky.

He went into the bathroom and flushed the toilet with the door slightly ajar so she might hear. He wouldn't like her to think he'd been snooping around. Back in the living room, she was putting two plates of linguini with tinned tuna, tomatoes and olives on top of the coffee table. She'd swept books, clothes and piles of paperwork on to the floor. There was a bowl containing salad and two tumblers for wine. Then he noticed she didn't have a dining table, though there was plenty of space. Clearly, Greta wasn't into entertaining much.

'Thank you.' He sat in his original spot on the sofa. She handed him a fork. He thought: what in the name of Christ, am I doing here?

They ate, side by side, concentrating on their plates. It was good, better than good; Matt realized he hadn't eaten a bite since his last dinner with Connie, and then he'd only picked at some veal. How could he have not eaten for nearly forty-eight hours and not even notice? The thought of Connie quickly dulled the edge of his appetite.

Greta pushed her plate away, she took a sip of wine. She'd barely swallowed four forkfuls of pasta and a couple of salad leaves.

'Greta, you should eat.' He couldn't help himself. 'You're far too thin.'

'I eat enough,' she said, lighting a cigarette. The pupils in her glazed, grey eyes had contracted to pinpricks. He realized she was quite drugged. Moreover, he realized that this was the routine, every evening, after she'd managed to get through the day's work. Her head was listing slightly.

'We have to get you to the airport,' she said.

'Aye, yes. In a while.'

'Call her. Call Constance. There's the phone, tell her I'm fine and you'll be home soon.'

'I will. I'll do that.'

He put his plate aside and reached for her, scooping her into the cradle of his arms. She was nothing but bones. He carried her to the bedroom, leaning down to sweep clothes from the bed, he could easily hold the weight of her with one arm. Her head lolled back.

Once he had draped her sideways along the bed, tucking a pillow under her cheek, he closed the roll-down metal blinds, blocking out the deadening evening sun. The room felt immediately cooler. He drew a sheet over her body and sat on the side of the bed listening to her subsiding breaths.

'Go and call her.'

'I'm just about to.' He didn't move, turning instead to stroke her hair. He was sure he could still smell lemon. That much at least had to be a good sign.

Her hand snaked up to his cheek, he could feel the rasp of her knuckles along days' old growth. He badly needed a shave.

'You don't look so different,' Greta said, pads of her fingers dipped into the grooves between his nose and mouth, 'except for these', she traced the laughter creases at the corners of each eye with her thumb. 'And these.' The movement of her thumb back and forth felt like a caress. He didn't want her to stop. As if reading his thoughts her hand cupped his cheek a moment longer before falling away.

'A little thinner on top too, but thanks for not mentioning.' He tried for a croaky laugh and it sounded slightly hysterical to his own ears, more of a strangulated gasp.

'I had to leave, Matt. I couldn't stay.'

'Why? Why couldn't you stay? I thought you loved me.'

'I did. But I could see what our lives would

be like. It wasn't what I wanted. I was fighting with my mother, my sisters, you were set on us getting married, you'd have followed if I said where I was going.'

'Where did you go?'

She chose to ignore the question for the moment. 'We were only babies ourselves. Seventeen for God's sake. We didn't know anybody else from the age of thirteen. After a year or so, I wrote to my sister, Rita. She'd write back and tell me about you, what was happening at the farm, at Mam's hair salon. Remember that?' She chuckled deep in her throat. 'That bloody salon. Parker's Perms, I hated everything about the place. That smell of peroxide, we could never get it off our clothes.'

Matt remembered because after an evening with Greta he would smell of peroxide too. And it wasn't from the age of thirteen, he wanted to say but didn't — that was their first kiss, they were hanging around together long before that.

'I asked Rita,' Matt said. 'I asked all your sisters. You've no idea how many times I asked. So Rita lied to me for years.'

'I made her promise. I was in London, I don't know — maybe ten years? Then I came to Italy.'

'You were in London and so was I.' It

seemed incredible to him that he hadn't sensed her presence.

'I know, I kept looking out for you. I was always on the lookout for people from home, funny, never bumped into anyone.'

'You must have been living a very quiet life.'

'Believe me, anything but. Rita never told me about Constance Bradley though. Connie, I should say, I'll get used to it. Maybe she thought I'd be upset.'

He didn't ask if she would have been, because he didn't want to hear the response. Her voice was drifting now, sounding faraway.

'Tell me you've been happy,' she said.

'Mostly, I have been.' And it was the truth. Matt couldn't say that he'd been unhappy, but it would also be true that a lot of the time, he was never quite sure. It wasn't a question he had asked himself periodically. There was work, the boys came along, there were fights with Connie, makings up with Connie. It was an ordinary, routine life, and until this weekend, he felt that on the whole, thus far, he could say he'd acquitted himself with a reasonable degree of integrity and, yes, maybe success, if you counted material possessions.

She was asleep. Now, he would call Connie. He would try to explain that for reasons quite beyond anything he could understand, he had felt compelled to spend a little longer with Greta. Plain old curiosity perhaps, wondering where she had gone when they were young. What had taken her son from her. He would make a sincere and heartfelt apology for behaving in this errant and uncharacteristic manner. He would tell her that he loved her and beg her forgiveness. Then he would call the airport and leave first thing in the morning.

Matt disentangled his hand from Greta's hair and crept from the room but he left the door slightly ajar in case she called out. Seconds later he returned to watch her sleeping.

4

Joe was already in the kitchen washing his muddy boots when Connie surfaced downstairs. She checked the phone in the hall in the unlikely event that Matt had phoned during one of her ten-minute snatches of sleep. Likewise, she'd already checked her mobile, then shook it, as though that might provide a message.

There were clumps of thick mud on the kitchen floor and all over the sink, water sprayed liberally from a flowing tap to bounce from the boots to Joe's chest to lie in a pool by his stockinged feet. He was using a dishcloth to scrub. Connie twisted the tap off.

'How many times? You use an outside tap for cleaning boots, just look at this place. How could anyone even think of washing something so filthy at a kitchen sink? A *kitchen* sink, Joe.'

Joe's face steamed to optimum level. He could stay puce for hours. He clanked the boots together to shake off any remaining mud clustered between the metal studs.

'What am I supposed to use in this house anyway?' He glowered.

'You could use kitchen paper. You could — '

'Oh could! Could you please shut up?'

Connie thought: you are unquestionably the most obnoxious, self-centred, arrogant little prick. She thought: you were more trouble as a baby than the other two put together. She thought: you could use that anger on stage someday, there wouldn't be any intellect behind it but maybe an audience wouldn't notice because of the cobalt eyes. She thought: Jesus Christ, where is your father?

She said: 'Joe, let's not get into one. Don't use the *kitchen* sink again, please. Was that a better way to ask you? Good. Perhaps now that I've asked you nicely, you might also nicely — listen.' She took a deep breath and exhaled. 'Okay. What d'you want in your sandwich?'

Dear God, he was pulling on the boots with the metal studs, on the kitchen floor. He was walking over the *wooden* kitchen floor, flying mud and water in his wake, to check what was in the fridge for sandwiches. She bit her lip.

While he looked blankly inside, he started a low rap under his breath. Something about taking a gun and shooting motherfos'. Connie took a sliced loaf from the bread bin. She felt older than a hundred, eager for the grave. Outside the kitchen window her life was hurtling by, she could peer and catch the tail end of it, if she could be bothered. *Look, there she goes. There, there! Missed it.*

'I don't think I know that one, Joe.'

'As if.'

'Eminem is it? One of them?'

'It's a guy called Shark. His best mate took a gun to their school one day. Shot six teachers right where they stood. Bam! Put it in his own mouth and pulled the trigger. Bam!'

'Right where they stood. Gosh.'

'I can see me doing that one day.'

'You can?'

'Specially Flintface. Oh yeah, I see that. Only I'd take him out real slow. Max-im-um pain levels.'

'You're pretty dangerous.'

He turned to gaze at her through narrowed eyes. That look, she thought, very Jude Law. Connie dangled two slices of white loaf. Only Benny ate wholemeal.

'Ham or Nutella, Joe?'

His head bobbled, debating.

'Nutella please.'

★ ★ ★

There was his bike to fix, the chain was loose again and the front right brake needed tightening. They could have had the argument about why he hadn't told her before or why he refused to learn to fix his own damn bike but she just wanted him out of her eyeline. Besides, he would have made so monumental a performance of such simple tasks she was better off doing it herself in a tenth of the time. She'd always been skilful that way with her hands. Her brother, forever stuck in his books, used to pay her to fix his bike which she sometimes broke just to get the money.

He was pedalling down the street when she remembered the tenner. She was about to call out then clamped her mouth shut instead. A puny victory, perhaps, but you had to steal what you could get from Joe. The phone rang and she ran inside.

'Hello yes?' Max-im-um gelid tone.

'Mrs Wilson? Just wondering if Doctor was on his way? He had an eight o'clock cavity this morning.'

It was Jennifer Copeland, the dental surgery nurse. She'd been with Matt for over fifteen years and still insisted on calling Connie, Mrs Wilson. 'Doctor' grated on Connie's nerves, too, the proprietorial way Jennifer used the term, he may be Husband to you but to me he'll always be Doctor. Connie felt she was taking a punch in the lower abdomen. She could hardly tell the stocky, pious nurse that Matt was at a dental conference.

'Oh hello Jennifer. Can you excuse me just one second, I have to give Joe something before he — football.' She covered the receiver with one hand as if the woman might read her thoughts which were flying just about everywhere, there was a chance one of them might plop down the line. What to say? What?

'Sorry about that. I have a huge apology to make Jennifer. I was supposed to call you last night. Matt's still in Rome, I'm afraid.'

'Rome? Nothing wrong I hope?'

'Just mild concussion, nothing to worry about.'

'Concuss — My goodness. What happened?'

'A bus. Clipped him. Ever so slightly. Really, nothing to worry about. But the doctor felt it would be best if — you know, a flight — for a while. He could be home today, tomorrow. Depends on the doctor.'

'Is he actually in hospital?'

'Actually . . . ' Think about that, think about it. 'No. They didn't think that would be necessary. Would you believe the doctor

94

turned out to be a friend of a very old friend of Matt's, so he's staying with him. I didn't even take the phone number, would you believe. It was all such a — you can imagine.'

'How dreadful. The way they drive in Rome, I can't say I'm surprised. But really, actually *concussed*, you say.'

'Mildly.'

'Nevertheless.'

'I know. Look Jennifer, can you get Martin to cover the most important — '

'There's a whole top row of veneers at two o'clock. Martin can't do those.'

'You'll have to rearrange things. He'll just have to handle what he can.'

'Well of course.' A loaded pause. 'Emm, you didn't think to leave your mobile with him then?'

'No.'

'Perhaps when you get a number you could let us know. It might be useful if we could get in touch, ask his advice and so on. Please don't worry about us, Mrs Wilson, we'll hold the fort. You'll be sure to tell Doctor that, won't you?'

Right after I tell him another few things, Connie thought, for a second she even felt a giggle rising up.

'Oh and Jennifer, we've decided not to tell the boys, what's the point in worrying them unnecessarily? We're telling them that Matt's at a dental conference in Rome if it's all the same to you. In case you're talking to them.'

'If I have a choice, I'd rather not lie, Mrs Wilson.'

Oh no? What about the big fat lie you told about your sister's wedding? The one that turned out to be a two-day shopping trip to Paris with the Eurostar tickets you won from the back of a Persil box?

'I don't expect you to lie, Jennifer. We're merely withholding the complete truth, for their sakes. It's what the doctor wants.'

'Yes yes, of course.'

Connie riffled fingers through her hair once she'd replaced the receiver. She drew the fingers all the way to the ends then let them drop again. Who next? What else had she to cover? Already she could hardly remember whom she'd told what. The versions of Matt were cloning at such a rate, she could hardly keep up. Where was the real deal though? What was he up to? This was getting beyond ridiculous, she should just phone the hotel and give him an ultimatum, return by this evening or she was changing the locks. See how he'd like that — worried about Greta, indeed. Why wasn't he worried about his sons? His dental practice? His poor wife?

She saw herself in ragged clothes, cheeks streaked with earth from the soil she was digging — no, *clawing* — to provide her family with something, anything — a potato. Rain beating pitilessly down on her head, her bleeding fingernails chipped and cracked. But just like Scarlett in *Gone with the Wind*, she would win the day and save them all even if it took her last breath. Up in the big house, Fred was probably sleeping, Joe was smoking while grunting into her mobile phone and Benny doubtless, was sorting through spare rags for anyone even poorer than themselves. That it should come to this! *Because he was worried about Greta.*

Connie stomped upstairs to get the hotel brochure for the number. This was the only way to deal with things, be firm, call a halt to this nonsense, stop indulging him. Really, it was time to get serious. At the top step an image of Matt tangled in bedsheets made her stop with one foot poised above the landing. His long legs carelessly spread on the mattress, sandy hair ruffled against a pillow, that easy, satisfied smile on his creased handsome face, a smile she knew so well, having placed it there herself on so many occasions. But her mind was playing nasty little tricks and now she could see Greta beside him. How close they seemed. How effortlessly intimate.

She had to hold on to the banister rail, her upper body doubled over as she rammed a fist into the base of her abdomen to counteract a crippling pain. She let out a solitary cry.

'What's the matter?' Benny was standing there with his head cocked to the side.

'Nothing pet,' she said, taking a deep breath and straightening her body vertebra by vertebra. 'Just wind, I think. Go on, I'll be down in a minute, get your muesli.'

She watched the copper head bob downstairs. How could Matt even think of leaving him for an instant?

Environment, she thought, clinging to the game plan. Something to do with the environment for Benny, he would come into his own and these shaky early years would be behind him for ever. For all anyone knew — the classmates that taunted him, the teachers who discussed him with those tight supercilious smiles — it could well be Benny Wilson who would end up saving the entire damn planet. Maybe not. She put a hand to her burning forehead.

He wouldn't let her intervene any longer. She used to go regularly to the school to single out boys she *thought* were giving him a hard time. The deputy head avoided her calls after a while. She would position her car at a distance from the school gates to watch him at break time. He never seemed particularly unhappy, just solitary. One friend, she used to pray, just one good solid friend for back up. She regularly invited candidates for tea, they ended up playing with Joe. Once she lost the plot a little, stamping hard on the foot of one young girl who'd mouthed something at Benny as he passed in the schoolyard. He'd extracted a promise from his mother to keep away after that. The deputy head had a few choice words to say to her too. Matt was furious when he heard (Joe told on her). 'You have got to back off, Connie. They'll be men one day, you have to leave them to fight their own battles.' It wasn't the first time he'd shouted that.

She found the hotel brochure and went downstairs again. The memory of Matt's hollow-eyed look, his haunted expression as he closed the door to her departing taxi, was more painful in a way than any fantasies about what he might or might not be getting up to with Greta. There was something else about him, too, which had taken all her speech away right at the very end. It was a look of disconnection on the gaunt, unshaven face. He knew how much he was frightening her and it didn't stop him anyway.

She summoned her brisk, woman-in-charge-of-family voice and punched the number out, growing in resolve and determination with every press of her finger. What a ridiculous situation to put her in — having to ground her own husband. She would deliver her ultimatums but, as she would with Joe, dangling the carrot of forgiveness at the very end. It would all be just fine, her natural optimism would see them through. The receptionist who spoke perfect English informed her that Signor Wilson had checked out the previous day. No, he didn't leave a forwarding address.

In the kitchen Benny was sorting green glass from clear glass, part of his weekly recycling routine. The bottles and jars clanked horribly. Connie held on to the hall table for a moment. Her eyes closed and immediately she was hurtling through black empty space the way it used to happen when she was a child tentatively trying for sleep for the umpteenth time. Moving so fast it was making her dizzy, making her breath catch because she knew when she finally came to a stop, the darkness would come hurtling right back at her.

No no, she was not going to go *there* again. That was another Connie entirely, someone she'd left behind in Consett and long forgotten. That was the Connie who'd lost her sense of humour for a while. There was no room for her in this house.

Benny called that they were out of organic milk. She called back that she would do a proper shop on her way home from work. He'd have to make do with wholemeal toast instead of muesli, amuse himself for a while and maybe Fred might take him for a swim if he asked him nicely. She ran upstairs to change; if she got lucky she could holler her goodbye from the hall again without having to look at his sombre, trusting face.

In all the years she had tried to articulate her worries about Benny to Matt and subsequently the psychologists and so-called child experts, she had never once voiced her deepest fear. That Benny reminded her of the girl she used to be. Quietly withdrawn, a watcher, constantly in a state of foggy anxiety. Not sure if she ever fitted in, or if she could fit in. When she saw him laboriously lining up green-glass bottles or clear-glass jars or making drills of baked beans at the side of his plate, she couldn't help but think of herself lining up the endless photographs she was always taking. As if a pattern might emerge and suddenly the world that was out there and not in her head might suddenly let her in on the secret. That was how it felt, that there

was a general secret that everybody understood but her. Now that she had morphed
into the adult-lite version of herself, the last
person she wanted Benny to bring to mind
was that lonely young girl. But he did.

'Bye, Benny. Bye Byeee.'

★ ★ ★

The Alternative Card Company had started
as a bit of a joke. Neither of the women took
it seriously at first. Mary was a freelance
graphics artist at the time. She'd had a few
gallery exhibitions of her own paintings as
well and a couple of features in the
Richmond and Twickenham Times in the
'my Twickenham by prominent local artist'-
type slot. Connie had gone back to work part
time, after trying a period at home with
Benny, at a design company which had a
section that did greeting cards.

She found the work mundane and
uninspiring but the alternative was full time
plus a daily grind to London to an ad agency
full of bright young things. Besides, she'd
been at home for a couple of years and felt
certain she'd lost her edge. Thinking up corny
Valentine ditties didn't exactly require a
razor-sharp mind. They were having a laugh
about some of her more saccharine lines. To

my dearest husband — the keeper of my heart. Be mine, sweet Valentine. Love is a flame and I'm on fire.

'You didn't write that, did you?' Mary had spluttered. 'Love is a flame and I'm on fire? Dear God.'

'That's what they want. What have I been saying? You do realize if you tell anybody I'll have to kill you.'

It was a Saturday afternoon, they were sipping coffee as Mary idly doodled on a pad with watercolours. Connie looked around at the clutter so inconceivable in her own house. How Mary managed to find her paints was a mystery. She never seemed to throw anything out. There were stacks of newspapers going back years, half-finished canvases, cardboard boxes supporting crusty, dried-out palettes and numerous unwashed mugs with rings of tea scum. The entire ground floor of the small mews house was devoted to Mary's studio. The floor above contained a kitchenette, two tiny bedrooms and a cubicle bathroom. The mess was everywhere there, too. It almost filled Connie with envy.

Their talk meandered to cards in general. How trite 'with sympathy' seemed when someone had died, yet what else was there to say? Happy Christmas when invariably it was an unhappy, frazzled period for most adults but what was the harm in saying it anyway?

'There should be cards you could send to people you hate.' Connie laughed. 'Crappy Christmas and a Crappy New Year.'

'Or a picture of the grim reaper to your ex and inside — Have a good one!'

'How's this for the man who can't commit? Roses are red, violets are blue, pissy-beds are yellow and so are you.'

Mary put a splodge of yellow on her brush and in seconds there was a giant dandelion on the paper. She fiddled around until it resembled a Van Gogh sunflower. They both stepped back to look, and that was how it started.

They worked every weekend for months after that, Mary creating skewed versions of famous paintings while Connie worked on appropriate slogans. She found a local printer to make a batch of samples at a good price. They put the cards in clear plastic bags with colourful sealing labels to denote who the recipient might be. On the back was another label signalling the inside message. And then they schlepped to every upmarket and independent stationers', first in their own area until gradually they spread out to cover most of London.

Orders were slow in coming at the beginning but then a large repeat order came from a store in Knightsbridge. Aggrieved first wives had snatched up the first batch apparently. The quirky Valentines sold out that February. Another repeat order came from a shop in Kensington, misused au pairs had bought up the pithy goodbye cards for their former employers. City staff liked the puns on stocks and shares for their tyrannical bosses. Ambiguous goodbye cards for unpopular members of staff sold well in Westminster.

Each card was a limited edition, signed by Mary. They were expensive but people were tickled by the idea of sending something warped in the guise of something innocent. And what could be more innocuous than a greetings card? Happy Birthday! Happy Christmas! Bon Voyage! Congratulations! Good Luck! Get Well Soon — cardboard clichés to cover unwritten letters, unmade phone calls, door knockers unknocked. A once-a-year platitude salved a once-a-year conscience. If anything, provided the brief wasn't to go too heavy on the ascerbity, a card from the Alternative Card Company was a bit of a backhanded compliment, signalling aforethought and some not inconsiderable expense.

They expanded into song lyrics and poems, taking care that the slogan was only vaguely redolent or just had the feel of a certain well-known line without bringing them into issues of rights. Connie set up a website and individual commissions began to trickle in. Wealthy people with axes to grind. Mary began to design her own compositions, entirely bespoke one-offs. They could charge hundreds for those.

A Sicilian woman contacted them, she wanted something for the ex-husband who had dumped her for a piece of fluff. It turned out that he was big in the local mafia and had reneged on their private, unspoken agreement that she would turn a blind eye to his leching provided he never turned a blind eye to their marriage. She was a big woman, spitting fury. She wanted a goodbye card for their decree nisi, something faintly threatening, something he would understand implicitly, just enough to worry him. Mary came up with an all black card save for one small white, luminous dot in the middle. It brought to mind the fading light on an old-fashioned turned-off television, or it could have been a spirit travelling towards the light. Inside Connie came up with one word: *Ciao*. They deliberated over adding an exclamation mark but the woman wanted it to keep it plain. Ciao. Let him look over his shoulder after that.

There were other women, the occasional

man, too. Connie and Mary would sometimes become enmeshed in their personal life histories and often kept in touch with many of them. It was nice when people let go of their bitterness and rang or called in to say they'd moved on. Often it seemed in hindsight that the commissioning of the card was the catalyst for that move. It signalled closure.

It wasn't all despair and angst. There were happy assignments as well, barmitzvahs and weddings, birthdays and anniversaries, people wanting to say things in a different way.

There was enough money coming in after a year for Connie to give up her part-time work. Mary concentrated on the cards and her own private paintings, gradually allowing her freelance graphics to dwindle to nothing. The company was able to support two salaries plus their overheads and they were happy with that. There weren't any plans to go global, after all. Besides, Mary was habitually more at ease with sufficiency rather than largesse: too much, and her Catholic guilt struck up with the persistent tick of a metronome. For a person with a very cluttered home, she had a remarkably uncluttered mind, Connie often thought with admiration. For her own part there were shadowy pockets in her head she didn't dare explore for fear of tripping over old, long discarded bric-a-brac.

⋆ ⋆ ⋆

The second day of Matt's absence passed with Connie trying extremely hard to push him, if only for those working hours, into a corner of her brain to join the rest of the bric-a-brac. There was a comfortable silence in the studio as Mary worked on a pastiche Constable landscape and Connie got on with orders and invoices and bills to be paid. She handled all the office side of things.

'You're white as a sheet,' Mary said now, looking at Connie from under her lashes. 'Didn't you sleep last night?'

'I told you that first thing when I got here this morning. Somebody's not listening.'

Connie busily shunted a pile of papers into a file. She gave Mary a droll look to soften that harsh last note which had crept into her voice despite her best efforts. You couldn't afford so much as a stumble with Mary, she'd be in there like a shot. It was very unlikely she'd missed the fixed, overcheerful smile on Connie's lips as she answered the phone all morning, or the deep sighs that involuntarily rumbled up from her belly once she'd checked her mobile phone for messages, or the lack of, as it happened.

'Any word of Matt?' Mary asked.

'Sorry?'

'Last night, did you get to speak with him? Any better idea how long he's going to be?'

'A few days maybe.' Connie pulled her mouth down to show it really wasn't something she was thinking about, to tell the truth.

'What's happening with his patients? It's so unlike him to leave them in the lurch. All that rescheduling, I'm surprised at Matt really, people take time off to get to the dentist.'

'Well *tough*.'

Connie bit her lip. Mary turned with her palette knife suspended in midair.

'I'm only saying,' she said.

'Since when did Matt's patients bother you anyway?' Connie tried to inject a note of mild exasperation coupled with amused tolerance at her friend's busybody ways. It was an ambitious mix to attempt and she failed miserably. Now, she just sounded cranky and Mary was sucking her teeth, a sure sign she sensed something was up.

'I think I'll finish early today,' Connie said. 'There's a shop needs doing, and things.'

'Okay doke.'

'And Mary?'

'Hmm?'

'I think I might take a sleeping tablet early tonight. You know, catch up.'

'Okay doke.' A little pause. 'I wasn't planning on coming round this evening in any case. William's up in London.' William was Mary's part-time lover. A horrible little schnit of a man, to Connie's mind, whose wife understood him only too well. Mary didn't seem to care for him all that much either but he was company, she said, from time to time.

'Well, that's me then.' Connie jangled her car keys. She dithered by the desk for a second, hoping Mary would ask the questions she obviously wanted to ask, hoping that she wouldn't. She felt a spurt of love for the back of her friend's head, the paint streaks, the wild hair; why couldn't everyone be more like her — content with whatever came along — why the complications, the unnecessary self-erected obstacles placed on the path to happiness? 'Right,' she added, slapping the pockets of her jeans for no particular reason, the keys were already in her hand.

Mary was craning around, eyebrows up expectantly. Connie opened her mouth then clamped it shut again. It was pathetic, even with your best friend, someone you'd entrust with your children's lives, there was a role you played. There was the Connie she'd moulded over the years. Mother of three boys, wife to

110

their father, sister, daughter. You gritted your teeth, you went on, you got up each day, you put your clothes and mascara and lipstick on, you said 'Fine thanks and you?' If you lost that self, the one you'd made, there was no knowing who you might find to replace you.

'Forgotten something?' Mary asked.

'What? Oh just doing my shopping list in my head.'

Mary, she wanted to say, how unhappy d'you think Matt's been lately? Have you noticed anything different, has he said something to you? He has a respectable career, he has three lovely kids, he has me, he has our dream house. He has, in fact, everything I've ever wanted.

Am I bad? she wanted to ask. Am I bad but somehow assumed I was good?

When he comes home, she thought, we'll sell up, we'll buy a farm in Durham, near his father maybe, we'll make love every day and grow things. Marrows and things. Drugs mightn't be such a temptation up there for the boys, they'll meet nice down-to-earth girls who know how to make blackberry jam. Matt will be in his element walking his land each evening. We'll go to church and exchange pleasantries afterwards with people the way they do on vicar sitcoms. Huge Sunday lunches to cook with Louis Armstrong crooning 'We have all the time in the world' in the large farmhouse kitchen filled with sedimenty aromas of beef and gravy. Animated chatter with their new closest friends around the traditional solid oak table, heads thrown back in mid-laughter, not a grunt or a burp or a solitary sarcastic put-down.

'See you,' she said to Mary, swinging the strap of her bag over her shoulder. She would paint the farmhouse kitchen the colour of egg yolk and fill it with jam jars of primroses in spring. Already she was decorating a candy-stripe future in bold, primary strokes, really — she couldn't imagine any other way it might be done.

They would all be happy. It was entirely possible.

5

Greta took Matt to Tivoli, a lively town on a hill about twenty kilometres from Rome, to show him the house where she used to live. That was the first surprise of the day. He'd just assumed she'd always lived in Rome. The second surprise was the size of the villa. Set in a residential area, a good walk from the centre of town, the white three-storey building was an elaborate affair with long casement windows and an arched mahogany double-doored entrance. High wrought-iron gates protected the house from the street. There were two cars parked in the drive, one was a Maserati. It was the fourth day of Matt's absence from his home, his life.

They stood at the opposite side of a wide, poplar-lined avenue, looking across. Greta seemed to be at pains not to be seen. Her eyes scoured every window though most were shuttered to keep out the midday sun.

'It used to be yellow,' she said. 'Yellow with white shutters. All white now,' she added thoughtfully as if he couldn't see.

'When were you last here?'

'Two years, roughly.' She shrugged. 'I

walked out once we'd buried Sandro. That was it.'

'How did he die? Are you going to tell me?' Matt reached out to touch her cheek but she turned her head away abruptly. His hand hovered for a moment batting air until he allowed it to fall. Whatever she would tell him, he knew instinctively that it wouldn't be the truth. Not the whole truth at least. It was one of her traits that used to infuriate, exasperate and excite him all at the same time. 'Of course I love you,' she'd say when he pressed down on her, forcing the admission, then the crooked smile, ' — at least I think so.'

She told him she loved his dog, Ed, a simple, useless mutt more of a hindrance on the farm than anything else but Matt had raised him from a puppy. Ed went everywhere with them until Matt noticed one day that the dog didn't follow them around any more if Greta was there. If she approached him, he loped off towards the house, looking for Stanley presumably. The reason became apparent some months along when Matt caught her kicking him. She laughed, her eyes sparkling with delicious spite when he remonstrated. How could anyone want to hurt poor old Ed? There never was a more inoffensive, bumbling creature. It was the first

114

time he'd wanted to strike her and make love to her and pull her hair really hard.

Looking at her deciding how much to respond to his question, made his hand itch to claw a handful of her hair, twist it in his fist, force her head back — for a moment he felt nauseous with desire. She was capable of such petty cruelty, for no other reason than her own amusement. Cruel and beautiful, she was like looking at the sun.

'If it's too painful for you,' he began in a voice so steady he could hardly believe it belonged to him.

'Of course it's too painful.' Her head snapped up. 'He died in a fire. That's why the house is white now. I couldn't get to him on time. Let's go. It was a mistake — a mistake.'

She moved to stride past him. Matt's hand snaked out and caught her hair, he tugged so hard he could feel follicles loosen their grip. She tried to pull away but he twisted harder, drawing her close.

'Greta, why did you bring me here?'

Her head gave an almost imperceptible shake, she stopped resisting, burying closer into his chest.

'I don't know. I thought — maybe I thought you could help.' The brittleness of her affected him. She had been fickle, ephemeral, moods carrying through a smoky laugh from worldly scepticism to girlish frippery on the length of a cigarette, never brittle, never vulnerable.

'I'm trying to help,' he said. 'Little things, I don't know what else to do.'

For the last few days he'd cooked for her, tidied the apartment, ran her bath, monitored her medication. She was down to one sleeping pill a night, two Prozacs by day. When she went to work he wandered the streets of Rome, wondering if he was going mad. If a sudden lightning bolt of insanity had struck that first moment he'd clapped eyes on Greta in the American Bar. There couldn't be any other explanation. Unless, of course he was quite simply a heartless shit, much to his own surprise. Certainly it was excessively callous behaviour towards the family he loved, completely at odds with the man he would have once considered himself to be. The more he tried to analyse what he was doing, the more confused he ended up. There was nothing in his past, no bench-marks to look back upon to say, yes, that might have been a telling moment presaging the cruel shit to come. It had been a steady life. He had been a steady son, husband, father. So who was this Matt? For the world, he couldn't come up with a solitary credible answer.

Yesterday, he'd walked for hours, seeing nothing, lost in his thoughts, imagining Connie's face, his sons. He'd lifted the handset of a public phone, inserted coins and listened to his wife's voice say that she was sorry there was nobody in to take his call. When he tried to speak, just a sob broke from his lips and he quickly replaced the phone. Stood there, shaking and sobbing like a baby. Like a goddamn baby.

He'd gone back to Greta's apartment, packed his weekend holdall and sat there waiting for the turn of her key in the door. When she walked in with a childlike smile, eager to see him, and saw that he was preparing to leave, the smile faded but only a little. 'Of course you must go. Of course you must.' She'd gone directly to her bedroom, perhaps to wait for the definitive click of the door signalling his departure. Instead he'd followed her, covering the distance between them in a few long strides to kiss her for the first time since they'd lain as teenagers together. The taste of her was exactly as he remembered. Such a soft, velvety texture at odds with the jangly creature she'd become.

They stretched out on the bed while he stroked her hair and murmured her name. It was the only thing that made sense. It seemed to him at that moment, just before she fell asleep, that it had been playing like a mantra somewhere in the deepest corner of his brain for all the years they'd lived separate lives. She had no idea, no more than he, that he'd kept her, growing older within him alongside his own viscera, an incubus he wanted to punish and nurture all at once. Greta Parker, such an electric, dangerous girl — a turbine of contradictions invoking in him a reciprocity of contradictory responses. It hurt him to see her so tamed. Through the night he held her and wanted her and wanted to be free of her, all at the same time.

Then this morning, he'd walked into the bathroom while she was showering. He was fully clothed. She blinked but didn't say anything. The soap glided under her armpit, along the contour of her breast accentuating tiny, silvery stretchmarks around the dark erect nipple. Down to her stomach which was almost concave, she was so thin. She rubbed shampoo into her hair, allowing the force of the water to wash it through. His eyes travelled to the triangle of hair between her thighs, there was grey mixed with oily auburn, the thick gleaming hairs matched her striking eyebrows. He stepped under the heavy spray of water, holding her from behind, crossing his hands over her wet, silky breasts. He couldn't remember when he felt

118

so hard. She pressed back against him allowing her body to stand limply receptive while his hands slid down her waist and buttocks, fingers burrowing through the crack of her thighs until they plunged into wet, slippery darkness, again and again until she uttered a cry and her breasts shuddered. He licked the side of her neck, she tasted of lemon. They stood for a long time, not saying a word as water ricocheted from their mutually bent heads, beating down across their shoulders to trickle through Matt's fingers once more splayed over Greta's breasts. They were completely lost he realized — nothing would ever be normal again.

★　★　★

Now, they were standing outside a place which had once represented normality to her. Her face was pressed against his chest, as though if she could get inside there might be something approaching peace. Without realizing what he was doing his fingertips were tracing a lumpy line of old scar tissue along the back of her scalp, it snaked all the way down to a hollow at the base of her neck. Residue from a bicycle crash that had left her for dead. Another crash and she certainly would be the doctors had warned: her head had become a fragile place destined to be eggshell frangible in tiny vulnerable sections for the rest of her life. He let loose his grip on her hair and a few silky threads remained twisted around his fingers. They floated away on a single breeze.

'All right?' he asked. She nodded, reminding him of a child rendered malleable and languid after a crying jag.

'I always thought you were too good for me.' She stepped back giving him a lopsided smile, she was mocking herself. 'Remember that twenty pound note? Twenty *poond*, man. We all thought you were daft. I'd have kept it in a shot.'

A laugh caught him by surprise. That damn twenty pounds, how well she remembered it, his moment in Gethsemane battling a thorny conscience. The first time he'd had to measure natural wholesome greed against his father's face. It was a lot of money in those days to find frittering in the gutter outside the local post office. Matt had picked it up, looking around, sensing a practical joke. Back at the farm he told Stanley and Greta, who were elated wanting their cut. Later, he'd said. Tomorrow, he'd promised. Under his pillow it remained flattened into dried-flower crispness for a week. Two years before, his father, Arthur Wilson, had been made redundant. He hadn't worked since. There was talk of the Company Works closing down, rumours spread like liquid paraffin just waiting for the match. Batches of men were being let go in the steady dripdown towards ultimate decline. Matt knew in his blood as much as in his heart that the note he'd found belonged to a dole packet. Counting fingers, a whip of wind, somebody's tea not on the table by the end of the week. He imagined how his father would feel, can't keep a job, can't keep the paltry substitute.

After a week he went to the post office and handed in the note. As it happened a man he knew, who had once worked alongside Arthur, had told the clerk of his loss, not expecting reparation in a thousand light years, simply so that he could tell his wife that he had informed him. Informing a bloke with a job of his own impotence, an irate wife would insist. The man told Matt's father, who came to his son with a peculiarly rigid smile and damp eyes.

Good though? It wasn't a word he would have applied to himself in particular. Certainly, he tried to live a reasonably honourable life, no more no less than the next man he would have thought. He had acquired a set of morals but then people did, just to survive. Perhaps he was as good as the tests that had come his way thus far. He didn't like to point out that if he were really a man of virtue, then what was he doing here with her?

Though in a vague way, in an as yet not fully formed thought, he understood that there was something else, perhaps that was what she meant — he had, without thinking, adopted responsibility for her, much as he had with Connie since the day she'd fixed him with rounded, tentative eyes. 'It could be me then, could it?' She was fifteen, part of the fixtures and fittings of the farm for years. He'd never looked at her in that light until the day, a year after Greta's sudden eclipse, she'd awkwardly reached up on her toes to kiss his cheek and instinctively he'd moved his lips on to hers. He was lonely, more than that, it was something akin to grief and Connie was warm and uncomplicated, the ardour of her kiss surprised him. Why yes, it could be her, someone to make happy. But good? Well, he might have described himself as tall.

His thoughts were interrupted by a car coming through the gates of the house next to Greta's. She immediately stepped to the side of Matt so she would not be seen. All colour had drained from her oval face, she looked spectral. The long black car passed and her eyes followed for the longest time.

'Somebody you — ', Matt began to ask.

'Please. Let's go, Matt. Please,' she said. This time he allowed her to walk away.

★ ★ ★

Greta remained silent and withdrawn once they returned to her apartment. She poured a large whisky and sat by the window with her head turned to the side. Matt tried to ignore the pills she was popping at regular intervals but he was growing concerned that she had lost track. When she absently thumb-clicked the pill dispenser for a fourth time, he swiped it from her hand.

'No more, Greta. You could easily overdose.'

She seemed to think that was amusing, a crooked smile split one cheek but quickly faded. Instead she appeared angry.

'You know they're a low dosage. Give me my pills, Matt. I know how much I can take in a night.'

'Some night you might forget.' He moved towards her seated figure and placed a hand on her shoulder. 'Talk to me about Sandro. Tell me about him.'

Her face turned away further from him, fingers scrabbling in a packet of cigarettes. She dropped one which he picked up and put

123

between her lips. He had to hold it steady to give her a light, her mouth was trembling so hard. She inhaled deeply.

'I can't,' she said after she'd considered for a long time. 'I just can't. Not tonight.' Her voice dropped so low he had to strain to hear. 'I know he's gone. I do know. That I'll never ever — ' A hand drew down the length of her face. 'Just give me my pills, Matt.' She lunged but he held them out of reach.

'No.'

'Give them to me!'

'No.' He shoved them into his jeans pocket and pressed her back into the chair, kneeling before her with his hands on her thighs. 'Greta, Greta. This is no way to live. You can't just seclude yourself from the rest of the world.'

'Why not?'

Because — what could he say in truth? Whatever she did, nothing was going to make her feel better. It wasn't anything on the same level but when his mother had died a few years ago, while the grief was at its sharpest in the early days, he had found some solace in work, in the everyday routine of family life. Aside from work, Greta was almost a recluse.

'You were always a social creature.'

'People change. Or things change them,' she said flatly. Of a sudden she was angry again, her face twisted and her thighs made a jerking motion for him to remove his hands but he kept them in place. It was difficult to tell if her mood swings were a reaction to seeing her old house earlier or the drugs. Possibly a combination of both. 'You don't have the right to tell me how to live,' she snapped. 'Why don't you call your wife? Your family must be demented with worry. What kind of behaviour do you call that?'

He took it on the chin because she was profoundly right. 'Cruel and selfish behaviour,' he responded with a grimace. 'Turns out it's much easier than I thought.'

'I never had any difficulty in those departments,' she said. He could feel the limp fade of her anger. At times he thought he was looking at the husk of a human being and the prospect of leaving her like this made his heart contract.

'I got through to the answering machine yesterday,' he said. 'Couldn't speak. I don't know what to think to be perfectly honest. What to make of myself. Don't know if this is the real me, someone I've been masking all my life. Or just a cheap excuse for a break with reality. Some penny annie midlife breakdown — Christ, how I used to despise men like that, looking to be young again, chasing their youth. Maybe I'll take up wearing a ponytail next. Get myself a big shiny Harley. Nothing would surprise me now. It could be all or none of those things. Or maybe — '

'What?'

'Maybe it's you.'

She turned her head from the window and looked at him then. I love her, he thought. So that's it. Very simple really. I've always loved her. Would be with her now if she hadn't run away. Dear God, what use was that information to him now? What use to his family, to Greta herself for that matter? There was no comfort in the first clear, unambiguous thought he'd managed to form in the last few days. No comfort at all. But there was a burst of joy he found himself unable to tamp down.

Looking at the evening light slide across Greta's shiny hair, turning it rust then mahogany, the way her teeth bit into pink lower lip, the blue pockets of shadow beneath inscrutable grey eyes — there was nothing about Greta that he did not want.

'Is it me?' she asked.

'Yes, you.'

He couldn't say more because where would that leave them? He couldn't tell her that, yes, it was her he wanted, very much yes. All day he'd had to wrap his arms around this new

126

strange body of his, shuddering with desire for a woman other than his wife. He couldn't tell her that she'd invaded his existence so that when he wasn't in the apartment inhaling her scent, breathing in the white cotton shift she'd casually tossed across a pillow, he was suspended in a fog of opportunities lost, melancholy half-formed longings, as if there was a persistent echo of musical notes from both their pasts conjoining them now. Because if he tried to explain he would end up making love to her and then he would have to leave her. He had a family, it was not within his canon to make his life less. She was vulnerable, he hadn't realized that so, too, was he.

Slowly, they began to talk of other things. Subjects they could explore without causing pain, people, what had happened to them. They began to empty their memory banks of stored trivia, the landscape of Consett threading through their reminiscences like a slow, polluted river. She told him of her years in London, she'd worked in a topless bar, leaning forward as she served drinks from a phallic-shaped tray, to increase her tips. She played it for him and they laughed. There was a modelling stint, topless again, of course, though she wouldn't go any further. He suspected she was lying though he had to chuckle when she re-enacted those poses as well. Greta had always been as good at sending herself up as she had been other people.

He made her another very diluted whisky and poured a stiff measure for himself as she smoked and told him about the early years in Italy. She'd met her future husband in an Italian restaurant she was managing at the time in London. Of a sudden, she grew animated, leaping up to ransack a collection of CD's piled in a loose heap in one corner of the room. He noticed that she'd stopped asking for the pills. They listened to Jimi Hendrix on 'All Along The Watchtower', Creedence Clearwater Revival's 'Lookin' Out My Back Door' — Jimmy Buffet, Robert Johnson, Leonard Cohen — their music collection was practically identical until he it came to him that it was he who had informed her tastes in the first place. It was his own catalogue he was listening to. That made him smile, she had no idea. Next to sex, or possibly equal to, music was the intercourse of teenagers. Listen to this, she said, I love this — an obscure Neil Young he'd played for her over and over again on the huge, unwieldy cassette recorder in the farm kitchen.

The night drew down as they alternated

listening with rapid bursts of speech between music selections. In those moments she looked like she might explode with talk, busy hands weaving shapes, tapping air. The electric girl of his memory. At one point stopping to draw a breath, tucking hair behind her ear, she looked at him and a thin spray of complicity passed between them, of the steady thunking from chimney stacks, of bike wheels whirring through a smoky afternoon, of sodden vinegary newspaper holding fish and chips, of pink powdery snow besmirched by warm exhalations from foundries, of fingers and arms and thighs twisting into one unimpeachable knot — of remembered love. I know you and you know me, still, this is true. Matt leaned forward cupping her face gently to kiss her mouth. Before they pulled apart again, they poured their longing and sadness into the kiss, what might have been, what wasn't, what can't ever be.

As Robert Johnson struggled with his 'Cross Road Blues', Matt wondered what would become of her once he went. As though reading his thoughts she told him that she had been thinking about returning to London. She checked his reaction and when he didn't say anything she nodded, deep in thought, yes, maybe that's what she would do.

While his back was turned changing the

music, he sensed a limpness come over her again. He glanced over and saw that she was struggling with tears.

'You're worried that if you speak with her, you'll have to go,' she said in a flat voice, adding, 'I suppose you can't run away from your conscience for ever,' though she made it sound like a question. He didn't respond. 'It was good — you, here — but you have a life to go back to. Connie, your boys. They must be missing you so much.'

Matt swallowed what felt like a boulder, he saw his sons faces racked up in front of him, their innocent incomprehension. He wondered what Connie was doing right this minute, if she would ever forgive him. Would he forgive her if circumstances were reversed?

'Phone her.' She reached for the handset. 'I don't want to be that kind of bitch. Call her before I ask you to stay.'

The object rested between them, a slim black challenge. Punch the numbers and he could be transported back to a life without self-recrimination, a purity born of numbness, of going on because he was halfway there already, might as well see it through, the faint sense of ridiculousness he felt each time he shrugged into his dental whites, of Connie's infectious giggle and his sons' implacable belief in their father and their

130

father's devotion. He'd made them; somewhere along the line, he should have explained that life was insanely complicated. That striving to be good didn't necessarily equate with doing good. That murkiness was everywhere in everything and the simple ABC tenets of childhood didn't amount to a crock of moondust.

'Would you ask me to stay?'

She stared out of the window, a nimbus of gold streetlight delineating a cameo profile. The cigarette tip glowed hot and fierce when she took a long suck. He realized she was engaged in an internal debate, slight shake of head changing her mind about something, lips compressing over the cigarette once more. Evidently she'd decided to hold her tongue. Both arms crossed her midriff, holding herself in.

'Greta?'

Her eyes squeezed shut as if suddenly stung.

'What d'you want me to say, Matt? That I regret the whole of my life — that I should have stayed with you? That you would have made me happy — though I don't think I would have made you happy. I hardly ever thought of you. That's the truth.' Opening eyes swivelled in his direction gauging his reaction, whites refracting amber light.

Briefly, he found himself suffused with the old rage at her betrayal. He could have struck her, yes, a woman. What did that make of him? He'd nearly lost his mind to rage the year after Greta left. Using any girl in town that allowed him. Walking away, zipping up without a backward glance, loaded with contempt for their affected cries and mewls, hating them and him for the movie magic pretence; whatever way you looked at it, against a factory wall a shag was a shag. He launched out on Friday nights looking for a shag or a fight, whatever, any communication of touch would do. Until Connie sheared him with her innocence.

A mercenary thought flitted like a light singed moth — fuck her, just fuck this woman and have done with it. What do you know of her, who is she now after all these years, she wants it, you want it, so what? If only it could be that simple, a trying-to-be-good man doing something other people might deem wrong, no big deal in the weft of things, a surrender to instincts, to passion — that cheap novella word he loathed.

No, it wasn't about a spurious passion — what was earnest and true once would be the same again and then he would have to leave his wife, his children; he understood that with prismal clarity. What do we love

132

when we think we love, he thought. Greta was riddled with flaws, as he was, as anyone was, maybe it was that, perhaps we fell in love with the flawed, ever hopeful, ever lonesome, humanity within ourselves.

He realized that she was about to continue and that he should stop her but somewhere buried in his subconscious he'd been waiting all these years to hear these words.

'But when you walked across the bar towards me the other day,' Greta was saying, 'you know what I thought? — instantly, without even a second's hesitation — I thought *fuck*, I've lived the wrong life. Imagine that? How simple. I've lived the wrong life.'

She gazed out of the window again, reliving the potency of the moment. 'There was so much I wanted back then, you can't know when you're a kid that you might already have what you need. I wasn't bullshitting when I said you were good. You are. Kind and honourable and just plain old-fashioned good. It wasn't a commodity I was interested in then. I wanted flash, lies, pretend thrills. But Connie saw the man you'd become so she deserves you. That's all really. That's all I have to say. We can't live lives other than the ones we've lived.'

A rueful smile and she was transformed

into the old Greta, the 17-year-old, clicking her scarlet-tipped fingers, blowing smoke rings within smoke rings already formed by the perfect circle of her mouth. A girl dancing backwards in a blue cotton frock. Full of bristling impatience to get out there and hunt down what the world might have to offer. Whatever she might say, she still carried that girl inside her as he carried the boy within him.

'Soon, I'll go,' he said, 'soon — but not yet.'

6

Connie's heart plunged when she saw the crowded aisles of the supermarket. The shop was going to take twice the time she'd allowed. There was absolutely nothing in the house to eat, so the boys had been saying, growing in stridency over the past few days. At first she avoided their plaintive cries by pretending to be swamped at work, she avoided Mary by pretending to be sick, then she avoided everyone by really managing to get sick enough to buy a couple of days closeted in her room with the curtains drawn so they wouldn't notice her puffy face.

After a week she told Fred that his father had called that morning while he was in school and would try to ring later that night but it was difficult to make phone calls at night. She couldn't think of an explanation as to why it should be difficult so she just shrugged that one off — 'He didn't say.' And he didn't leave the number of this new hotel he'd moved to, either. Fred had taken to giving her long searching looks. She wouldn't be surprised if he suspected murder.

To Mary she said that Matt had moved on

to Budapest to a *twin* conference, but not to tell Fred. She couldn't think of an explanation for that coda either and where Budapest came from, she had no idea. Maybe she'd got a postcard once.

To the dental surgery, she said that Doctor's condition had deteriorated, he was in great pain from that clip by the tram, sorry bus, and wasn't fit to travel. He wasn't fit to speak on the phone either but she'd be happy to pass any messages if they wanted. It turned out that they most emphatically wanted to pass messages. She wrote them down with painstaking attention, which patient required which treatment and who was it again was having trouble with his right molar? The second she put down the phone, the messages were thrown in the bin which was placed beside it now for that sole purpose. When they rang back for responses she said that Matt was having difficulties with his concentration levels, all patients should be postponed until further notice and any in severe pain should see Martin. Or some other dentist.

She slung a bumper pack of oranges into the trolley and thought about what she might say to Stanley if he called again looking for his brother. Did he get the bus or tram or conference or Eastern European story? She couldn't remember. This was the eighth day of Matt's absence and not a word. A part of her hoped he was dead because if he wasn't, he deserved to be.

Apples, two melons which Fred loved, kiwi fruit excellent for vitamin C. A lemon for gin and tonics excellent for getting drunk.

It was the smell of Matt she missed the most. His musky scent in the bed beside her each morning. Hands massaging her breasts lazily, making up his mind if he wanted the full works or just a grope. She had always wanted him even through their worst rows — she could never get enough of him.

For some reason she couldn't fathom, when she wasn't brooding on his absence these last few days in particular, she couldn't get that taxi driver and his dead wife, Linda, out of her mind. She invented a whole life for Linda, gave her a wardrobe, a set of pearls and an emerald ring with a cluster of tiny, crystalline diamonds, she could see that ring with X-ray precision. She gave them children and named them Bob and Sue. She imagined Linda's blue bedroom then redecorated it in cooking apple green, they discussed the duvet cover at great length and settled on a muted sage with a narrow stripe of cream down by the bottom. Yesterday, they'd made pastry together, and this time, Linda got it exactly right. It hurt, almost unbearably, when she realized that she would never get the chance to meet her now. Linda was gone, unimportant and gone.

Giant lumps of cheese, mild cheddar and extra mature for Joe, he liked any food with a tang, he could eat whole red chillies without so much as a blink. What next — yoghurts, little pots of fromage frais, big tubs of ready-made custard for Benny, he ate it straight from the pot. Meat, at some point she must get meat, pork chops, a chicken, sausages, veggie sausages, pork chops, burgers, veggie burgers, thin steak for ciabatta sandwiches, pork chops. God she loathed shopping. She used to have dreams of driving them all to a pump attached to a supermarket, filling them up for the week like petrol.

Cereal, crates of sweet pap, she didn't need to bother with Matt's special muesli. Perhaps he didn't bother eating muesli anyway these mornings, perhaps he was too busy eating Greta.

The endlessness of shopping, the repetition, stacking the trolley higher and higher, emptying it at the checkout, filling bags, putting bags in trunk of car, taking out from trunk of car, emptying bags into fridge and freezer and cupboards. Looking in fridge and freezer and cupboards two days later and there was her shopping — like Linda — gone. Back to supermarket, mild cheddar for Fred and Benny, extra mature for Joe because he likes things with a tang. Pork chops.

The first time she laid eyes on Matt it was raining.

'Can I get at the sausages please?' a woman asked by the chilled meat section. Connie's trolley was blocking access and clearly had been for some time, there was a number of people backed up waiting to get at sausages.

'Pardon?' Connie glanced up realizing too late that her face was streaked with tracks of black mascara. 'Of course you can,' she added, moving the trolley. The woman shifted her weight from foot to foot, she bit her lip.

'Are you all right?' she asked.

'Of course I am.' Connie beamed. She lined up her full trolley beside the chilled cabinet, patted her shoulder bag, twice, and walked away.

It was dusk, the streetlights were coming on. Connie was eleven, about to start secondary school. She was on her way home with bags of shopping for her mother. Tucked in a shop doorway sheltering from the rain were Matt and Greta. She knew Greta well enough, she lived in the next row of houses along, they'd played skipping on the street together in a large gang of girls when Greta was younger.

Matt was sitting on his bike, a great hairy lump of a dog by his ankles. Both the dog and Greta were looking up at him. He was laughing. She noticed his big white teeth. Sandy hair he wore straight and long, curled wet against the dark upturned collar of his jacket. He had big ears, too, that stuck out through the hair. He had kind, shy eyes with deep hoods that cut into deep laughter lines even back then. Brown she thought but couldn't tell for certain, they danced liquidly in the dim light. It was a full nicely shaped mouth holding those big teeth. She would have bet anything that he'd grown to fit his smile, that once it might have been too large for his face. He was tall and lean with straight, jutting-out shoulders. His hand reached up, curving around the back of her neck to pull Greta's head closer, it was a long kiss. Even on the telly Connie had never witnessed one quite so passionate. She looked around in embarrassment. Was it all right to kiss like that in a shop doorway?

Greta straightened, she swept her long wet hair over one shoulder. She tripped away from him, dancing backwards, wagging a finger in a teasing gesture. Connie noticed he stayed motionless for a while watching her progress down the street until she'd rounded the corner. With a start, Connie realized that she herself had been standing still for a long time. She moved just as he did, their paths crossed in the centre of the road. One of her bags of shopping fell and he swung a hand down from the bike to give it back to her. He was smiling but his eyes were looking over her shoulder. He was cycling away with the dog loping after the wheels of the bike, barking with sheer exhilaration. She should have said thanks. She should have said something. There was a track on the road where the rubber from his wheels cut through the rain. She looked at that until a car angrily honked her to the other side.

★ ★ ★

Joe was trying to browbeat Benny out of his turn with the remote control in the living room. Connie had to negotiate a passage through the pile up of coats, shoes, rucksacks and what was that buried under a hoodie at the foot of the stairs? Oh, Joe's skateboard, perfectly positioned for someone's quick skid into a waiting ambulance.

'What are you? Loser. *Loos-err*. There isn't even anything on you want to watch, you just want your turn. Baby wants his turn. What if

I take it off you, gonna cry baby?'

'Stop it, Joe,' Connie said in a weary voice, stepping into the room. Fred stepped in right after her, he was shadowing her so hard these days that she'd turned around a couple of times and actually bumped into him.

'Fred, will you please stop creeping up behind me like that.'

'What? Can't I walk into a room?'

'Mum — did you get some food?' Benny asked. He didn't say 'something to eat' or ask if she'd got anything nice as he usually did, things were getting pretty basic now. They were looking for food.

'Actually Benny, I didn't. We'll get another takeaway tonight.'

Joe was up and out of his sprawled position on the sofa with a howl of outrage. He even forgot to put on his fake cockney accent.

'What the hell is going on around here? You go to the supermarket and come back with nothing. Zilch. Tell me you really didn't come back with nothing.'

'Zilch.'

'Mum, the problem is for me, I can't eat most of the takeaway stuff,' Benny said in a plaintive voice. He was right, she felt sorry for him. He could have beans on toast.

Fred's pupils were pulsing like strobe lighting in a disco.

'This can't go on,' he said in that middle-aged tone he adopted when he was at his most disgusted. She waited for the word 'disgrace', it couldn't be far off. 'Just look at this place,' he continued, waving a hand at the filth of the room, the one room she'd always managed to keep pristine. He was working up to a right lather. 'We've been on takeaways and toast for the last week. There isn't a clean school shirt between us. Have you seen the wash-basket upstairs? Well, no, you can't because there's clothes piled high to the ceiling. You haven't even opened the post. There could be *important stuff* in that post. Don't you care? The phone could be cut off any minute for all we know. You missed my parent-teacher meeting yesterday afternoon. I was sat there waiting through every appointment, you might've told me you weren't coming — '

'Was that yesterday?'

'Yeah, it bloody was.'

Joe and Benny were sitting back to let Fred get on with what he did best. They gave little grunts of approval, however. There was nothing better than a good bollocking from Fred if it wasn't directed at yourself. Connie sighed and rolled her eyes.

'Excuse me? What's the sigh for? The big rolling your eyes? We have rights, you know.

We didn't ask to be born. We didn't ask for
— Don't cry. Please don't cry. Okay, what we
could do here is this, I'll take on the washing,
Joe here can do a small shop — '

'I won't know what to — ' Joe's angry
protest was stifled quickly.

'We'll do a list. A *list* moron. You know
what a list is? Right, where was I? Okay,
Benny — you clear up the hall and we can
take it in turns to cook for a few nights.'

'I'm only doing veggie things,' Benny shot
in firmly.

'That's fine.' Fred flexed his jaw and
rubbed a finger around the neck of his school
shirt. Truly he would be a Colossus striding
back and forth across the courtroom. He
would strike terror into recalcitrant defen-
dants and lazy, sloppy judges alike.

'All sounds great Fred, make it so,' she said
after Captain Picard in *Star Trek the Next
Generation*. 'It's just for a few days, until
your father gets home.'

'That's the next subject — '

'Mum, where *is* Dad?' Benny asked,
advancing to the heart of the matter with a
speed she couldn't deflect. They weren't
stupid, her sons, for God's sake. Their father
was missing for eight days without a word,
the same father who had never stayed away at
any conference anywhere before. Who might

144

have spent, at most, a night or two in Consett visiting his father without them. There was no food, the place was a tip, her face was a constant black and white minstrel show, she wasn't checking homework or that vitamin supplements had been taken, the telly was on night and day, there wasn't even toilet paper.

'Budapest,' she said. 'I have to go upstairs now boys. I may be some time.'

She could hear Fred's strangled tones as she fled. 'What the hell is he doing there? It's a bloody *disgrace* is what it is.'

★   ★   ★

Connie continued to turn pages of her old photo album, humming quietly under her breath in a valiant attempt to drown out the pounding insistence of Mary on her bedroom door.

'C'mon Connie,' she bellowed. 'I know you're not asleep. This has gone on long enough. We've all tiptoed around you waiting for the truth but we've had enough.'

Tiptoed, Mary? Connie didn't think so, though she had been remarkably restrained by her standards. There was only the tiniest semblance of a gulp at Budapest.

'Connie? Fred's called me over here. He wants a family conference.'

145

A family conference? How exactly were they going to have that without Matt?

'And Connie? He wants to know where you've buried the body.'

Okay, that was better.

'C'mon darling. You've got three frightened boys downstairs. Open up. I've brought a lasagne and two bottles of that Rioja you like, I'm holding a glass right now — it smells like a sewer, filthy little beast.'

That did it.

'Mary, I just can't talk about it,' Connie said opening the door to yank the glass from Mary's puckered lips.

'Well, I *know*.'

'He'll be home in a few days and I just don't want anything blown out of proportion. We have lives, Mary. Lives we'll have to get back to once this — this episode is over.

'Of course.'

'It's just — if I talk about it, things might be true that aren't true at all.'

'*I know*, darling.'

'What? What do you know?'

'That whatever you're saying is right.'

'Maybe I'm wrong.'

'Maybe you are.'

'Mary oh Mary, *he's the love of my life*!' It was a wail, coming from somewhere down by her toes to creep up along her legs, into her abdomen, shooting through innards until it pierced right through her heart, on its way to her mouth.

Mary blinked. She grabbed the glass back from Connie and took a hefty swallow. She bit down hard on her bottom lip. What was happening to her eyes? Connie cocked her head to the side to take a better look. Yes, yes, they were filling up, a pearl-like tear perched in one corner by the bridge of her nose. Mary's face was suffused with colour. She looked like she was about to explode like the cartoon characters when they've just swallowed the strongest curry known to man. A tiny sound tore from her throat. Oomp. Her shoulders began to rock up and down.

Connie could feel the same imperative that had directed the wail to her mouth take her over. Her own shoulders began to heave. She had to bend forward to let out the longest wheeze. The sound rocketed Mary off. They each had to hold on to the doorframe as spasm after spasm of helpless laughter racked their bodies.

Everything was going to be just fine after all.

They went downstairs to face the family conference. Fred had taken the phone in the hall off the hook so there wouldn't be any interruptions. Joe was grunting on Connie's mobile, appropriated from her bag, when they stepped into the kitchen. Benny was lining up leftover baked beans in straight drills across his plate, which tugged at Connie's heart. He was so young, so horribly innocent.

She wished she'd listened to him better when he suggested that she recycle plastic bags by bringing them back to the supermarket for her shop. How easy it would have been to please him but at the time she'd just thought, one person, what real difference could one person make? She wished she had banned all aerosols from the house at his quiet request. And checked the sources of her veal at the very least if she was going to remain a carnivore. She wished she had got him that puppy he was desperate for and to hell with the dog hairs on her sofas. He cared so deeply about things that, really, passed her by. Benny was a living, breathing, walking conscience. What could possibly have afflicted him so?

'Joe, off my phone please.'

He gave her the hand, palm facing to her, imperious little git.

'NOW!'

He finished the call in a hurry and glared at her all the while. The phone was tossed on the table when he'd finished. His arms were folded tightly across his chest to let her know how much he did not want to have this conversation. His father might have been the sole, lonely resident, picking his nose, of Mars for all Joe cared. Connie felt an unreasonable rush of sympathy for Matt.

'Right,' she began, 'there's been talk of Budapest and such like.'

'What talk?' Fred interjected. 'Yours.'

'Well, yes.'

Mary was pouring herself a full glass of Rioja. When she'd taken her first sip, it was considerably less full.

'Boys,' she said, 'and that includes you Joseph — your mother has been under a lot of strain lately. She's been battling like a trouper and putting up a good show.' She had to have another deep swallow after that one.

'How come we're starving?' Joe, of course.

'Hardly starving. I've ordered takeaways,' Connie protested.

'That's not proper home-cooked food.'

'We're all bored with proper home-cooked food!' Connie waved an arm taking them all in.

Joe was glowering, itching to get at her phone again. Fred sat with his chin propped in the cup of his hand, twin engines pulsing away, a giant suppurating spot perched on the tip of his nose. Benny was still lining, this time a necklace of beans around the perimeter of the plate. She knew he was counting under his breath, too, he'd stopped doing that aloud because it upset her. Oh for God's sake! They were all going to leave their wives now, they loved their father and that's all they would know. She looked into the future, alone, three broken sons coming for Sunday lunch. Three daughters-in-law avoiding her calls.

'Your father is having a touch of a crisis,' she began soberly, then stopped.

'Might you expand somewhat?' Mary prodded gently after a considerable silence.

'He's not himself at the moment.'

'If he's not himself then who is he?' Joe barked.

'That's what he's finding out we can only assume.' Connie had to mentally nail her feet to the floor she wanted to flee so badly.

'How long is this going to take?' Joe asked.

'I've no idea and that's the truth.'

There was another long silence while they digested that. Fred was looking really frightened now. A reciprocal shiver of fear feathered down Connie's spine.

'Mum, are you saying might he never come back?' Benny asked in a whisper so low they all had to strain to hear him. How could she answer that? What could she possibly say?

'Well, where is he exactly?' Joe asked.

'In Italy still. As far as I know.'

'You mean he never did phone that morning you said he did?' Fred blurted.

'No. He didn't. I'm sorry Fred.'

Joe fisted the table so hard they all jumped. He stood up kicking back his chair. He stuck his livid face right into Connie's.

'This is crazy man! I've never heard anything so — '

'Joseph!' Mary remonstrated. 'You're upset, understandably, but there's no point in taking it out on your mother. She's quite enough on her plate. It's your father you need to address.'

'Address?' Joe whirled on her. 'I think you've missed the point, Mary. Duh! He ain't here, is he? He's in Italy *she* says.' He jabbed a finger in Connie's direction.

'Don't you call me *she*!'

Fred was on his feet now too. He could tell that Joe was going to go all the way this time.

'Calm down Joe. We're all angry but it's not Mum's fault.'

Joe thumped his brother away when Fred came too close. Fred's eyes narrowed, he would stomach one thump, not another.

'You had a huge fight, didn't you?' Joe turned on his mother. It could never be his father's fault. His great big calm old man. Of all his sons, Joe was the most protective of his father, aching at his inarticulacy whenever his mother was letting rip with the verbals, stepping in, telling her to ease off whenever he felt she was taking advantage of her advantage. Getting a silent, affectionate pull on one of his lugs from his father afterwards. Got me out of the soup there, son.

'We did not have a fight,' Connie enunciated slowly, though she was simmering ready to boil now, too. 'He didn't want to come home. Just yet.'

Fred moved towards Joe, his second mistake; Joe's fist lashed out in a sideways swipe that caught his brother bang on the ear.

'Boys please! Mary for God's sake help me.'

Both Mary and Connie jumped in to pull the brothers apart, Fred had his hands locked around Joe's throat, his eyes were practically rolling back in his head with rage. Mary hauled at Joe while Connie prised Fred's fingers loose with the greatest of difficulty. Joe's foot lashed out looking for Fred but caught her instead painfully on the side of her thigh.

'Joe, Joe!' She whirled around. 'Your father is in Rome with another woman!'

Benny stepped across to where they were all standing in a shocked tableaux. He handed Connie her mobile phone, they'd never heard it ring in the melee.

'Mum. It's Dad,' he said quietly.

7

There was a day when he'd considered the smallness of teeth. He was peering into the reluctant maw of a young boy needing several fillings, possibly a crown. They were weak teeth, outer enamel easily eroded; on a small, individual scale, it was important for the boy's future that he sort his mouth out. He would need a good firm bite, a strong chew for his food, a reasonably white smile to attract a mate, something to grind in his sleep, something to sever that pull of sellotape, excise that toothpick of skin on his cuticles, perhaps in time might even need to be identified by his dental records. While out there were other universes, galaxies spiralling into existence. There was busyness of an inconceivable scale, futures beginning as pasts imploded across the whirling matrix of the heavens. It was happening all the time, comings and goings, hugeness, while he filled cavities and noticed one day, quite by chance, that teeth were small and he was growing old.

Connie had paused for a much needed breath.

His wife who blushed so prettily when

someone commented that they must have been childhood sweethearts. How nice, how extraordinary really, people seemed to think. She always brushed such comments away with a wave of her hand — together since she was fifteen and he eighteen, romantic you think? Could be they were just too unadventurous to find anybody else, maybe they were just stuck with each other like old habits they'd never outgrown. She joked in her way but secretly he knew she was pleased. She liked being referred to as childhood sweethearts.

On the phone, even her voice sounded strangely unfamiliar. There was the him anchored to her gutsy and most reasonable anger and the him freefalling through space. There could be moments after all, days even, when he didn't have to feel responsible for Connie.

'I'll be home soon,' he said into one of the few gaps of silence.

'Soon? What the hell d'you mean, soon?'

'Connie, all I can say is I'm really sorry. Truly. Though I know that's not much use to you right now.'

'Damn right it's not much use. How can you do this? What makes you think you can do this? We're your family. We need you. I don't care if Greta's lost a dozen sons. D'you hear me? I don't *care*. And what am I supposed to tell them at work? The doctor's temporarily taken leave of his senses but normal service will resume *soon*? Soon? You bastard.'

'Connie — '

'Your sons are killing each other. We're living on takeaways. But that's okay because you know what — it's just occurred to me — we're *all* on holiday. Matt takes a holiday away, his family takes a holiday at home. I'm not sure I even want you to come home. I'm not sure I even know you.'

'You know me.'

'Are you sleeping with her?'

'No.'

'Is that supposed to make me feel better?'

'I don't know. Does it?'

'You're not lying?'

'I'm not sleeping with her.'

There was a gusty sigh on the other end.

'I suppose it does make me feel a bit better. Just enough so I don't stab you.'

In spite of everything he could sense her relief.

'Can I have a word with the boys?' he asked after a long silence.

'I'd rather you didn't. I took this in the living room so I can think what to tell them.'

'We could tell them the truth.'

'They're too young.'

'I'm not sleeping with Greta.'

There was a shivery intake of breath from her side.

'Maybe not. But I bet you're thinking about it. All the time. Watching her every breath. The way she smokes a cigarette. I bet she still smokes, doesn't she, Matt?'

'Aye.'

'You see, I remember. I do remember.'

'Those days are gone.' Even as he said it, a tug in his lower abdomen felt visceral.

'She left you. I didn't. Just you remember that.'

'I do. I do, Connie.'

'Leave it much longer and there won't be an us to come home to.' He could hear the catch of her sob and a hurried 'Goodbye Matt', before the line went dead.

He stared at the replaced handset in Greta's apartment which had just opened up his old life with such brute force. It had come rushing at him the moment he'd heard Benny's tremulous voice, then Connie's. What was he doing here when they were there? How had that happened? He felt he could drown in guilt. Felt that he should, it was more than he deserved. The ring of the phone cut through his thoughts and he automatically reached for it.

'I just did ring back to get your number,' Connie said. He could tell she had been crying. 'All I want to say is, come home. Please come home. We need you too. And — and — just that I love you. I still love you.' Abruptly, she was gone again.

He had to get out of there, walk for a bit and try to sort his head out. He left a note for Greta saying he would be back later and quickly left the apartment. Outside, he pounded the pavement like a man possessed.

For Connie's sake he'd chosen dentistry instead of becoming a vet which was his first choice when his prodigious exam results became known. He'd studied hard certainly but even he was surprised by how well he'd done; school had always come easily to him, he was streets ahead of the class from infant years. His brother had to swot, watched over by their then redundant father, a man on a mission to make sure his sons didn't encounter his own dead-end. But good grades came easily to Matt who managed to keep up the same steady pace balancing farm work with his nightly studies. Balance, steadiness, even-handedness — these were the words that characterised that section of his life; it could be said nothing much had changed until now. Unlike most of his contemporaries he was singled out for higher education from an early age. A rare beast, indeed, in a school where the majority of students gave up at sixteen to join the Iron Works, first chance they could, until that option was denied them from the late seventies.

When the college offers came in, Connie chose London because she didn't want to go to Glasgow as he did. He said they'd think on — there was at least a year's hard graft in any case to raise money for the first year at college — but he knew in his heart that her wish would prevail. This was someone he could make happy. He could make her eyes light up just by talking about their future together. He indulged her choices, why not? After Greta, it was Connie who had nursed him back to a life she was holding out like a ring of safe steel for him to step into.

He had done well for himself, for his family. It was a good life. And it was waiting his return. All there, waiting. He walked on.

★   ★   ★

'He said he was thinking about things he hasn't really thought about for years.' Connie blew her nose, pressing the pads of her thumb and forefinger against puffy eyelids in an attempt to stem any more tears. They coursed down her cheeks in relentless procession in any case. 'You can't imagine how strange he sounded, like he doesn't hardly know me.'

'He's having a breakdown, you know that's what it is,' Mary said with too much conviction. Connie's head shot up.

'Think so?'

'What else is there to think?'

'It bloody well better be. Now the boys think I'm the crazy one, telling them their father's with another woman one minute, taking it back the next. Oh he's just with an old friend who happens to be a woman. Me being over-dramatic *as usual* — Joe, the little prick. Proper home-cooked food. I've a good mind to check into a hotel. Why do I have to be the one here dealing with the crap — I haven't done anything wrong.'

'You believe him when he says he's not having an affair with this Greta person?' Mary licked her lips, trying to steady a course between casual but not overly so; it didn't do to smatter a person's worst fears all over the canvas like a Pollock painting. Connie looked stricken.

'Maybe I'm a fool but I do believe him. You see, to him it would be the biggest thing. I could do that. Casual affair, make me feel good, lose a bit of weight, so what? For him to make that move — well, he'd be lost to me.

Here I am, actually wishing he didn't have such moral spine, wishing he could just — then come home and lie to me and we'd fight and he'd go on lying to me and everything would be fine.'

'He's not in his right mind just now,' Mary said in a voice she knew sounded nannyish. 'Who knows what triggered it off, you hear of people, perfectly happy people, coming across something from their past by chance and suddenly they're — ' She stopped, Connie's eyes were slitting. 'Okay okay, I'll bin the pop psychology.' Mary thumbed through Connie's photograph album trying to keep her expression light, the way her friend would want, but a rigid scroll of frown stood out on her forehead.

'I thought he was happy,' Connie said.

'Listen to me, maybe he is genuinely concerned about an old friend. She's lost a child you say?'

Connie nodded rapidly.

'Think how you'd be.'

'I am thinking. I'm thinking how that makes her dangerous because she's got nothing to lose.'

'His whole life is wrapped up in this house, he's a family man. He *adores* his wife and kids.' Mary waved an arm expansively. Connie wrinkled her nose.

'Mary, are you going to leave no cliché unturned?'

'All right. Tell me about Greta then.'

Connie drew the photo album on to her lap. She turned a page, Mary craned to look. There was a photograph of a stunning young girl with long auburn hair flying in the wind flicking Matt's neck and chin in a light graze. He was smiling, looking down at her. The girl faced the camera with a frank, almost disconcerting stare. There was body language between them instantly palpable even through an old, fading portrait. It wasn't a Matt that Mary could recognize, even his smile looked hungry. His hand hung loosely over the girl's shoulder, casual though possessive too, long fingers practically cupping one of her breasts. Her legs stood slightly apart, it was clear that she was pressing her lower body back into him. If they hadn't just made love, they were about to. Mary almost had to lower her eyes the lust was so tenderly obscene; she had no right to intrude.

Connie tapped a finger over the girl's face.

'Greta,' she said in a low voice, half to herself. She looked up at Mary, a hot flush steaming up from her collar-bone. 'It's not about whether he's sleeping with her — I honestly don't know if that means all that much to me to be brutally honest. I've been asking myself and I don't know, sure I'd be angry, it would be a betrayal — that stuff of course — but it's more. It's Greta. There's no way to explain — it's Greta herself. I should have known she'd never really leave us.' Unconsciously, she was worrying her thumb back and forth across Matt's face, needing to draw comfort even from a photograph of him. 'You know how he looked when I left him, Mary? Haunted is the only word. And you know what else — young. He looked young and I hate him for it.'

Mary gazed at the girl's pale oval face in the picture. It was true, she did have a haunting quality. More than that, there was something she could only describe as immoderate, it was there in a sullen curve of mouth, candid knowing eyes, an almost foreknowing gaze, the scornful hauteur of beautiful youth — an expectation of excess.

She badly wanted to go downstairs to pick a fight with Joe, it would do them both some good.

*   ⋆   ⋆

Mary couldn't sleep, filled with the sort of unease a person feels on hearing their room might be haunted. Since she'd known Connie and Matt they had been her template for normal, sometimes chaotic, sometimes contented, sometimes discontented family life. Even when they rowed there was always an undercarriage of closeness between the couple, they shared more than a marriage and three sons, they shared a childhood. That was what set them apart to her mind. Until this Greta, of whom she'd never heard one word before, intruded into a photo album to turn Mary's template on its head.

She had grown to love Connie and Matt over the years with the ambiguous, critical love she had once felt for her own dead parents, with the crystal purity she would have felt for her own children, had she been blessed. She was forty six, admitting to forty-two. Connie was well aware of the four lopped years sometime around her mid-thirties but held a surprise fortieth party in any case, on Mary's forty-fourth birthday. The years came but children didn't, she wasn't expecting further surprises.

She couldn't pinpoint the source of this unease at first. Perhaps it was simply the circumstance of Matt's unusual absence; he wasn't a man prone to fits of intemperance, if anything the adult he'd become had elided with the overly mature young man she'd first encountered. He caught up with himself so to speak in later years. Connie's gay, wispy

164

humour complemented his sobriety. Mary had often watched them in company marvelling at the quiet, harmonious way they fielded and batted, inclusively protecting one another from harm. She couldn't help but wonder if Greta was a harm from which there was no protection. A hot spurt of resentment shot through her for this woman she'd never even met and hopefully was unlikely to meet.

The prickles across her scalp had begun as Connie talked her through the album. Portrait after portrait spanning a number of years, Matt with his dog, Matt with his brother Stanley but, mostly, Matt with Greta. A couple of images in particular arrested her attention. They were stretched out like babes in the wood under a canopy of trees, limbs entwined, twisting around one another, it was difficult to tell in the picture who owned which body part. There was an empty bottle on the ground, it could have been whisky, alcohol at any rate. A light dusting of what appeared to be pink snow coated their clothes, banking up in a heavier drift either side of their supine bodies. Mary peered closer, something lying between them had caught her eye. There was a ribbon, possibly black velvet on one end.

'Her pony tail,' Connie had explained. 'Don't ask me why. He loved her hair but he cut it off before he passed out. I was there when they sobered up. She thought it was a great joke — can you believe that? She had the most beautiful hair. He felt terrible and she was only laughing. He threw away the Swiss army knife after that.'

Another moment snatched in time captured Mary's eye. There was a bike flung on grass, front mudguard grotesquely twisted where it had hit a solid object, the trunk of a tree she figured, at some distance a lifeless Greta was draped across Matt's hunkered thighs as he held her, blinking uncomprehendingly into the camera. The scene had a peculiar Pieta resonance. Greta's skull had been split, Connie had explained, she'd spent three weeks in hospital, the first in intensive care. She would bear a potentially fatal fault line down the back of her head for the rest of her life. Matt refused to race their bikes after that, though Greta was all for swinging right back into action just as soon as her stitches healed.

'I felt really bad for taking this picture,' Connie had gone on. 'I just turned up the way I did back then with no idea what had happened. I'd taken the picture before I noticed the bike and realized. And I feel bad about telling Matt that I don't care about Greta's dead child. She was my friend once, after all. You wouldn't wish that on anyone, not anyone in the world.'

The album was cluttered with other pictures, too. Connie picking blackberries with her mother, she must have surrendered her precious camera to her brother for once. There was something about the images of her friend as a child that felt at odds with the happy-go-lucky woman she knew now. Not that she was unhappy precisely, more that she looked somehow out of place. Ill at ease in her posture, uncomfortable before the camera in a way she clearly wasn't once she was doing the clicking again. A surprisingly sombre child, Mary was curiously reminded of Benny.

It seemed to Mary that what she was really looking at as the pages flipped over was Connie as the lens through which the story of Matt and Greta was gradually unfurling. It came to her, a vision of a copper-haired young girl stalking something she couldn't quite understand but was nevertheless ineluctably drawn towards. If the sexual halo surrounding this handsome couple was discernible in a simple photograph years on, what strange ether-altering vibes must they have emitted to an innocent child allowing her camera to take in what her eyes could not. How lonely Connie must have been waiting on each new batch to come out of the dark room, to slip into her hand, slick, shiny chronographs of someone else's love.

Oh yes, Mary knew that loneliness well, old friend, dogging the dark, shearing Sundays into cups of tea, now that biscuit, now that bath, a word with Fr Alexander perhaps two if he could spare the time, checking the clock for the countdown to lunch and company, melting with waxy relief into the organized chaos of Connie's kitchen.

There were portraits of Greta on her own unmindful of the arresting lens. Head turned at a slight angle, eyes fixed on somewhere distant, a crooked smile as though enjoying a private, inner joke. Mary could see with her artist's eye that Connie had taken great care with these compositions, she'd waited for a certain fall of light, for the right angularity of head to profile delicate, ridge-like cheek-bones. To be so meticulous, Mary understood but didn't say that there had to be an element of infatuation for the subject by the artisan herself.

That impression swelled as Connie spoke of the girl with silken hair she cared so little for she'd only laughed at her own scalping. Greta had a habit of talking through an exhalation of smoke from her cigarettes. Words came out in little visible gusts, she could weave the burning fag through the fingers of one hand without dropping or scorching, how sophisticated was that — Connie chuckled, remembering. Greta danced backwards when she was addressing you so that it always seemed that she was teasing or flirting or both. She had perfect legs, no, almost a parody of perfect legs, they went in and out in exactly the right places with exaggerated precision, ankles slim as wrists. She carried herself with a cheeky swagger making a skirt swish from side to side like a swathe of loose material caught in a gentle breeze.

Then, those clothes sent by cousins in America which had caused Connie to catch her breath with longing. A pair of Levi's jeans in particular which curved around her thighs with the definition of tights. Those jeans were the envy of the neighbourhood, faded on the knee, on the buttocks and in little fanning out creases around the crotch to a shade of denim blue that no one else could get exactly right. American blue it could only be.

When she was being nice to you there was a sound she made at the back of her throat, just one beat of a suppressed laugh, almost a hiccup, it made whatever you were saying seem more amusing than it was. The same sound could be derisive if Greta raised an eyebrow while giving you a cool look. She clicked her fingers and talked right over you if she thought you were being boring. It was funny how everybody went along with whatever she was thinking. The same on the streets of town when they played as a gaggle of girls — skipping, tag, just talking about boys or clothes or the top twenty records chart, it was always Greta's court with even the older girls kowtowing to her. How did she get that power? Why did they hand it to her so unprotestingly? Connie couldn't recall a single challenge.

She'd seen her once in London in one of the clubs Mary had taken her to. For a moment she thought it was an apparition or a trick of the subterranean gloom but it was Greta all right, dressed in clinging black from head to toe, her hair grown long again glistening with a sateen polish under a spotlight as she swayed to a slow number. Connie had suggested they leave soon after, she'd never said a word until this instant to Mary.

As Connie spoke, Mary had begun to feel strangely usurped. She had thought of her relationship with Matt and Connie as a special triangle. Only to discover that a triangle had existed long before her. She was nearly six foot and no skirt of hers had ever swished as though caught in a gentle breeze. How could she possibly compete with Greta?

In a curious way she felt cheated of the paradigm Matt and Connie had held up to her, robbed of her own position and an unshakable conviction in their permanence. She knew it was churlish, inappropriate in the light of Connie's pain but she couldn't help but stare wide-eyed into the darkness above her bed, thinking: you two can't split up. What about *me*?

Horrible, *horrible*, to be faced with someone else's prior claim on her greatest friends and the possibility that her own connection to the family really might be as fey, airy and inconsequential as she had played it, though in her heart she had believed there were unspoken depths, silent ties that bound her to a family she considered her own. They were all she had.

She wanted to sob with the same swampy fervour and voluptuous outrage as the day when she'd first looked up at those forbidding gates of boarding school in Lancashire, a million miles away from her Sussex home. Stiff retreating back of her mother, you'll thank me one day dear, wave to Papa now, there's a girl. Chair legs screeching on wooden floorboards in an otherwise silent dining room, rows of bowed heads with steepled hands under chins, mounting hysteria of her own stifled sobs, doleful clang of bell for evening mass, again for bed, unfamiliar body rustles turning in for the night of unfamiliar bodies. Visceral ache for her mother who, in spite of her stoical words, had had wet eyes as she turned her back. For the best, dear, like my parents did for me. Mama, I'll be good. I'll be so good. I'll do better. Seven years old, still warm and slick from the womb. Had she been blessed with a child, Mary would never have left it. Not for a moment.

Those years themselves put to bed, replaced each evening by Connie's welcoming smile, pop of a wine cork, scent of something churning in the oven, Matt's absent-minded spousal kiss to both women, the boys gliding against her body, barely noticing her bulk, her presence, she was *that* familiar — had she got it all wrong?

Sleep was out of the question, Mary decided. Abso-bloody-lutely way out of the question. Usually she prayed to St Anthony when she was troubled. She imagined a kindly, worn face, head at a slight tilt. This is so petty, Mary dear, come to me with a proper problem. Really, I've been up to my neck in war and poverty and quite a lot of cancer recently too, ordinarily Francis or Jude take those but there's this new jobshare thing going on. I'm snowed under. Get a life, dear.

She got out of bed feeling suitably chastened. A gentle ticking off from St Anthony usually did the trick but she felt a touch miffed at the same time. Petty to him maybe, easy for him to say. She was a big girl but the space she was occupying was steadily reducing. He didn't have to be quite so cross.

It was a warm night with a distant rumble of thunder. She donned a wash-shrunken ruby kimono and padded to the kitchen. Maybe she would just stay up all night and sleep tomorrow.

William's last visit had unsettled her, too. Diluted love-making in the watery hours of early evening, the hours before a man has to return home. He hadn't even stayed the night after all. Who was she kidding — love-making? She could almost feel her hips give a resonant flick of echoing disdain. He probably felt that he was doing her a favour, forty-six, big girl small life. While he had invented an alter-life simply by dint of his affair which made him romantic, questing, to his own mind. She despised his self-delusion and felt sorry for his gullible humanity in equal measure. Poor William, she wasn't much of a concubine.

He'd left a half-empty packet of cigarettes

on top of the microwave, which he would remember on his next visit. She hated that, the way his eyes would flicker for something meaningless he'd left behind; it couldn't be far off the day they'd flicker for her the same way.

A hiss of rain against the kitchen window. Come back Matt, she thought, come back and make us all safe and normal again. Come back and be loved.

8

Their father was barely two-thirds the size of either of his sons by their mid-teens and he disciplined with only half a heart, it was more his way of telling them to get out of there as much as anything. He was obsessed with them getting the education he'd never had. The farm was worthless, the town around them closing down, closing in on itself as if by general consent. It had been like the Wild West once with embattled locals fighting Irish famine refugees, men so impoverished they couldn't afford ideals. They broke strikes in the pits for tuppence, the same pits which were to lead to Consett's steel industry. The same Irish who by turn were to lead to the town's strictly demarcated population.

To this day, there were family names his father could remember as blacklegs in the year long strike of 1929; passed on to him by his own father, the bitterness never faded. Then came the seventies and eighties and profits plunged at the Works. It had been set up in Consett because of the town's proximity to raw materials, once those materials were exhausted Consett's location had become a liability. Whole swathes of a community in Company brick houses were made redundant. Matt's father, after forty years graft, being one of them.

It was lodged in his mind with mica clarity the day Arthur Wilson came home from work for the last time. He'd washed and changed as normal then sat to supper with his hands resting, fingers curling up on his lap. He said ta hinny to his wife, Enid, when she placed his supper on the table. Matt was in another corner of the kitchen, studying or pretending to be engrossed because they were all watching Arthur surreptitiously. His father looked thin and defeated. He used one hand to eat and lift the mug of tea to his lips while the other remained curled and useless on his thigh.

In the melting shops, years before, Arthur had seen his cousin fall into a ladle full of molten iron. They said that one of the chains had been loose and he tipped in. Arthur only took the time off that was needed for the funeral. The Works was an incredibly dangerous place, deaths and serious injuries went with the territory, every man understood. Arthur was a labourer, initially working at the blast furnace before he moved to the Coke Works where he worked on the wharf, a horrible job dealing with the hot coke but he never complained. And now it was over, all the years of smoke and heat and roaring noise, for nothing. Looking at his father's stooped shoulders, Matt was overwhelmed by a sense of helplessness: Arthur was suffering and there wasn't a thing any of them could do or say to alleviate his pain. All over town, men sat at similar tables with their lives taken away from them.

Yes, it was grim up north in those days, people down south, gentler, cosseted, with years of padded contours behind them, really had no idea. When he first arrived the ready smiles and unguarded greetings made him suspicious but it was impossible not to be seduced by the easy careless chatter, the softer way of communication, the unaggressive entryways into conversations.

He could not get over how easily words came to people. His own armoury seemed painfully inadequate, he was constantly tongue-tied and chose to say less and less for fear of sounding stupid. That was a trick of confidence being a southerner lent you, the permission to say stupid things on occasion, it was all right, you were amongst friends, just shooting the breeze, few too many beers maybe. You didn't dare take chances like that if you were from Consett, the side of your head would be booted in if the stupid thing

177

you said happened to make someone else look stupid too. It had taken Matt a decade to not see every other man as a potential combatant. The male of Matt's childhood and teenage years wore imaginary wing mirrors on his shoulders to watch his back.

As he walked on into the night and into an area that looked less than salubrious, memories of the farm, of things that never seemed important neither then nor since, insisted across his brain. Farm was really a rather grand word for the cluster of outhouses around a central white manse facing on to the main road into town. Most of the acreage was wooded with a few broad, sloping fields which they tilled. His mother kept hens and a handful of milking cows, occasionally she added a couple of pigs which they slaughtered themselves. It was never a viable concern, the farm, more something that was in the family and had to be used. Enid did her best with it the long years Arthur grafted at the Works but she didn't take to the life, she loved her books and needlework, quiet indoor pastimes. She was a morose woman prone to dark, lingering moods which reflected her surroundings.

Closer to town, it was a black-and-white landscape with giant slagheaps scarring the earth lightly dusted with snow, deep scores of intermittent darkness cutting into white, running down from a flattened top. Straddling the town itself, side by side two fat, curved chimney stacks rising up to a monotonous talcum sky. They towered above tightly pressed layered rows of company houses. Your first kiss in Consett was with those stacks behind or in front of you, they went in at the waist like a woman. Your first real fight with fists and drawn blood was accompanied by the constant thunking sound from the steelworks and mushrooms of belched smoke shrouding a million orange fiery sparks. There had even been a time when he believed every town had stacks sending overblown mushrooms into the sky.

Other images he'd long forgotten, stupid, inconsequential things, played on his mind. Pink snow drifting down from the iron ore in the atmosphere. The wheels of Greta's bike whirring that day her brakes gave out and she lay lifeless in a flaccid heap at the bottom of Snoot's Hill. He'd run to her, certain she was dead, certain that he'd lost her for ever. Connie had a photograph of him cradling her inert body. It was the strangest portrait, his face only registered mild surprise looking directly into a camera he had had no idea was there.

Funny how Connie had managed to

179

capture so many seminal events of his youth. What image would she garner now as he briskly walked through street after anonymous street? The endless grafitti? The soft muted lights of Rome spread out like a sequinned blanket beneath him? The naked concrete, balcony-less apartment blocks either side of this street? What street? What was he doing here? He walked on. A lone taxi passed and he was tempted to hail it but his feet were still itching to move on.

He thought of Greta, before she left, indulging Connie on the farm one day like she would a pet lamb, kicking her away verbally, as she physically did Ed, the next. Yes, she could be cruel. No doubt about that. But when she was good, like Matilda, she was very very good. And soft like a favourite pillow.

Up ahead, coming out of a seedy block, three youths moved in his direction. They had been chattering animatedly but had grown silent at his approach. Instinctively, he unslouched his shoulders and drew himself up to full height.

Strange how it had never occurred to him before how chain-like their adolescent relations were, linking, breaking — forging together again. *Could it be me then, could it?* Connie's little heart-shaped face.

Matt had always loved the way she dealt with her sons, his own mother had had such a dark, ruminating nature. Connie jumped in, waded in if they resisted her. She shouted, she pleaded, placated, cajoled — it had taken him years to realize how subtly and skilfully she adapted her own responses to suit the different nature of each boy. He observed the way they looked at her too, three sets of eyes following her around a room. They were measuring themselves, the men they would become, in the reflection that came back at them from her pupils.

He believed she was about as perfect a mother as he could wish for his children. Though there were times under her benign stewardship when she forgot that he was not in their number — her constant maternal chivvying could be wearisome. Times when he had wished she would look to the side a little, soften her oppressive focus on her sons' futures. Sometimes he got the impression that when she returned from work or shopping or anything that took her out, she had to check and recheck that everything was in its proper place within her home as if each time she expected to come back to find nothing there. As if her own existence was melded with the bricks and mortar of her house and without it she might herself dissolve and disappear. It only now occurred to him how insecure she was at heart. How could he have missed that all these years?

The youths were just ahead, walking with all three heads bent. They were older than he'd first thought, in their early twenties. Three bent heads and silence could mean trouble he knew from his own fighting youth. He squared his shoulders to full breadth, slowed down his own gait so that he didn't appear anxious to pass. He knew not to make eye contact if a head should raise. From what he could see they had small, mean, pointy faces. Brothers perhaps, or cousins. They were alongside now, one of them stepping off the pavement to facilitate the pass. Matt made certain that his path didn't deviate in what might look like his giving way.

There was a high mesh wire fence to his right. The sound of a large dog barking carried in the still night air. A car's headlights caught all four male figures for an instant then moved on. They were behind him now. The soles of their shoes were all rubber, another bad sign, so that he couldn't tell with any accuracy how far behind. One of them had muttered something to the other two just as they'd passed him by. Matt wasn't about to turn to check if they'd travelled far. He kept up a steady gait and wished the goddamn dog would stop barking so that he could listen better. Then he heard it, the sound he'd been intuitively waiting for. The whooshing noise rubber makes hitting pavement at a rapid pace. Two sets of feet, he figured. The other was probably hanging back on lookout. He slid his hands out of his jeans pockets, automatically clenching his fists as he slowly turned around.

★   ★   ★

Benny was bringing a new boy home from school for tea. He got one chance with the new boys and only asked them to please her, Connie understood, but she still felt ridiculously hopeful. You never knew this could be the one. She pictured a serious nerdy face, spectacles perhaps, books under his arm — how she longed for such a vision to walk through her door. Both boys cloistered in Benny's bedroom debating global warming or the Amazonian rainforests or the texture of Bird's Eye new veggie burgers at the very least. Two shiny caps of heads pressed together in serious congress poring over an atlas or something, their immediate bond forged then sealed for ever over the chocolate cake with frosting she was making right this moment.

She'd called Mary earlier, she wouldn't be in today, a million things backed up to do and bloody Benny had just landed a friend round for tea — careful not to say 'new' friend though Mary would instinctively know and realize the momentousness of the occasion.

Also, she'd said far too much about Greta.

She'd spent the morning shopping and this time made it to the checkout. She would make two home-made pizzas, well, home-made insofar as she would slather a jar of tomato purée over ready-rolled dough bases, adding pre-sliced meats and peppers, topping off with pre-grated cheddar from a resealable pack. One of the pizzas could be vegetarian but there would be an option if the boy didn't share Benny's vocation. Of course he wouldn't, she was only dreaming, he'd have said already if he didn't eat meat, still, he was somebody coming for tea — she'd have served him blinis and caviar if he'd put in a prior request.

She popped the cake in the oven and stepped out into the garden. It was her favourite month, the flowers still ringing with newness before July would wilt petal edges and throttle beds with weeds. The wide fenced plot was entirely her territory, Matt only ever cut the grass, lawn-moaning as he called it. She would get Fred to do it later so

184

that it would be one less thing for Matt when he got home, doubtless he'd have to play catch-up at the surgery for quite some time. He'd have to do something about that loose fence post though, one bad wind and the whole panel would collapse. And there was the shrivelled wisteria up by the top windows to cut back, she didn't fancy any of the boys going that high on a ladder.

Connie stood taking a deep scented breath. All in all it promised to be a good year in the garden. She'd managed to tame a wild, prickly shrubbery into something sedate and countrified. Every year she wondered about a water feature but Matt said the tweeness would be the final nail in his coffin, he just about stomached two fat cement cherubs either side of the white wicker loveseat which caused him to wince every time he passed. Okay, so she was passé — Connie turned a full circle in the centre of her own Eden, clean sun after the rains of last night bathing her face with tender warmth. Who the hell cares, she thought, I made this — it's gorgeous.

To cut or not to cut was always the question. Would scaled down flowerbeds pay her back by tempering their show if she filled the vases (lined up by the kitchen sink as it happened, waiting with water and a drop of bleach). No, it was a lovely day, it would be a charming evening, Matt had finally called. The garden she decided would be faithful, loyal and true, keeping up a good show no matter that it would never look quite the same after pruning. Everything had to evolve, experience change, diminution, but a different view might be no bad thing from time to time, no less for a garden than a marriage. She went for the secateurs.

Purple lupins, two blood-red peonies — any more would be plundering — a handful of ivory arum and custard-yellow day lilies, sweet williams and a couple of gladioli which she regretted sowing from corns, they seemed to stick out with a coarse vulgarity in her delicate planting scheme. Tiny nuggets clustered on both apple trees she noticed with satisfaction. She cut some dark green background foliage from the vibernum and realized that she was humming.

Fred was on his early day from school, stepping out to join her with a pint glass filled with orange juice — a whole carton's worth — the sugar, the expense, she couldn't be bothered upbraiding him.

'You look nice,' he said.

'Do I? Thank you.' She cut a last arum lily, resting back on her heels to shuffle different arrangements together by vase size. Fred took a long swig of juice, which left a scrim of orange over his top lip where there was a line of downy first moustache.

'So what's the deal with this 'friend' of Dad's then?' he asked.

'Hmm? Oh Greta you mean. I vaguely remember her to tell the truth. Been down on her luck poor thing, your father wanted to help her out, you know what he's like.' Connie decided against the gladioli they didn't seem to go with anything or maybe if she stuck them on their own in the hall they mightn't look so ugly in dim light. Fred downed the rest of the juice. He licked his lips.

'He's not having an affair with her, is he?'

'Certainly not!'

'Is she pretty?'

'Not that I remember especially. Look Fred, you must have homework to be getting on with.'

'So where did he bump into her or did he know she was there and he looked her up? How did it work? And why didn't he call and let us know where he was? You can't say that's normal behaviour. You said he was crying in those thingy gardens that evening. What? Crying for her?'

'Why would he cry for her?' The secateurs

187

flew through air snipping stem ends at a furious rate.

'You tell me — because she was down on her luck?' Fred persisted.

'What is this — an inquisition? Look, he hadn't even bumped into her at that point. I'm sure I imagined the crying, my head's fuzzy about all that. He met her at the dental conference, okay? They started talking, olden days, so on and so on. It turned out she'd lost a child. I think — I think her husband hadn't been as sympathetic as he might. So Dad just thought he could help them out a bit. He'll be home any day now. End of story.' A film of sweat coated her forehead, a bead trickled all the way down one cheek.

'She's a dentist?'

'Hmm?'

Fred's mouth curled with disgust.

'Mum — the dental conference was something you and me made up, remember?' He turned on his heel, she could hear him stomping through the house, up the stairs until one resounding slam of the bedroom door. Connie winced. She had to swallow a mouthful of bile. Damn! She all but chopped the top of a finger off.

In the kitchen she put the flowers into the line of vases, cramming them in any old way, even the gladioli. She took the cake out to cool, mixed the frosting and started on the pizzas. By the time she was finished Benny's key was turning in the front door. He wouldn't let her pick him up from school any longer, insisting it was only around the corner, though she'd monitored his progress from an upstairs window for the first few weeks. You couldn't be too sure these days, was that man parked in that same car yesterday as well? Sometimes when she closed her eyes at night, all the accidents and potential calamities she'd *never* thought of whisked across her mind.

She wiped her hands on a dishcloth saying a silent prayer for Benny's friend. Dear God please — a nerd, a geek, someone who'll make Benny look good. This day that had started out with such promise was shredding her nerves into liverish ribbons. Her son was standing by the kitchen door. He looked pale and nervous, anxious green eyes darting over her face, willing her not to say anything embarrassing.

'Hi bun-Ben-neee!' Not the most auspicious of beginnings. He jerked a thumb over one shoulder, for a second he looked like a frozen rabbit.

'Sebastian's just using the loo.' Sebastian? That was promising. She looked at Benny, he looked at her, they both knew this was going to be a disaster.

'Well now, what d'you think Sebastian would like? Milk and biscuits? I know you'll have fruit.'

'I suppose you'll have to ask him,' Benny said dubiously.

'Thank you, I will.'

There was a flushing sound. Benny's shoulderblades went up to his ears. He half turned as a lock shot out of its bolt, cheeks dilating with panic.

'Sebastian!' Connie cried. 'Welcome!' A blond Adonis with gelled hair towered behind Benny. He was a magnificent sports specimen right down to the skateboard trainers. Shoulders genetically designed for rugby, a white smile brimming with confidence. Connie felt a little faint.

'Hiya.' He bounded into the kitchen. 'Is Joe home yet? One of the boys who came home with Benny once told me about him. Can I have a go on his skateboard? I heard it's like well heavy.'

Benny's eyes were so wide she thought they might well drop out — boring into her — not the skateboard, anything but that. Connie beamed at Sebastian. ''Course you can. In the hall. Under the stairs. Off you both go now.' She shooed with her fingers, turning to pour a glass of water to ease the parched, arid zone in her throat.

Later, she could hear the monotonous roll of wheels followed by the double thwack of the board coming off the pavement edge. Joe had joined them shouting instructions, he could never resist an opportunity to show off superior knowledge but in a way she was pleased, one iridescent son might provide cover for the non-sparkling variety. She stepped out to call them in for tea. Sebastian was gazing up at Joe with a worshipful mien, hanging on every word of instruction in some technique or other.

'And like then you lift your left heel, yeah? Twist of the shoulders, like this, like this, yeah? Knees bent and — '

No sign of Benny. She went upstairs. A guilty start when she opened the door, he was cross-legged on the bed reading an old *Marvel* comic, he bought them off the internet using her card, faithfully reimbursing her from his weekly pocket money.

'Benny, your friend — Sebastian — is wondering where you are.'

'No he isn't.'

'Well, he just said to me. Seems like a nice lad. You can have him round again. Anytime.' Connie peered over his shoulder at the comic, an ancient Spiderman meshed in bold black lines over lurid blue and red. The colours of those early issues were almost obscene.

'Did I tell you about Valda?' she asked.

'*June and Schoolfriend* the comic, yeah, she was the one with the precious crystal that gave her powers. The Christmas one that went on and on but you had to keep reading but you were only six and girls a lot older couldn't understand about Valda and your mum came in and took the comic off of you but in a nice way 'cause you were half asleep and your head was like this — ' He dropped his head on to one shoulder. It was all by rote, mechanical, why couldn't he just say, boring boring boring, or even imply it? Joe would and by turn she would have wanted to cuff him. Benny's detached recollection of stories she'd told in an effort to get through to him seared more than Joe's impatient contempt or Fred's stolid interest. 'And your mum said 'Night now hinny, them eyes'll be out like eggs of the morning'.'

'I am Valda,' she proclaimed of a sudden.

'You're Mum,' he countered. 'That's okay.'

'I have special powers.'

'I don't like skateboards.'

Connie noticed the creeping rash rising up his neck for the first time that evening. Nerves because of the guest he'd only invited to please her and now he felt that he was failing miserably. When he tried to act normal, at any rate *her* rendition of normal, he ended up with spots, a blanched face with a blue worm of vein wriggling on his temple. She forgot herself and let out a deep sigh, his eyes widened and he pulled the comic closer.

'Jesus Benny, I'm sorry pet.' Though that was the wrong thing too. She slid backwards closing the door again with a quiet click. Stocks and shares, unit trusts, investment funds, forget it, she thought, if you could bank a parent's sense of failure, if the dividend was commensurate with the capital invested — there was your pension fund all set up ready for the denoueument deathbed scene, sorry about that time, yes and that, there's money in the kitty for the therapists, don't get ripped off, if a woman starts a sentence with 'I'm not having a go now' she's going to have a go. That's all, the rest of it you can figure for yourselves. As much as I did anyway. So long then, I'm off.

Connie stood in the landing gazing up at the perfect cobweb she'd preserved for the sole purpose of *not* having a perfect house. Each silver thread was illuminated by a corner downlight. Furious Eminem harangued in Fred's room. The door had remained steadfastly closed all evening. Downstairs in the hall, Joe and Sebastian were kicking a ball back and forth.

'Outside!' she shouted down. The ball clattered against the front door, bounced back, then whacked against the door again. They were ignoring her. She jumped up to annihilate the cobweb but couldn't reach, there was a book on the floor and she flung it but still no success, a broom on her mind, Connie stomped downstairs barging past Joe to the phone. If she had to scream at someone it might as well be someone who deserved it. With a finger in one ear to drown out the continuing racket in the hallway, she picked out the number for Greta's place. The ball struck the hall table sending one of the newly filled vases crashing by her feet. She slammed the phone down. Words tumbled out of Connie's mouth:

'Piss off outside Joe and take that traitorous little bastard with you!'

There was a stunned silence. Sebastian's lower lip began to wobble. Connie had to close her eyes. Dear God for all his girth he was only nine.

'I'd like to go home now please, Mrs Wilson.'

'Oh there's no need for that Sebastian. Look, let's have some chocolate cake. We could have it before the pizza.'

'If you don't mind — '

'Please Sebastian, I'm sorry for what I said.'

'I want my mum!' he wailed, knuckling his eyes.

'You've really gone and done it this time.' Joe glared at her accusingly.

Connie was spinning around.

'Is there a jacket, no? Joe, he lives two streets up, walk him home.' She ran to the kitchen and returned with a package wrapped in paper towels, 'Here, half the cake, take it with you Sebastian. Have you got brothers, sisters? No? Well all the more for you. Tell your mother I said you were excellently behaved.' A hand on his back guiding him to the door, Joe was scowling, she nudged him with the other hand. 'Any time Sebastian, any time at all, we've *loved* having you.' She yanked the door open, pushing them both into the sturdy frame of Jennifer Copeland, the surgery nurse, who was standing with a finger poised, just about to ring the bell.

'Go!' Connie commanded, the boys ran. Jennifer looked startled.

'Mrs Wilson, if it's not a good time — '

'I don't know Jennifer. What's a good time? There isn't a good time. I have no idea when he'll be back. No idea whatsoever. I understand things must be very difficult for you and Martin right now. I'm sorry, what

can I say? That's all I keep saying — sorry
— over and over and all I'm trying to
do is — Would you like some cake? Tea
maybe?'

Jennifer took a step backwards.

'I think maybe I'd better leave you alone,'
she said.

Connie compressed her lips and nodded.

'I think maybe that would be a good idea,
Jennifer.' She closed the door and slammed
her back against it, breathing in deep gusts.
Me too, she thought, I want my mum. *I want
my mum.*

'Fred! Benny! Downstairs now please.'
They couldn't hear with Eminem crashing
through the sound barrier in Fred's room.
She ran up, pounding first on Fred's door,
wrenching Benny's with a violence that made
him blink. Joe's school rucksack lay on his
bed, she emptied the contents on to the floor,
ignoring the packet of cigarettes, a lighter,
catalogue from the Erotic Print Society (so
that's where it had gone) and Matt's new
Swiss army knife which had cost them all a
weekend of searching.

'What're you doing?' Benny asked.

'Here.' Connie tossed him the bag. 'Just
cram it, anything, underwear — for yourself
and Joe — socks, something to sleep in.
Quick pet please.'

Fred was peering sullenly from a crack of doorway.

'What's — '

'Fill a bag, Fred. Essentials — underwear, hair gel — downstairs in two minutes *please*.'

She was galloping back down as Joe stepped through the door.

'Wait by the car, here, you might need a jacket, take one for Fred and Benny, too. No questions — just wait by the car.'

He stood holding three jackets as she ran from room to room, shutting doors, locking windows, crunching shards of broken vase under her shoes along the length of hallway. Fred and Benny joined Joe in sour, mutinous file by the front door. Connie grabbed her bag, a jacket, and pushed them through, which amounted to a rugby manoeuvre with one shoulder in Fred's case, he was that solid. She double-locked the door and ran to the car.

'C'mon, get in. All in the back please. I don't want anyone rabbiting in my ear beside me. Yeah, I know it's a hard life. Tough. You can leave me to die, alone and neglected, when the time comes. For now, just get in the bloody car.' The doors were flung open awaiting them. With the greatest of reluctance and eyeing her with a certainty now that she was well and truly round the bend, they obliged. Connie pulled away in a jerk of steering wheel, forcing a passing car to halt with a squeal of brakes and a hand slamming down on a horn, the sound carrying for ten seconds until she rounded a corner at the top of the road.

'My skateboard's still out.' Joe's voice rose in panic. 'Mum! My skateboard.'

'I'll get you a new one,' Connie said. 'And Joe? Here's your pack of tabs, light one for me will you?'

9

A line of streetlights winked sending out rotary blade beams along the wide main street. It looked like she was driving through a phalanx of illuminated windmills. The town was asleep. Some new shops but no substantial changes, mostly two-storey, brick-fronted buildings with two or three rectangular casement windows on the top floor. Connie's car swished past the old Woolworths with the flat top, once an Aladdin's Cave where she bought all her Christmas presents and eyed longingly for weeks in advance the camera which was to be her tenth birthday present. Rows of plastic pick 'n' mix tubs, sweets and shiny wrappers gleaming with precious gem allure, how her fingers used to itch. Further along no need to stop at the zebra crossing, there wasn't a sinner about. Her stomach rolled with a mournful echo of childhood, lonely for herself.

There was the corner shop where she'd first seen Matt kiss Greta. She'd made it her business to find out all she could about him. His mother hadn't invited Connie's mother to help herself to blackberries, Brenda Bradley had sought permission on her daughter's prompting. She'd arrived at the farm to discover that he was still taken.

She turned left, the car climbing up through densely packed terraced houses either side. They'd made one pit stop, her sons munching through cardboard fish and chips in morose silence. They were angry with her and a little frightened she could tell but thankfully they'd kept their thoughts to themselves. Rain then, for the last two hours, windscreen wipers chugging out a mechanical beat almost in time to the light sounds of sleep within the vehicle. Rumbles and lip smacks, a tinny whistle from one of Benny's nostrils. For a while she'd thought she would drive for ever, how would that be — to never stop except for food and to use the toilets of a thousand grey, anonymous service stations, to just go on and on independent of past, unburdened by future because there wasn't going to be any — only a woman in a steamed-up car with three sons, deliberately going nowhere.

Rain had dissolved into a persistent cling of mist now, yellow dashes shimmered across the street under her solitary headlights and the streetlamps above. Curtains drawn, houses plugged out, a dog's half-hearted bark as she indicated to the right. A few yards along, she pulled in, resting her head for a while on the finally still steering wheel. She turned the engine off expecting the boys to stir into life but they remained in convinced sleep. Joe moaned aloud, doubtless dreaming of the skateboard they both knew she could never really replace, he'd customized that one to such a degree. She lit the last cigarette, adding her own brand of pollution to an interior already fogged by unspoken fears and boyish doubts. We were happy, she wanted to assure them, it wasn't an illusion. We were happy, your dad and me.

She peered through an almost opaque windscreen. Long tunnel of darkened windows facing on to one another along the silent street. She could hear the steady tick tick of wheels revolving on Matt's big black bike, panting breaths and a pink rasher of tongue as the dog kept pace behind. Where was he now — her lovely boy with the shy smile, swooping down to pick up a fallen bag of shopping? How could so many years have passed, and so quickly? She wanted them back, every last one of them. She wanted them back, only this time she would savour them. They were supposed to grow into gentle old age together, hand in hand, all the battles and petty anxieties behind them with the final lag of the journey yawning ahead, extending that ultimate genteel courtesy of seeing one another out. To think that she had once let everyone believe that it was his brother, Stanley, whom she fancied. She had never not loved Matt.

Connie got out of the car, not a sign of movement when she peered back inside. Three houses up the street, she lifted a door knocker and brought it down in one tentative thud. All around she imagined whispers, mumbled protests of sleep-interrupted neighbours. She knocked again, twice this time in quick succession. Who's that yammering on Brenda Bradley's door? Reminding herself that her mother wasn't as nimble on her feet as she used to be, Connie stepped back to see if a light had come on in the first-floor window. A moment of panic, maybe Brenda wasn't there, maybe she'd gone away somewhere but surely she'd have said, besides, she never went away. Connie hammered the knocker with full force, an echo reverberated across the street. She was overcome with a desperation to get inside.

'Stop up,' her mother's voice commanded behind the front door. 'Who is that, this hour of night?'

'Mam, it's me. Connie. Open the door please.'

It took a while, Brenda was a one for locks. A light came on in the hall as the door peeled open. Connie's mother held her thick candlewick dressing gown tightly by the throat. Her head craned out looking left and right before she focused on the woman standing limply in her doorway.

'Constance?'

'Don't ask me now, Mam. I've got the boys in the car. Can you keep us for the night?'

'Well, go and fetch them in pet.' Brenda gestured with a flying arm, her head still checking for neighbours.

Connie ran back and shook the boys awake. While they grumbled and stretched, she pulled out their bags from the boot realizing too late that she'd forgotten to pack anything for herself, not so much as a clean pair of knickers, she'd have to borrow one of Brenda's motherfo's. A giggle caught in the back of her throat — her mother's small, pointy face, screwed-up eyes not quite believing what they were seeing, could be some new type of robber imposter got up as her daughter. Oh thank God, Connie thought, I'm back in the land of mistrusting forbearance.

When they were all safely inside Brenda greeted her grandsons with a pinch to each cheek. Already there was a familiar smell wafting from the kitchen. She thrust blankets and pillows at Fred and Joe.

'Roll out your mattresses in the attic room. Don't leave on the light when you come back down.' She turned to Benny. 'You can stop with your Mam. Brenda, I says to myself, they'll be wanting soup.'

Connie followed her mother to the small kitchen at the back of the house. There was a folding formica table with three leatherette-topped stools, nothing was built-in. Along a top shelf the length of one wall stood a drill of full blackberry jam jars, neatly labelled in Brenda's tiny writing. Lamb's meat and bones were frying in a huge, dented saucepan with two handles. Connie sat resting her elbows on the table, chin propped on her clasped hands. Benny sat beside her in a similar pose.

'It'll be jam and cut loaf for you lad,' Brenda said over her shoulder, signalling Connie to the bread bin with one wagging finger. Finely sliced carrot, potato and onion were going into the pot, she always sliced like that, directly from her hands straight into the stock. She added water from the boiling kettle and beads of polished barley. Saliva poured through Connie's cheeks.

As Benny ate, chewing with his own intense deliberation, shifting the glutinous mound from one side of his mouth to the other, Connie stared past her mother at trickles of moisture running down the four-paned window both inside and out. The fringe on the solitary overhead light shade still hadn't been tacked on properly, hanging loose since she was a girl. Soup began to bubble sending up gusts of aromatic steam. Fred and Joe returned standing either side of their grandmother not knowing where else to put themselves. Connie felt for them, they looked tired and apprehensive. Brenda filled two bowls.

'While they're supping I suppose you could make up your bed,' she said to Connie.

The bedroom reeked of damp; flowery wallpaper peeled into little curls up by the ceiling. It was a big event, choosing that paper, Brenda had brought book after book of samples from the haberdasher's before they settled on posy clusters tied with ribbons. It looked fresh and dewy back then, much like Connie herself. She caught her reflection in the mirror over the plywood set of drawers her father had made before he died, according to Brenda. Though Connie had always suspected that Brenda had rustled them up herself in between the two jobs she managed and her market stall on Sundays. Exhaustion etched deep grooves under

Connie's eyes and twin channels from nose to mouth. She made the bed then pinched her cheeks to add some colour but they just looked like pinched cheeks.

Fred and Joe passed her on the stairway on their way to the attic room which used to belong to her brother.

Joe said, 'You do realize we've got school tomorrow?'

'I'll call them.'

'How long are we going to be here?'

'Just a short while. I wanted my mum. Can you understand that Joe? Fred?'

Joe nodded wearily, she hated to see the fight sucked out of him like that. On impulse, Fred stepped back down and pecked her cheek. She'd forgotten how he towered above her these days, it was all she could do not to lean into his reassuring bulk. Instead she leaned over the banister rail to call for Benny. When he was safely tucked up — nervous eyes following her every move, almost flinching when she bent to kiss his forehead — she went downstairs for soup.

A steaming bowl awaited her on the table. Brenda was busy washing up after the boys. It felt like distilled goodness going down Connie's throat. She could have wept with gratitude. A thousand days of childhood in every mouthful — stamping gritty snow from shoes in the hallway, hawing on ruddy hands, unwrapping scarf from a stiffened neck, early winter dusk falling on the street outside, steamy succulent gloom of her mother's kitchen and soup waiting for her every day after school. Silky globules of barley sliding all the way down to her stomach. Heat glowing from within, turning red fingers white again. There was nothing, nothing on all of God's green earth that she could have wanted more in those days. It was funny how in times of distress, the experiences of a lifetime could contract to simple, basic fundamentals, the essence of memory, all things superfluous cleared away. The scent of a kitchen. A bowl of soup. Home.

'Thanks Mam.'

'Well now.' Brenda turned, wiping her hands on a dishcloth. 'That'll do you good.'

'It's buggering fantastic.'

'It buggering is.'

'Mam — '

'Get your soup.'

'I'm getting my soup.' Connie took another mouthful. 'Matt's in Rome with Greta Parker.'

'Well now. I suppose that's bad?'

'It's not good.'

Brenda nodded, mouth pursed with deep thought. She was a short, thin woman with dark triangular eyes caused by overhanging flaps of lid, a cap of peppery hair which she'd always worn in the same cropped, mannish style. Aside from the eyes she had the smooth, unlined skin of a much younger woman. She had determined to marry late and did so, being nearly forty when she had Connie, her next birthday would see her seventy-eighth year. Connie's father had been close on fifty on his wedding day and had died of a sudden heart attack when both his children were little. Brenda had managed in her indomitable, unflappable way to take everything in her stride. It was precisely that stoicism that Connie longed for now.

'Bella Parker's lass?' Brenda asked after a while. Connie nodded.

'So Rome's where she ended up. I did wonder. Her sister Rita's still in the house but she'd tell you nowt, not that I'd ask mind. She's put the front room back in after the salon, made a pig's ear of it to my sights, no nets on the window, you can see right through. Has he left you, d'you think?'

Connie scraped up the last of her soup.

'She lost a child. Matt says he's not with her in that way. Only to help like.'

'How help?'

'He says he'll be home soon but I don't

know. He sounded strange on the phone.'

Brenda's lips were pursed in thought again. She folded her arms, leaning back against the sink. Connie held her breath.

'If he says he's planning on coming home then that's what he'll do. He's not a man to say a thing and do owt otherwise.'

'You think so?'

'Aye. I do.' Brenda nodded vigorously. 'It's wor Matt, another man I mightn't be so inclined. There now, you'll need a serious word with him, of course, when he arrives. And stop at home. This is what comes of going off foreign.'

Connie gave her mother a grateful smile. She should have come here days ago.

'Will you stay a while or are you going up?' Brenda asked.

'I'll stay a while. And yes, I'll check the doors and remember to turn out the lights.'

Brenda paused on her way out.

'Would you credit who's next door now? Peggy Humpish's daughter come all the way home from Australia to buy the old place off the Council. Imagine that — at fifty-odd year of age with an accent. It would appear, Constance, that we're gone bijou now. I won't be worth a light in the morning if I don't get on my bed. I'll check the front door locks in case you forget.'

Connie stayed on a long while in the kitchen, not forgetting a great many things.

★ ★ ★

Sometimes, if she got lucky, Mary could catch Fr Alexander before he left for the night. She could tell from a dim glow through stained glass that he was at the altar or in the small sacristy behind, preparing for the morning. She considered him diligent and properly earnest, if a little wet behind the ears. But if she hammered on the solid oak doors, he would allow her in, to light a candle (which she would, of course, extinguish before leaving) and to say her evening prayers. It was a filled silence in there at night, kneeling in the first pew, different to the silence waiting at home.

'Pray for me, Mary,' he always said, opening the door, allowing her in. A slight touch of the evangelical to her mind, the serious demeanour, belaboured piety. Why should she pray for him? He had his own direct line while she was way down the pecking order.

'Pray for me, Mary,' he said tonight, forced to step aside as she blundered past him in her anxiety to get in.

With her head down she practically ran up

the length of middle aisle pausing to genuflect before sidling into her habitual pew, for a moment she felt like an exposed, giant crab skittering for safety. She pressed her forehead on to her clasped hands and began to pray. Dear Father in heaven, please bring peace to troubled regions on earth, look after the sick and needy and those that need you most . . . She went through her usual checklist ending with the Lord's Prayer and three Hail Mary's. That out of the way, she turned to St Anthony. Dear St Anthony, I realize you're very busy but I'd be greatly obliged if you could get Connie to phone me. There's nobody at the house, the car is gone, the phone just rings out and she's not answering her mobile. The front door's been double locked and I only have a key for the top lock. *I can't get in.* I'm locked out. That never happens. It may seem a little thing to you so please don't be angry or impatient with me — but, you see, she always tells me if she's going to be out for the evening. Always. And really, I'm not sure what to do or even if I should be doing something, so if you could just give me a moment of your time —

A hand squeezed her shoulder making her head snap back with irritation.

'Mary, I must lock the doors now,' Fr

Alexander said. She thought his smile a touch patronizing.

'If I could just have a moment, Father.' Mary lowered her head again. The hand lifted then lowered in a tighter squeeze.

'Do you have any idea of the time?' He gave his watch an ostentatious frown, raising one arm while pulling his mouth down, doubtless as he'd seen in the movies.

'Please just — '

'Really, I can't,' he cut across. Mary let out a loud frustrated sigh. She made a sign of the cross and rose about to head towards the rack of candles, twenty pence piece already in her hand. Fr Alexander blocked the way, even though he was smiling both arms rose either side, quite firmly, Mary thought, unnecessarily firmly. She was a giant crab again being shooed up the aisle away from her place of refuge. Fr Alexander stayed close behind and for a second she contemplated letting loose on him with a deadly pincer. She whirled around at the end for a final genuflection and to cast him a withering look. It didn't seem to bother him, that silly beatific smile remained on his lips.

'Goodnight Father, I hope you sleep well,' she spat as he closed the doors in her face.

Mary checked her phone again but there was only a message from the server telling her it was time to top up. She drove back to Connie's for one last look. Not a light in the house, so unusual, even when she went away, Connie always put a couple of lights on a timer for safety. Mary sat in her car for a long time, waiting for her phone to ring, waiting for St Anthony to get back to her, waiting for something good to happen though nothing good ever happened unless Connie and her boys were around. Maybe they really were at home and just didn't want Mary's evening visitation. Maybe the car was parked by an unfamiliar kerb somewhere and they were huddled in candlelight around the kitchen table at the back of the house, closing ranks, immediate family only, no trespassers.

You see, dear? St Anthony finally spoke, you're not blood, in the final run of things, you're not of their blood. Go home, get some sleep, you look like some ridiculous stalker. A stalking, well, crab, in fact.

'That was mean and cruel,' Mary said aloud, turning the ignition. 'I'm not sure I like you any more. This is all that horrid Greta person's fault, why don't you be mean to her instead of me? I'm going to find a new saint if you're not careful.'

She looked back over her shoulder at the silent, darkened house. Remembering games bell, unsullied kit, not picked for the team again, huddles of girls whispering behind hands aligned sideways to their mouths, a trim of brown paper pinned to the hem of the skirt she'd outgrown so quickly, a brush swirling in water before dipping into blocks of colour again, alone in the dorm, painting her loneliness.

It couldn't be true, Connie, her sons, Mary's family, huddled in the dark against her? Get a life, St Anthony said, though not unkindly, get a life, dear.

'Will you stop saying that?' Mary shouted. 'I'll tell you which life I'd like to get. That witch in Rome. *My* Rome, I'll have you know. She even thinks she can have that. I wish on all the saints in heaven above that she would just drop dead. D'you hear me? What do you have to say to that? Eh? Eh?'

But St Anthony didn't have anything further to say for the night. Perhaps he had been shocked into a reverberative silence. Mary turned the ignition off and slumped over the steering wheel, nostrils filled with the sweet gardenia scent of her mother in a way she hadn't remembered for years.

10

A pale, watery light crept up the walls of Greta's living room. It took Matt a couple of moments to focus on her anxious face peering down at him through the early morning gloom. He was still stretched out on the sofa where he'd closed his eyes for what he'd thought would be two minutes, the night before, once he'd returned.

'Are you all right?' she whispered. He could tell that she'd spent the night keeping vigil. The dark circles under her eyes had taken on the colour of ripe plums.

'Aye. Fine.' The knuckles of his right hand ached and he could feel a tiny cut by the corner of his lower lip. Other than that he was pleased to think he'd acquitted himself pretty decently for a guy no longer in his prime. Childishly pleased, in fact.

'Are you sure you shouldn't see a doctor?'

'No need. But one of them might have to. I cracked his nose good.'

The second he'd heard the rapid running, he'd turned with flaying fists. They were going to try to steam him but he'd caught them by surprise. He could see immediately the idea was for one to distract him with an elbow to the head while the other quickly slipped a hand in his pocket for his wallet. He wasn't carrying his wallet as it happened, only loose notes, which when he thought about it, he should have just surrendered.

'You could have been knifed,' Greta said, echoing his thoughts. Her finger traced the little cut by his lip. She was looking so tenderly at him, he could have happily endured another attack. As it turned out, with his height and streetfighting experience from youth, he was well able to handle them. Only an elbow connected with his face while he'd managed two juicy punches. They weren't up to much, taking flight as soon as they realized that he was going to stand his ground. But God, it felt good. Nothing like the clear swing of a fist to cut through unambiguous thoughts. Nothing confusing about a fist either dealt or received. He'd managed to hail a taxi after that and despite the fact that Greta was worried out of her mind at his absence so late in the night, he'd crashed out practically immediately on the sofa.

'I'm getting old,' he said with a rueful smile, flexing the fingers of the injured hand. 'Worried about my hand for work.'

'Yes, work,' she said thoughtfully. 'What took you walking in that area anyway? It's not safe by day never mind at — ' Her voice trailed off, intuitively she understood without him having to say. 'You phoned Connie.' He nodded, both taking in the implication of that for a long silence. Greta sat beside him on the sofa, palms of her hands pressed together, sandwiched between her knees.

'Okay,' she said, beginning to rock slightly, back and forth. 'Okay.'

He couldn't take his eyes off her. Adrenaline and testosterone were still surging through his blood, he wanted her so badly he had to clench his fists to stop his hands from pulling her to him. All he could hope was that some day he might be able to look back on this time together as a pleasant interlude, a chance happening, his temptation in the desert. In deeper time he might even grow grateful for the opportunity of closure with Greta. In great old age, if he lived so long, her face might not even form in his head, instead, he might find himself on certain days, compelled from some mundane conversation, the evening geriatric cocoa perhaps, to stand outside staring up at the sky; rheumy eyes watering and blinking under a great fireball of dying sun, a gnarled visor of hand shielding the long gamma splinters. And he might find to his surprise, for no immediate reason he can think of, that he is smiling.

Out on the balcony, a blackbird greeted the morning with a flourish of song. It carried regret into the room, for loss, for time passing, for pain endured and pain inflicted, for lives not turning out the way they had once been planned with breathless anticipation, for the chance moment gone when all things might still be changed. Tears brimmed in Greta's eyes and Matt could see his own reflection shimmering for an instant before it slid down her face. He wiped a tear with a thumb and licked the salty taste.

In an instant, love passed between them, not reciprocal, or reflexive — you love me because I love you — simply there was choice, person to person, a forgetting of self, the belongings of self, of what had been accrued and had sufficed very well but now looked diminished — family, house, garden. He realized with the shock of someone finding they're capable of murder for the first time, that he was, in fact, capable of making such a choice. It could all be gone, in a smile, the time it takes for a heart to beat, the time it takes from being sentient to dead. The time it takes to breathe.

Greta, too, appeared shaken. She let out a long sigh and rose to her feet.

'Can we get out of here for a while?' she asked.

'Greta — '

'You have to go. Just the way of things. Let's get coffee and croissants and pretend for a while that you don't.'

★ ★ ★

They sat in Piazza Navona sipping coffee, watching street hawkers peddle rubbish to tourists with the splendour of Bernini's Fountain of the Four Rivers as a backdrop. Matt tried to get Greta to eat the croissant she'd suggested but she couldn't face it after all, she said. They took a taxi to Pyramide and a train from there to Antica Ostia, the ancient port. She wanted to show him around, she said, not adding — before you leave, but it was understood.

Spread out in every direction were the ruins of the commercial city once home to over fifty thousand inhabitants. Original plaster destroyed over time to reveal the intricate redbrick skeletons of the buildings. Temples, baths, basilicas, a vast rounded theatre gave way to warehouses, tall apartment blocks, private residences, fullers' workshops, tanneries and flour-mills. They passed shops and civic offices, panels of black-and-white mosaics signalling the commerce within, the butcher, the baker, the candlestick maker. Cargo-laden vessels entering harbour, amphorae being unloaded, a river with a bridge of boats. Inscribed slabs named the various guilds of the city, the dealers in oakum, rope, the tanners.

When he closed his eyes Matt could hear the echo of a thousand conversations, trundle of wheels over cobble of the mule driven carts ferrying food and provisions and cloth to the denizens of Rome; working-day banter flying back and forth between people who couldn't have imagined someone standing on the space they occupied, imagining them, a couple of thousand years later.

He felt that he was gazing at the perfect embodiment of capitalism unfurling, there for anyone to see, the self-perpetuation of want. There wasn't any *need* for coloured togas yet a thriving guild of fullers set up to fulfil a want, generating employment, taxes, by turn generating a new set of wants which generated another.

'It's the prototype for Disneyland,' he said, half laughing.

'You're right. We haven't improved on it,' Greta responded.

They stepped through an arch into the cool interior of a tavern wine-shop which once served food and offered overnight lodgings on the upper floors. This one had three airy rooms, the central opening on to the street with a wide counter at which passers-by could buy a drink, sitting down if they wished on stone benches flanking the entrance. Behind the counter were shelves where the tavern-keeper would display his fare; beneath, basins for washing dishes and tumblers. Further inside was a cupboard and more shelving with the remaining plaster of a still-life painting advertising the sort of nibble customers might like with their drinks: eggs in brine, grapes, olives, a radish or two. Tapas, Matt thought.

As they moved along the main thorough-fare, lined either side with flat-topped stone pines, Matt grew more convinced that these people had not really left at all. There was too strong a feeling of them everywhere, in their gardens, their marble-floored villas, the communal latrine which once had revolving doors and flushed with running water. The plethora of baths where they bathed and steamed and could step into annexed suites for massages or beauty treatments. The idea of talk, of commerce, of intercourse, of how could this possibly be all over, was absolutely overwhelming. He felt certain in the dead of night, alone and hiding, if he strained to listen, the level would reach a pitch the same frequency as his own hearing. Greta was smiling at his pleasure, at his wonder.

'Funny how history sort of immerses you when you lose someone,' she said. 'I mean, of course I did all the tourist bit when I came here first. But it was a suburban life mostly, Rome was the city nearby where I came to shop, meet friends at an art exhibition, curse all the intruders in high season making it difficult to catch a taxi. While you're never unaware of the beautiful things around you, how could you be — still, you're just a person living a life which happens to be near Rome.' She pulled her mouth down and gazed into the distance.

'Then Sandro,' Matt probed gently. 'Tell me.'

'I walked out of my house the day of his funeral. Just bags of clothes, possessions, enough to take me out of my life.'

'Tell me,' he insisted, squeezing her hand. They were alone, on the final approach to the Porta Marina beyond which stretched the ancient foreshore of the Tiber, long since changed course so that the port was actually on dry land now. Greta stood still for a moment and looked at him.

'I have a daughter, Matt.'

'A daughter? But — '

'Let's sit.'

They settled on a diamond-patterned brick

wall of a synagogue ruin, facing into the building at four still erect marble columns. Afternoon sun beat down on their heads, lending a sheen to Greta's cheeks. Her eyes were dry, gritty. Matt waited.

'Gianna, after her father's mother. Seventeen now. I haven't seen her for two years.'

Greta's hands were folded limply on her lap. She couldn't bring herself to look at him again but stared straight ahead, focusing on the pillars as if she were talking to them.

'I have not lived a good life, Matt. I want to tell you this so that you can really know me and go back to your own life.'

'Greta?'

'It wasn't a happy marriage, not particularly unhappy either to tell the truth. Tommaso had his flings, he travelled a lot, it was pretty much separate lives in those last years together. We were polite, went through the motions, got on with it. There was plenty of everything, I wanted for nothing. I can't even say I was rich but unhappy, bored maybe, too much time on my hands. There were affairs, Matt. Nothing serious — I liked to flirt, to get that breathless feeling, feel my heart pumping faster. The pretending to fall in love until things turned sour. That's how trivial it was, a trivial life.' She continued to stare straight ahead, her face impassive as the brick around them.

'A family moved into the house next door. We got along very well from the start. Dinners, you know, barbecues, drinks in the evening. They had a young child. The day in Tivoli when we stood outside my house, their car came through the gates, if you remember.'

'You didn't want to be seen. Aye, I remember.'

'The husband, Paolo — it was a long flirtation. Eyes lingering just a second too long as we'd pass food, a little extra squeeze saying goodnight, that sort of thing. I don't think you'd be too familiar with all that, would you?'

'No. I can't say that I would.'

'We became lovers. Absolutely nothing in it other than a mutual thrill, mutual flattery. We enjoyed playing naughty children. It was cruel to his wife, they weren't that long married, she loved him deeply.'

Matt felt a spur of anger, remembering Ed the dog and Greta's wilful kicks. The way she used to spurn Connie as though the younger girl didn't even exist. She would, of course, have carried that dark streak of cruelty into adulthood.

'I don't want to embellish, you understand,' Greta continued, face still hewn from granite. 'Make it sound as if it were some great love story we couldn't resist. It was what it was.'

'Go on,' he snapped more sharply than intended, adding, 'go on, Greta', in a softer tone.

'Tommaso was away. So was Paolo's wife with their little girl. I left Gianna in charge of Sandro and went next door.' Her voice had taken on a dull, lustreless timbre, speaking by rote what she replayed every day in her mind minute by minute, second by second. She coughed and shuddered before continuing. The shudder racked her body from the feet up, rising to her neck, so violently, Matt thought he should stop her in case she broke in two. A hand shot up, fingers splayed when he moved to touch her.

'What I didn't know, was that Gianna had taken to slipping out of the house late at night herself. To meet a boyfriend. There was a power cut that night. All of Tivoli was out.' For the first time Greta craned to look at him, no light in her eyes, nothing, not a flicker, she, like Tivoli, had been put out. A tiny moan escaped Matt's lips as he realized what had happened. For no apparent reason it came to him fully fledged and he was certain in an instant that he was right.

'You didn't know,' he managed to speak.

'You didn't know because you were already in candlelight.'

She nodded, once, then stared ahead again. They sat in silence while late afternoon shadows dipped in and out of the synagogue's ramparts; flat, dead heat drumming on their heads, Matt's now bent, as though in prayer. Greta made odd, heaving sounds intermittently but did not cry. He understood she did not want to offer herself the momentary release of tears. All too clearly, he could picture the rest. A boy waking to find himself alone in the dark, creeping downstairs, calling for his mother, the drawer in the kitchen where the candles were kept, a struck match illuminating the beautiful face he'd seen in her photographs, a taper of yellow light gliding up along the stairs until stilled and upright by a single bed. A sigh of breeze tickling muslin curtains through a crack of open window. Stronger sigh until muslin tickles flame.

'It rained. All day long, the day we put him in the ground. Gianna was in hospital, they'd had to sedate her. She was the one who came back to find smoke — They said he'd died of smoke inhalation. Maybe they said that to make us feel better — *better.*' Her voice cracked on the word. Another deep rumbling shudder and she wrapped her arms around

226

her body in an attempt to quell it. 'He was — he was the most beautiful boy, Matt. Gentle and good-natured. He loved to walk with me, simple ordinary things, if I forgot for a second and my hand holding his grew slack, he'd curl my fingers tighter. I used to look at him and think, thank God, none of me in him. I wish you could have known him.' She turned with those dull, quenched eyes again, looking straight through him to a place he could not travel with her. 'Why wasn't it enough just to have known him and loved him? Why?'

She wasn't expecting an answer and Matt didn't try. There was no answer. She had made her hell and now she was burning in it. They sat on while the sun beat down on their unprotected heads. Matt felt, for the first time since he was a young lad, that he should say a prayer, or remember one, or something like it. Sweat had parted Greta's hair along the back revealing the long coiled snake of scar tissue. Her shoulders moved up and down in those dreadful heaving sobs that made her shudder dryly in their wake.

They sat on until the sun lowered in the sky, a late breeze fanning the tops of their bent heads while the ghosts of Antica Ostia went about their business, buying, selling, making, mending, unaware that their time had long since passed.

★ ★ ★

It was early evening by the time they returned to Greta's apartment. She immediately ran into her bedroom where he could hear the tears she'd pent up all afternoon. She was stretched across the bed with her head hanging over the side when he stepped in. She could hardly breathe she was crying so hard. A sob would start at a pitch and work its way down to a juddering growl, the sort of judder a ship gives when it dips from a crest descending to the bowels of a wave. A couple of times she gagged and he thought she would be sick. He went to her and lifted her head gently to place her face against his shoulder. His shirt was wringing wet in an instant. 'Sweetheart,' he said, over and over again because there was nothing else to say. She was trying to say something but each time a sob would take her over. Finally she managed:

'I want to be dead.'

'No Greta please — '

'I dream about it. Sometimes I — and then Gianna — what I've done to her already. I keep away from her so she doesn't have to see me — It's the best I can do for her. But if she heard something happened — she'd have to carry that, too. I can't even finish this — this existence. Can't even go to him. And then another day comes. And another. The way it will be — until I die. Why can't he come back? Why can't he come back my darling darling boy?'

He cupped her face, lifting it to his lips, kissing her salty cheeks, forehead, chin, wishing he could obliterate some of her pain, knowing that nothing could. He kissed her as he would a child, raining down fiercely, possessively, battling with the pain, trying to make it relent, give her a moment's peace.

'I want you to know I love you, Greta.' He kissed her mouth drawing her air into his own. 'Whatever's happened. Whatever's going to happen. I want you to know and believe that I love you.' His tongue flickered against hers and she made a small mewl-like sound. He could feel the waves of heat coming from her body, of wanting to be touched, penetrated, to know a moment of not being alone in her skin with so much pain. But her hands pressed against his shoulders trying to break his tight grip. Her mouth struggled to unlock from his and for a moment he thought he would lose his mind.

They rolled on the bed, tumbling over and

over, her groin arching up to meet his as he lifted her T-shirt to kiss her breasts, one hand fumbling to unzip his jeans. She helped him draw his own shirt over his head. Their fingers tugged at clothes, pulled and finally ripped until he was suspended above her, elbows taking his weight as he looked deep into the swollen grey eyes. Blood surfed through his eardrums, constant thunk from the Iron Works, pink snow on white skin, Greta spread beneath him, that first time, that first time when he had closed his eyes before driving his body and mind and soul, all the way home, all the way to the heart of the sun.

'I can't stop this time,' he said, 'you know that, don't you?'

Her eyes never left his as he slowly lowered his mouth on to hers. Inside, sheer brightness, tongue circling tongue. His thigh nudging hers further apart, this couldn't be wrong, how could it be wrong — he said her name, a prayer, a benediction, a rememberance — before he entered her.

11

Nothing had changed in Brenda's small living room since Connie was a little girl aside from the addition of framed photographs of her grandchildren lined up either side of the cast-iron fireplace all the way to the ceiling. A hexagonal brass mirror hung from a rusted chain with a horizontal line of wood block miniature prints of Paris above that. Brenda had never been to France, but if she fancied going anywhere, it would be Paris. On the mantle stood a prayer set in china made out to look like an ancient scroll, two flowery china vases with one dried rosebud apiece, the colour of oxidized wounds. A brass fish with open mouth, brass lady in ballgown that concealed a bell. Empty brass letter holder and a brass letter opener with a curved ornate handle. These last items had been polished quite recently.

In front of the fire stood a guard with a picture of a ship from the Spanish Armada battling a stormy sea. Either side, more brass accoutrements and two high-winged arm-chairs with tapestry seat cushions. There was a gateleg table folded up against one wall with

231

four dining chairs in a rigid alignment facing into the room. The small mock leather sofa where Connie sat had to be pressed up against the window when the table was extended, but that was only on Sundays and Christmas Day.

Looking around in the dim morning light, Connie envied her mother's saturation. The room was full, could hold nothing further, contained all that was required and aside from a lick of fresh paint from time to time, there was nothing that Brenda would have seen fit to change. The room was done, leave it. No, not saturation, Connie thought, completion. The closed-door simplicity of completion so alien to her own generation.

She yawned and rubbed her eyes. It was only half past six and already she'd been sitting in the semi-dark for an hour, fully clothed, anticipating something but what she couldn't figure. A churning in her stomach making her restless and excited and apprehensive at the same time. Earlier, when she'd tried to sleep, each time she'd managed to get to dropping-off point, her body had startled awake and the dark had come rushing down on top of her the way it used to when she was a young teenager. Back then she would open her mouth thinking that if she could just swallow enough of the night, it might fade a little and give her some peace. But it proved increasingly restless inside her, too, so she would creep downstairs to sit on this same sofa waiting for the first spears of light. She understood perfectly well what was preventing her from sleeping but understanding didn't solve the problem. From the age of fourteen until her departure for London with Matt, sleep proved as elusive as the holy grail.

Brenda was in the kitchen, doubtless making a huge pot of porridge which the boys would eat though silently gagging. They generally tended to treat their Consett relations with a deference they didn't always show down south. It was a curious mix of insecurity and inverse snobbery on their part in that wishing to humour their 'really real' northern roots, they were also unconsciously swallowing wholesale the thin-skinned northerner stereotype. Or worse, they were afraid they'd come across as poncey city boys. If they didn't want porridge, they only had to say — though Connie never told them that, partly because porridge was good for them but mostly because there had to be some small recompense in life for a parent. Getting the odd one over on your kids was up there. She closed her eyes and allowed herself to drift for what she thought might be a few minutes. When she opened them again, the room was filled with light and her three sons were stooge-like peering down at her. Their worried expressions were so comical she had to laugh.

'I'm glad you find something to laugh at,' Fred said, a little peeved. She got the impression that he would have appreciated a touch more of the tragedienne in her performance.

'I nearly always find something to laugh at,' Connie responded breezily, reaching out for a quick squeeze of Benny's hand, which he placed behind his back when she was done though he flickered a smile and wiped an imaginary speck from one eye.

'So what happens now?' Joe asked. 'What're we supposed to do around here all day?'

'C'mon.' Connie jumped to her feet. 'Let's go see your granddad.'

'Not the farm,' Joe groaned.

'Yep, the farm. Good for you to get in touch with your roots. Today, we're mostly going to do good things.'

'Oh for fuck's sake,' Joe muttered under his breath. They were huddling out the front door. Connie called to her mother not to bother with lunch, they'd eat at the farm, but the scent of soup was already coming from the kitchen.

'I heard that, Joe.' Connie elbowed him in the ribs. 'Mind your language please.'

'Piss and shit,' Joe muttered all the way to the car.

'How was the porridge?' Connie dryly asked of them as she wrenched the car door open.

'It had lumps,' Benny responded, seriously considering every mouthful of breakfast until she wished he would stop. A few hundred yards along, she knew he was still giving the porridge his full attention. *That*, that was the thing that bothered her sometimes. It was just a throwaway question, laden with a degree of sarcasm the other two would pick up instantly. How was the porridge? For God's sake, Benny, it wasn't what do you want to be when you grow up?

'But otherwise it was okay,' he added after some time.

'What's he on about?' Joe snapped.

'The porridge,' Connie answered in a deflated voice.

She took a fleeting glance over her shoulder and her heart lurched. Benny had his head down and he had squashed his body into a tight huddle by his side of the car. He caught her glance and immediately stared out of the window as though the passing fields were of huge interest. A worried frown flickered on his brow. He didn't know what the hell was going on, no more than she, and she could have happily murdered somebody's granny to eke a smile from him.

'Come on, Benny. It's a day off school.'

'Yeah!'

Did he have to look quite so geeky putting on that false enthusiasm?

'There's one thing I have to say about your so-called friend Sebastian,' Joe was cutting in. Connie tried to dart him a look.

'Yeah?' Benny said, already rounding his shoulders for the put-down.

'He's crap on a skateboard. Total crap. I'd drop him if I was you.'

Connie could sense the lift in Benny. One throwaway remark, though by no means not deliberately well intentioned, from his older brother, and he could hold his head up once more. She didn't even want to correct Joe's grammer. Joe, she thought, I temporarily take back everything I've ever said about you. You're a star.

Arthur Wilson greeted them from his tractor. Connie had wondered in the past if he sometimes fell asleep at night astride the great noisy beast and just chugged into action again at daybreak like a little wind-up toy. He was such a small, grizzled creature to have produced the giants he had. A squat rectangle of a man with sad, molten eyes and a mouth that had a way of twitching when he smiled as if a smile in itself was a sure way of asking for trouble. But in the way of wiry shortness, he was resilient and strong as a horse, even now in his eighties. The boys strolled across as he climbed down, hands thrust in their pockets, wry grins on their faces in the manner they'd seen their own father greet his father many times. Fred and Joe clapped Arthur's shoulder then shook his hand. Connie felt a swell of pride. They would be fine men.

Arthur held a hand out to Benny which was shaken after a tiny hesitation. No kisses, nonsense, trill of exclamations, this was the Alamo where men were men and boys were men in waiting and thus could entirely dispense with sentences of more than one clause. Similarly, emotions were, in general, best avoided. If you absolutely had to have them then best keep them to yourself. If you couldn't manage that then best go to London or some other big city where people spoke a load of drivel and grown men could cry into their beer.

Everywhere she looked, from every age, Connie could see Matt. Diligent son, quiet farmboy, lover of Greta. But Greta had gone away, spurred into harum-scarum flight after the bicycle accident, never to return at least not to Matt's knowledge, while Connie had stayed the course, had staked her claim and waited until he'd turned to see that she had been standing there all along. Here, in this place and in the red dusty air of the town, their histories had forged together, no less than the constant forge of steel in the casting bays up in the Works itself. She saw why she had come here, to remember who they once were so that she could return, armed with that knowledge, to who they had become. She was gathering herself, all that she knew of herself and Matt — perhaps for battle, perhaps for forgiveness.

Feeling clearer in her head than she had for many days now, Connie stepped out of the car to greet Arthur.

'Well, this was *not* expected.' He closed two hands over hers and pumped vigorously. 'Wor Matt not with yous then?'

Connie shot her sons a silencing glance.

'He's in Rome, Arthur. Helping out an old friend — but never mind that, it's good to see you. You look so well.'

'Aye, I'm champion, me. Rome you say. Who would this old friend — '

'You wouldn't remember.' Connie pulled her mouth down. Joe was approaching and she didn't want him blundering in. 'Arthur, would you mind if I made us all some lunch in the kitchen? Tell you what — I'll get on with that if you want to set the boys to work. All those jobs you must have backed up, well, here's your answer! They're always on about how much they enjoy a bit of hard graft on the farm. Isn't that right, Joe?'

Joe issued a look that might have felled a less robust constitution but Connie was feeling curiously elated. Even Joe couldn't remain churlish in the light of his grandfather's obvious pleasure at the prospect of three strapping lads for an afternoon's labour. Arthur pulled at his nose while his pale blue eyes danced with keen anticipation. She was instinctively speaking his language, what passed for small talk — it wasn't his way to sit around asking how was whom and where was what — any questions would gradually trickle out over a bale of straw or a gathering rake. Usually Matt was up on that tractor before Connie and his sons were even out of their car.

'You can bet your boots I won't say no,' Arthur said. He walked off with a hand resting lightly on Joe's shoulder. Already there was a scrim of crud around the ground-scraping hem of her son's overlong designer jeans. Connie's frisson of spite felt good enough to eat.

She found ham and eggs in the kitchen and

started frying. A hen wandered in to keep her company and she shooed it out to raucous protests. There, by a ceramic bread bin, was Matt's old radio/cassette player; she put on a local station and began to hum while cracking eggs. Like her mother's house, nothing had changed. The kitchen smelled of manure, carbolic soap and sourish milk. How many nights had she sat at that slab of table with Matt, planning their future together? Leafing through college application forms, shivering with excitement at the grown-upness of it all, the unknowable prospect of anything and everything yet to happen. Sometimes, it grew too much for her to contain and she would launch herself at him, a hand clutching either side of his face, lips hungrily devouring his. And afterwards, that shy almost perplexed smile cracking slowly across his face at her spontaneous shows of affection.

An old Jimi Hendrix number was playing on the radio, which she took as a good omen. She went out to call them in for lunch. What she saw made her bend over in silent peals of laughter. In the distance, Fred was up on the tractor, weaving perilously across a sloping field. She actually saw him hit a tree at one point, reverse, then hit the tree again. Joe was gingerly carrying a bale of hay in the crook of one arm while the other hand remained steadfastly, though by his definition, coolly, in his jeans pocket. His immaculate white trainers picked a trail through chocolatey muck, delicate as a newborn colt's first unsteady steps. Benny was chasing after a rooster, hunkered forward, like one of those maniacal Cambodian soldiers in a war movie, with his arms spread wide — what exactly did he think he was going to do if he actually caught the old bird? As it happened, the rooster must have come to the same conclusion because he turned of a sudden and the chase resumed in the other direction. Benny was sprinting towards his grandfather with the mangy cockerel in hot pursuit.

Tears streamed down Connie's face. God, she wished Matt was here to see this. She didn't even have to worry about her youngest who was neither more nor less adept in this place than the two polished Londoners ahead of him.

To the right of the house was the old bicycle shed. There, up against the far wall, was Matt's old black bike with a triangle of cobweb between the handlebar and brake. It took her a while to get at it as she had to negotiate a path through mounds of junk. She lifted it out into the open ignoring the pitiful clattering sounds. The rear mudguard needed adjusting. Connie remembered the toolbox on a shelf in the shed; she was on her knees tweaking, spinning wheels, tightening the chain, which needed oil, before she knew what she was doing. The brakes squealed in pain when she pinched, more oil and a touch of corrective screwdriver and all the sounds subsided. She felt like a surgeon testing the operated-on patient as she swung one leg over the crossbar. The saddle shifted down a bit but the bike was strong and sturdy and just begging for a run.

Connie half cycled, half tiptoed her way around the other side of the house. She knew exactly where she was heading and didn't want the boys to see. At the bottom of the long steeply sloped field she got off and pushed the bicycle all the way to the top. It took nearly ten minutes by which time she was covered in a sheen of sweat and her back ached. Up at the top, looking down on the manse, the outbuildings, her sons like Lowry stick figures darting here and there, the humpbacked stone bridge over the river to the right of the property and the main road from town slicing almost to the front door of the house, she told herself not to do this. Sheer (in every sense of the word) madness with the earth still pockmarked from rain and the grass much longer than the days when Matt and Greta plunged down. She tested the brakes. They would hold but if she hit a recalcitrant hummock, all the braking in the world wouldn't stop her somersault. Still, her eyes were picking out the route they used to take. Straight down the centre of the field where the ground was the smoothest, though there was that tree to avoid almost towards the final ditch which had scuppered Greta.

The sky was a shade of vanilla streaked with spumes of charcoal grey. Rain had finally stopped in the middle of the night, she being awake to hear its petering out, missing the sound when it was gone. The reek of sodden turf was still spicy to her nostrils, it would slow descent but equally would suction rubber wheels making the going extra-rigorous. She had never attempted this, neither as child nor teenager. It was a crazy idea. She was a grown woman for heaven's sake. Exhilaration coursed through her blood.

Connie swung her right leg over the crossbar. For a second she thought something grand like her life flashing before her eyes should unfold but nothing so grand as that occurred. A gurgling empty stomach reminding hunger. She lifted and spun the front wheel the way she'd watched Matt do it. She raised it higher and higher, leaning back with the weight of her body to the back. A blackbird called from a stringy bush behind.

Already her vision was blurring. You can still stop, a cautionary voice in her head attempted to plead. Mentally, she said: bugger off. The front wheel whined in expectant rotation, sound of a stirred hornet.

For a second Connie squeezed her eyes shut. When they opened again, the boys were standing stock-still at the other side of the ditch at the bottom of the field. Arthur was shambling as fast as he could towards them. Someone had pointed out her position. Connie let out a holler and surged the bike into the air to set up speed. She landed with a quiver and pretty much everything after that was a quivering blur. A third of the way down there was a stretch of smoother ground and the wheels obliged by picking up a really decent pace. Connie splayed her legs and shouted with glee. Wind filled her lungs and whipped through her hair.

The trick she'd seen with Matt over and over again was to resist the urge to squeeze on the brakes too early. Just a touch, followed by another, about two-thirds down. The front wheel hit a hummock of earth and sailed into the air. She could hear the boys shouting up. The wheels landed again with a bone-shaking tremble but she mastered the wobble and was picking up speed again for the final descent. A long primal scream curled out of her mouth. Feet back on the pedals — that tree was looming closer, faster than she'd thought. First squeeze of the brakes, but the pace didn't slow significantly. Trying to veer off course at this stage would be lunacy, the bike would go into a spin. Second tip to the brakes, a little slower. She could pick out markings on the trunk of the gnarled old oak. Losing her nerve, she braked too hard, too quick and the back wheel lifted off the ground. It took every concentrated muscle in her body to right the wobble this time. The bike was zigzagging. All the way to the tree, Connie gritted her teeth and applied pressure to the brakes in a series of tiny movements. The bike stopped with a final quake about three feet from the oak.

She got off and let the wheels clatter to the ground, pedals still whirring. There wasn't an inch of her not covered in sweat, it dripped through her eyebrows into her eyes. Adrenaline surged through her veins making her dizzy now, there was no place for it to go.

'My God,' she gasped as the boys ran across the field. 'I did it. I actually did it.'

'Are you crazy?' Fred was shouting. 'Not even a helmet.'

Joe got to her first. He was grinning like a loon.

'That was.' He stopped and shook his head.

'That was like the sickest thing you've ever ever done. Man that was heavy. Me next.'

At first, her instinct was to baulk. Only a fortnight ago her instinct would have been to smash the bike into pound pieces to stop any one of them even considering such a run.

'Okay. But first we have to buy a helmet.'

'Two helmets. A smaller one for me,' Benny said. Connie grimaced, no no she couldn't do this. Not Benny.

'If you break every bone in your body, don't come crying to me.'

His head listed to the side, mulling over her words in his deliberate way.

'If I break every bone I won't be able to walk, so I couldn't come to you. You'd have to get a stretcher.'

'Whatever. Come on.'

Perhaps the seven or eight grapefruits she'd craved every day while carrying him had something to do with it.

★ ★ ★

All afternoon, once they'd got the helmets and executed their chores, the boys took it in turns to freewheel down the field. Connie sat by the base of the tree, watching. Their excited cries felt like nourishment to her soul. Even Benny seemed to throw off his mantle

246

of seriousness as he sped towards her with shining eyes, a wide, infectious beam splitting his face. Of course, Joe had to test the limits of the braking advice she'd given and ended up in a sprawl by her feet. It was strange yet somehow appropriate watching her sons flying down to her as she had once watched Matt. She could see him in each one of their faces and could feel his presence close by. The years hadn't passed and she was still a girl looking up a field at what she loved.

Later, after more soup and chunks of her mother's sultana loaf, Connie walked the boys around the streets where she used to play. Clusters of little girls passed, embracing summer with rolled milk-dough arms and heart-shaped sunglasses, tiny Lolitas with everything ahead of them, perhaps, even, love.

She showed her weary sons the site of the Iron Works, demolished now, impossible for them to begin to imagine how it had once dominated the town. Waking and sleeping hours it thunked like a festering heart over the town until the surgeon of change and time and commerce pronounced it ailing, critical, eventually dead. It was her heart, Matt's heart, and Greta's, too. That strange tubular carbuncle with black stacks reaching up to the sky, how she imagined a grim lonely outpost would look in deepest space.

They passed Greta's house; Brenda was right, you could see straight through now to the kitchen at the back. A wall that separated off the hair salon from the rest of the house had been knocked down. Four sisters — Rita, Marlene, Hedy and Greta, named after their mother's favourite movie stars. An exotic combination to have fussing over your hair. They chewed gum while they cut, blowing huge bubbles which splatted over their jaws, the constant sound punctuating the continuous chatter in the salon.

'Greta was the nearest in age to me and your dad,' Connie said. 'We were very close the three of us.'

'Greta?' Fred frowned. 'The friend in Rome?'

'Yes, her.'

'But I thought you could hardly remember her. Now you were close, you say.'

'It's both, Fred. The truth is, I've tried not to remember her. How can I explain? It's like something huge from your childhood, living on in a pocket deep inside you for the rest of your life. She was that huge to me back then. But I don't think she ever really saw me, though I wanted her to. So, strange as it sounds, she's still with me but I'm not with her.'

Fred nodded as though something had struck him but he kept silent. They were about to move on when the front door opened. Connie recognized Rita though she hadn't seen her for what seemed like a hundred years. Rita's eyes squinched up. 'I know you, don't I?' she asked, peering at Connie. Her sharp little ferret face was deeply scored from years of smoking. Long ridged fingernails in sugar pink tapped against one cheek trying to remember.

'You knew me as Constance Bradley.' Connie put out her hand. 'How are you, Rita?'

'As good as I can be. Are these your lads then? My, haven't the years gone by. Well, this is the damnedest thing — here is you passing my door and Greta on the phone not half an hour ago.'

Connie managed to keep a stiff little smile on her face dreading mention of Matt in Rita's next sentence but she was prattling on about Greta, how rarely she called, the coincidence of it being this evening. How she hadn't been doing so good not since the death of her son but she'd sounded more back to her old self on the phone. She was even thinking of taking a trip to London with maybe a view to going back there. Rita surmised that there were too many sad memories for her sister in Rome. It would be nice to have Greta in the same country again, she did so make Rita laugh.

Connie nodded, making interested responses with her face while her gut wrapped around her innards. The boys were hopping from one foot to the other with ill-concealed boredom. Fred's eyes were pulsing looking at his mother.

'Rita — I'll have to stop you there,' Connie managed to interject. 'We have to — we have to go.' She pressed Rita's hand again and left her in mid-sentence.

'You're okay,' Fred said. It took her a while to realize it was a question.

'Yes,' she said. 'Yes, I'm okay.'

When the house was finally silent later that night, she lay in bed trying to process Rita's information but every conclusion led to another the exact opposite. It could be a good or a bad thing that Greta hadn't mentioned Matt. It could be good or bad that she was sounding more like her old self. Would that make Connie seem pallid and insipid by comparison?

She hadn't meant to make of her life quite such a compact thing. As a girl she'd sometimes thought she'd grow up to be somebody important with a big life, though never with any great conviction. Years had

250

passed while she meant to develop a hunger for knowledge, an interest in politics, read the books she knew she should, show more of an interest in the outside world not merely acquiesce to what came into the house via a television tube — so that's the world, that's what's going on out there — put your own plate in the dishwasher, Joe, like I've told you a thousand times. The visits to art galleries with Mary were about it on her cultural calendar. Maybe she'd become stolid and safe and reassuring — boring in her compactedness.

But the simple truth was all she'd ever wanted was to marry Matt and have a family. She had been ashamed to admit that and when she had wanted more, it was really her frustration at herself coming through, that it was a miniature life, no more no less than she had anticipated and she didn't have sufficient vision or ambition to push herself harder. She'd got what she'd wanted and conversely was cross with herself for wanting so little.

Still, there was work, she hadn't done so badly there. People to meet, lives to briefly touch, the suggestion of intersections beyond her immediate domestic scope. There was also the pleasure of an empty kitchen on a yellow sunlit morning, everyone still asleep, scent of coffee percolating, pottering about her domain in her nightie. A feeling of satisfaction provided by a briefly full to bursting larder after a monumental shop, provisions for her family, meals racked up to cook. There was the scent of sheets crisp from the drying line, windows sparkling with vinegar, that first surge of growth in the garden in spring, newly planted pots, watching, waiting for them to suddenly take off. Her sons dawdling a pace behind her rapid footsteps through the shopping centre — faces coated with feigned nonchalance for fear someone might see them out *with their mother*. Impatiently looking back for her three stooges, stabbed with a spear of love for their transparency, their gauche incompleteness, their tender youth.

Had she made herself so small she had grown invisible to Matt's eye? Had she made herself so small that a big, full, grown-up thought could no longer find fertile ground? Could she find somebody to blame other than herself for that — of course she could — temporarily. Ultimately, blame homed like the fondest of pigeons.

She closed her eyes listening to the feathery breaths of Benny curled into a ball with his buttocks pressing against her hipbone. If she could just dodge the darkness pressing down before it captured her for the night, she might manage a few hours' sleep. Twinges from the bike mushroomed up and down her body. *The phone!* She sat up with a start. She'd forgotten to switch it on since they left Twickenham.

Scrabbling about the unplumbed depths of her bag in the dark it came to her that not only could Matt not reach them, neither could Mary. She would be frantic with worry by now. Seventeen messages — all from Mary.

'Mary?' Connie whispered. 'Sorry to call so late — '

'Jesus Christ!' Mary bawled down the line. 'Where the bloody hell are you?'

'I'm at home. Consett, I mean. It was a spur of the moment thing. Sorry, I should have called to let you know. I didn't even think to put my phone on. It's my head — I'm not sure what's — really, I am so sorry pet.'

She could hear what sounded disturbingly like sniffles the other end.

'Mary?'

'I thought maybe you were closing ranks against me. I thought maybe I was out of the gang!' Mary tried to sound jokey which only emphasized her anguish. Connie could have sliced off one of her big toes, she felt so guilty. Poor big shambling Mary — how could she have been so thoughtless? How random and biting was the whipflick of cruelty least intended. She thought of Matt, the at times, unintentioned detached tone of his voice on the phone.

'Are you all right?' Mary asked in a quieter tone.

'I'm not sure. How are you?'

'I've been praying to St Anthony. I think I might have to drop him.'

'Drop him.'

'Okay. I will. He keeps telling me to get a life.'

Connie smiled into the darkness.

'Tell him get stuffed. I had a life. It had a shape. From where I'm sitting it's all looking a bit blurred round the edges right now.'

'I think things will work out all right,' Mary said but there was a thread of worry in her voice.

'You know, it doesn't for most of the people we deal with at work. I thought I understood what they were going through but really I had no idea. It's all clichés, the anger, rejection, denial — but it's like you're outside yourself, watching the emotions flitting by exactly on cue. And they're almost an inconvenience really, you want to get to the nub of it, not so much how can this happen to me, it's more — to Matt — *Could you do this to me? Could you do this?* Ask your St Anthony that. How can you be toodling along one minute, living a perfectly normal life with a few abnormal bits and pieces and suddenly the possibility of the whole damn thing being taken away from you is something you have to face. I'd be a fool not to consider the possibility, don't you think?'

'I suppose,' Mary allowed after a long pause.

'It's nothing on a world scale. Not an earthquake or a war or the truly terrible things that people have to endure. Look, I could be sat at home drinking a cup of coffee and in the time it takes to put that cup down to answer a knock on the front door — life could be over — they've come to tell me that one of my sons has been attacked by that lunatic with the hammer. Believe me, I am trying not to wallow in self-pity, to keep a sense of proportion going. It's only a little life. But it's nearly always had Matt in it. You see, Mary, what I've come to see is — I don't know how to live my life without Matt. It's really that simple. And now that he's found Greta again, I don't know if he can live without her. Oh I don't mean in an overblown *I can't live without you* melodramatic way. Smaller than that, just small and simple and perfectly true. All the more lethal.

Maybe I was having my happy ending and just didn't know it.'

'Don't say that. Please don't say that.' Mary's voice tailed off as if she had turned from the mouthpiece. Connie couldn't hear the next sentence.

'Mary? You've gone faint — '

'I *said* I hope she drops dead with her next footstep. I do.'

'What would St Anthony have to say to that?'

'He wouldn't be thrilled.'

'Well, keep thoughts like that up and you'll burn in hell alongside me. Because there was a time — '

'Connie?'

'Her sister says she's thinking of coming to London.'

There was a long pause while Mary digested that.

'I'm not even going to say — this is a terrible thing to say, but — the truth is, I really do wish her dead. Maybe that's what she wants, to be gone, finished with it.'

'I think that's what Matt is afraid of.'

'Come home tomorrow, won't you?'

'Yes. Yes, I will.'

'It doesn't have to be a huge thing. Could all be blown over — this time next week even.'

'I've been trying to keep it small. Containable.'

'I know you have. Connie? Connie dear, here's a cliché — everything's going to be all right. And just for good measure — really.'

'He's never forgotten her. Not for a day. I don't think he even knew. I did though, I always understood. It's the way I feel about him. You can wish her dead all you like, Mary, she's been a ghost for years.'

★   ★   ★

A last pale shimmer of pink cut into deepening dusk as Connie pulled the car into their street. Benny was asleep while Fred and Joe continued to stare morosely out of the rear windows in a gloomy silence they'd managed to keep up through most of the long drive home. Connie's eyelids were beginning to bat dangerously.

'Mind how you go,' Brenda had said, 'keep stopping for cups of tea if your head goes light. Though it's mostly mugs they give yous in those places these days.'

'Bye Mam. Thanks for everything.'

'For what? Couple of bowls of soup is all. Have you remembered — '

'The jars of blackberry jam? Yeah, they're in the boot.'

'Last year's, of course. Maybe you'll come up in September and we can pick them fresh on the farm. Matt and the lads can give Arthur a hand while we do that.'

Brenda's eyes had held Connie's with concentrated penetration. At the mention of Matt she gave Connie's shoulder a quick though pincer-like squeeze. She nodded her head once then backed away from the car to wave them off.

'At bloody last,' Fred yawned, as they finally glided to a halt by the kerb.

There was a light on in the living room. Mary must have managed to get in after all.

'Fred, you'll have to carry Benny.'

Fred scooped his brother out of the car while Joe stood making loud grunts about the aches in his limbs, pins and needles in his feet.

'Joe, just shut up and come on.'

Connie was fiddling for the right key when the front door opened. Matt was standing there. His eyes briefly left her face to take in his sons. Fred was the first to move.

'I'm bursting,' he said, handing Benny over. 'Hiya Dad.' Then he was gone to the toilet. Benny's arms crept up to encircle his father's neck; though the hug was brief it was still a remarkable gesture for him. His face curled into Matt's chest, asleep again. 'My skateboard's nicked of course.' Joe was scanning over his shoulder; he glared at Connie. 'Thank you very much for that. Dad,' he added, bumping him in greeting on the way in.

Matt's eyes settled on Connie trying to gauge her reaction. It didn't seem possible to her right at that moment that he'd just managed to slip back into their lives as easily as he'd slipped out. She should be angry, combative, articulate at the very least but a curious numb sensation had taken her over. It was impossible to know if she was experiencing the lull before the storm or the calm after. Perhaps they were only poised on the brink.

He was thinner, light from the hall throwing cheekbones into gaunt relief. He wore a strange baggy T-shirt she'd never seen before. His look was tentative, shy, not guilty, a searching half-smile, shoulders moving up in silent query, a gesture so familiar it clutched her heart. Where do we go from here then?

'Connie — ' He stopped then repeated her name. It was hopeless: never a man armed with words, how could the right thing, an appropriate phrase, one helpful sentence, surge into his mouth at this very moment to carry them through.

Connie raised a hand, palm facing him

though he wasn't speaking.

'Is this you home?' she managed to get out. There might be plenty of time for her own words later, as many as she could spew but first she had to check. 'Really home, I mean. Not for talks or to get your stuff or whatever.'

'Really home — if that's all right,' he added hesitantly.

'I may have to kill you.' Connie was limp with relief.

'I realize that.' He broke into a sheepish grin and she moved a step closer. Without thinking she reached out to touch him, fingers stopping in midair inches from his face, slowly, slowly, his cheek listed sideways into the waiting cradle of her hand.

'Your father's looking well,' Connie said after a while.

'Good.' His head remained in her hand.

'I rode your old bike down the field.'

'Connie — '

She moved a finger to his lips.

'I don't want to know. I don't ever want to know.'

Benny snuffled in his sleep. Connie helped carry him inside.

12

It hadn't snowed for years yet already there'd been a couple of flurries in November and now a proper snowstorm in December, like the ones of Connie's childhood. Whiteout, a cleansing of the earth, until the street at the front of the house turned sludge grey with ugly car tracks and there were ruddy brown sprinkles of grit along the pavements. The garden was still pristine though, with bristles of grass sticking up through the white melting crystals making her want to shave it, if there was such a thing as a giant razor. She turned and Matt was standing by the kitchen door looking at her intently. She had no idea how long he'd been there. He was holding a box of baubles for the Christmas tree, streamers of tinsel spilling out.

'I thought there was another boxful,' he said, 'in the loft.'

'There should be.'

He pulled the corners of his mouth down. 'Unless I'm blind.'

'Actually, I sort of remember throwing a load of stuff out last year. The baubles were missing that thingy you hang them with. I'll get some on my way back from Mary's later.'

'Why don't we meet you in Kingston? We could get the stuff, have a bite to eat. It'd be kind of — '

'Christmassy?'

'Yeah.'

'Okay. Sounds nice.' Connie smiled with her eyes. 'It's a shame — the snow so early.' She turned to look out again, feeling Matt's eyes on the back of her head until he started a low whistle on his way back to the living room. There was the sound of laughter, busyness, a deep thrum of excitement, even teenagers grew nostalgic and childlike putting up the tree, tacking gaudy snakes of tinsel around the room. Usually she directed the performance but they knew well enough where everything went by now. More than that, she was trying to leave them be.

It didn't come easily but she had been making a conscious effort to loosen her grip on them all the past few months. Something Matt said some weeks after his return, once they'd really started to talk, had struck her like a fist. He told her that he'd felt an inexplicable resentment building up while he was in Rome. 'Towards me?' she'd exclaimed. 'While *you* were in Rome?' His expression agreed with her incredulity, shrug of his shoulders saying, go figure. He might have left it at that if she hadn't delved. 'I can't properly explain,' he'd gone on. 'Look, I don't want to hurt you any more than — it's probably just me.' Connie reached out and squeezed his arm. 'Please — I want to know.' He looked at her in a strange unfamiliar way and suddenly she wasn't sure she wanted to be on the vivisection table any longer but it was too late. 'The thing is, Connie, sometimes I think you need to own people. Of course, I know it's the people you love and you really just want to see them well and happy, I realize all that — just — it can be oppressive. I see it on Benny's face at times too.'

Though it seared to the last layer of her skin, she understood that he was opening up in the light of the soul searching they'd embarked upon at her insistence. She'd had plenty to say, too, much of it painful for him to hear, how she felt that he had been allowing his life to ebb, purposelessly, perhaps even hopelessly — so she couldn't very well censor the odd comment wrought from him. Still, it stayed with her like a misshapen nugget of coal deep in the place that also accommodated Greta.

At least they were communicating, not in that peculiar strangulated fashion of the first couple of weeks which had been characterized by a strain of high, giddy tension. He had gone to such pains to please, to be pleasant, to tell her how well she'd coped, that she'd felt close to hitting him a couple of times. His eyes were over bright, glazed on occasion, he continued to lose weight and she would suddenly turn to find him tapping his forehead with the long fingers of one hand, a look of complete distraction on his face. A guilty flush as the hand scratched instead as though that had been his intention in the first place. In his anxiety to do right having done wrong, he was overdoing everything from smiling and small talk (never his metier) to enthusing about work as if each new morning promised uncontrollable joy at the surgery. Did she want to eat out later or would he stop and get a video on the way home? What about a movie? What about — Connie's teeth gritted with irritation.

'What you did wrong,' she enunciated once in the early days driven to distraction by his ceaseless apologies, sorry my fault, sorry — completely slipped my mind, sorry to the doorframe when he bumped into it, 'was the not calling. That was wrong and totally unfair.'

'I'm very — ' he began.

'Matt! Don't say it! Just please don't say

that word again. Not for the rest of the day anyway. I suppose in a strange sort of way it could be argued that you're perfectly entitled to stay away to help an old friend out. Not letting your family know what you were up to or who you were with was cruel. I don't believe you to be a cruel man so it became doubly cruel. You might have trusted me to trust you.'

He was very pale, there were new jutting crags on his face from the lost weight giving him his old youthful angularity back. She knew that at any time she could ask a question and he would provide a truthful answer. That much hadn't changed. And in a way she could no more explain to herself than anybody else, that seemed to be the greatest cheat of all. She longed for quickfire lies, darting eyes trying to cover every possibility, retracing what had been said already, an involuntary frown at an obvious self-contradiction. A blatant lie you could catch between your teeth and gnaw until you drew blood. A lie so cheap and tawdry, becoming in an instant the thing you were angry about and not the cause. *It was the lies, Matt. Don't you see?* Just like in the evening soaps. But he didn't offer any lies because that wasn't his way and he couldn't offer any truths because she'd foresworn him. And simply, painfully, she was furious with him for not humbling himself enough to sling a whole slew of untruths in her direction. It was the least he could do. Then again, perhaps there was nothing to lie about. She had unwittingly created her own vacuum.

'She was my friend once, too,' Connie continued, picking a speck of fluff from his collar. He turned away.

'I trusted you the whole time,' she said. His head whipped back, their eyes locked in silent complicity. 'The whole time,' she repeated and caught his wince. 'Well then, that's out of the way,' Connie added, refusing to blink or lower her gaze for a second.

Fred and Joe appeared to buy the helping-a-friend-in-Rome scenario without question. There was no reason not to, Joe cared less in any case while Fred took his cue from his mother's response and as she herself was buying the full package for the sake of her sanity, any awkward questions which may have lingered in Fred's mind disappeared in the light of his father's returned presence. There had been moments when she'd even felt cross with them for going along the very path she was leading them. Cross that they were so wrapped up in their coddled lives that it was beyond their scope to imagine how close they might have come as a unit to annihilation. Benny sensed a change though. She could see it in the way his eyes followed Matt, she figured it wasn't anything he knew for certain, or even if he'd actually formed the words in his head but there was something, deep in the animal of him, the place where Benny kept himself apart. Matt could see it, too, and Connie could almost touch the invisible layer of protective, tender love he rained down on his youngest son. When he tried to extend the mantle to include her with pained, pleading eyes, she hesitated, torn between wanting to blindly run into his arms and the cautionary voice in her head telling her to hold back.

The first night was the strangest, both trying to feel their way, trying to pick up signals one from the other, how was this to be played out? It was all new unexplored territory and they couldn't as before tell each other where the footholds were. She had already consigned him to silence but there was a synchronous rhythm yet to be composed, how much silence, on which subjects, what was acceptable, if he didn't mention Greta at all wouldn't that imply guilt if not in actuality at least in his thoughts. While the boys were around they talked about the visit to Consett, the farm, Arthur and his tractor, Brenda and her soup. As though she were the one on the extended visit away. It got them through those first few awkward hours. Buoyed in measure by this small success, Connie pressed on to venture her meeting with Rita.

'Greta might come to London,' she'd said airily.

'Aye. It's a possibility.'

'A change might be good for her.' They'd dropped the subject until later when they were finally alone and Matt told her about Greta's son. It wasn't difficult to imagine the woman's guilt or to feel a spear of sympathy — Connie found herself asking questions, glad that she hadn't sufficiently demonized another being to the point where nothing in the world could elicit a compassionate response. She began to feel part of the story again, no longer ostracized, shut out. It was very odd, talking about Greta relieved her fears in some perverse fashion, as did making Matt talk about her. What she could not face was any talk of Matt with Greta, dinners, conversations, sightseeing trips, though she knew she should if they were going to carry this off. They were entering a spiral of what was not being said and a couple of times she came near to choking but pressed on regardless. Twice Matt froze in mid-sentence, hands with curled rigid fingers either side of his face as though trying to hold or catch something, self-contempt seething in the solid brown eyes before he exhaled with a tremendous blast, able to continue again. He described the apartment, the little boxroom where he'd spent the nights — a quick rapier glance at Connie — please please relieve me of this. She nodded her head urging him to continue in like vein. Defeatedly, he spoke about the mattress, how uncomfortable it was.

There was the big brass bed to face together the first night. They were courteous as strangers seeking shelter from a storm forced to share the same bed at the inn. Connie understood that he was mentally debating the pros and cons of what his next move should be. She understood that he was doing this for her sake and not his own. Should he reach for her — wouldn't that be the obvious course of action after time apart? Would it be a presumption too far that might unleash the fury she was at such pains to hide but which he knew was burning like a tiger in her taut frame. If her tongue was loosened, compelling questions she'd already made clear she did not want answered, where would that leave this design of damage limitation she had devised in a split second. *I don't ever want to know.* Then again, it was very late, they had both been travelling, under normal circumstances they would most likely wait until morning to make love in any case.

They lay side by side in the dark, the backs of their hands lightly touching, neither of them wanting to break the silence. The last thing needed at that particular moment was a string of hackneyed phrases, soap opera analyses, of talking things through. Her lack of strident recrimination so far was in its way more punishing to him than if she laboriously talked him through her feelings. She was aware of a small thrill of vindictiveness, impossible to quell. For the present, it seemed to Connie, the most important thing of all was to keep up a semblance of normality. To go through the motions so that the motions would take over and, in time, naturalize, become seamless, the interwoven tapestry of their lives once more. Gradually, she hoped, perhaps painstakingly, the years and hours and minutes of togetherness, their collective consciousness and memory, of love shared and bodies known to each other with orthodox intimacy would reassert and they might find themselves stronger for this brief acquaintance with the possibility of separateness. She held her tongue and pressed upwards into the darkness the elemental force of all those years and when Matt squeezed her hand, she was certain that he could feel it, too. He turned and she slid backwards into the waiting scoop of his body. They didn't stir for the rest of the night, shielded in a capsule of darkness and silence until morning light would show up all the tiny cracks and fissures again.

Once the initial feverish period had settled down and Matt stopped apologizing for taking up air, the process of going through the motions did take on its own momentum. He was busy at the surgery, three full sets of veneers in one month, some complicated crown and bridgework. There certainly wasn't a shortage of cheques coming in — they talked about taking the family to the Caribbean for the spring half-term. There were parent/teacher meetings, Joe taking a roasting for his consistently bad behaviour, Benny clearly perplexing his young, exuberant teacher by his quiet withdrawal and refusal to respond to her cajoling games. 'Childhood seems lost on him,' she'd laughed, instantly regretting when Connie's eyes turned to stone. Fred was a prefect with large opinions on almost everything and a propensity for sharing them. No bad thing, Connie had thought, quietly pleased. There were football tournaments taking up entire weekends. Takeaways with the usual Indian versus Chinese arguments. Sunday walks by the river after lunch, Matt and Connie leading a reluctant male procession. Benny, you can feed the ducks now. Why don't you just throw all the pieces in — they'll come for it. Benny, you don't have to feed each duck individually. Okay, we'll sit over there and wait for you.

In general there was a strained and delicate gentleness between Matt and Connie. He would catch her quietly studying him from time to time and that slow, hesitant smile would creep across his face. When she began to shake with fear at what might have been lost, he would know instinctively and reach out to wrap his arms around her; she would remain very still accepting the embrace or hit him away in a cloudburst of dark rage. Leave me alone, just leave me alone. Some nights she went to bed not knowing who she was going to be when she got up in the morning.

Even Matt's seemingly bottomless pit of contrite patience got on her nerves though she managed to pierce through on rare occasions. One night they lay under cover of darkness, the only true refuge they could enjoy together. It had been the sort of unspeakable evening for a woman when she pushes her own boundaries of bad behaviour, snapping at everybody with wilful extravagance because they were there, because she could, because there was a kind of delicious pleasure in being downright horrible, savouring the freedom while conscious of the guilt to come. Matt had touched her shoulder and she wrenched away deciding to be unspeakable for a while longer. Damn it, it felt good.

'Connie, listen to me, you know we can't go — '

'If I can, you can. Don't kid yourself, Matt. Anything can be endured.'

He groaned with frustration. 'For Christ's sake, listen to yourself sometimes. I know I hurt you but if you won't accept an apology and you refuse to talk things through — where are we, you're on your Via Dolorosa and I'm just the big bad boy what done it and ran away. Connie? Give it up now. I'm here. We have to start somewhere.'

She sat up in a fury.

'What? You think if you offload any guilty secrets that's all right then? Clean slate, fresh start — all that bullshit? I will not let you do that. I *will* not. We had to do things on your terms while you were swanning around Rome. Now it's my turn. Stuff your so called honesty and integrity. I hope you choke. You're a fake. It's all fake bollocks.' She didn't think he was disingenuous in the least but it felt good to whip him with, to his mind, the worst possible insult. She wanted him to be incendiary, driven beyond coherent thought, drag her to him roughly, heedlessly, force her to take back her wanton taunts with the thrust of his own body. Is that fake? Is that? She grew hot and moist imagining him inside her, angry, honest, carnal. But he turned away pulling the duvet over his shoulders.

'We'll get through this whatever way we have to,' he said in a dull hopeless voice. 'You want secrets, fine, whatever you want.'

It was his turn to be insensitive and she was shocked.

'That's as good as saying there are secrets! Now you've put me in an impossible position. You want me to say — tell me everything, tell me the whole shooting gallery. Well, I'm not going to be the rock you hone your precious conscience on. Let me tell you something for nothing — we all have our little secrets. We all have to live with them. It's just your turn to feel a bit mucky around the edges. Welcome to the real world, Matt. Think you can unload just to make you feel better — ' She mimicked his voice. 'At least I tell it like it is. *At least I'm true to myself.* Oh aye. Give me a break.'

The black cloud hovered between them

throughout every meal, throughout every household exchange; they wanted everything back, the bad as well as the good and the effort was killing them. The rare times they made love took on a desperation they had previously not known, each too eager to please, culminating in a curious kind of brinkmanship. That was good. No, *you* were good. They lacked the languor of familiarity, the casual use of another's body that grows with years. A version of Matt had returned and it wasn't the version who had left.

Connie would find him gazing up at the sky, deep in thoughts they could not share. His weight loss became a worry and she took to feeding him meals rich in heavy carbohydrates to find most of the contents of the plate scraped into the bin later. He mumbled in his sleep and took to fighting imaginary enemies in dreams that made his limbs thrash. She whispered soothingly until he was calm again. While he feigned pleasure at the simplest of things, a walk, a meal, a movie, there was a dull ring of emptiness about his person that she remembered of the time when his mother died. He was constantly distracted and constantly trying to conceal this distraction, which Connie grew convinced was making him ill. Sometimes she had to excuse herself in mid-sentence, half walking, half running down to the river to cry wretchedly on a bench for hours.

Other times, anger spilled out of her. She'd goad to the point where she thought, he'll have to react now, I'll crank it up just one notch further and he'll have to blow — decent, naked anger — anything was preferable to this trance-like state he didn't seem to be able to slough off.

'Matt!' She shouted one night. 'When are you really coming home? I'd just like to know because it's like living with a shadow.'

'I didn't realize that.' He frowned, genuinely perplexed. 'I'll try harder.'

'Try harder to what?' Connie spat. 'Pretend you want to be here?'

'Of course I want to be here. This is my home. You're my family. Where else could I be?'

Connie's fists clenched. 'You tell me, Matt.' She took a step closer. 'And while you're at it you can tell me something else.' But even as she glared at him the question dissolved on her tongue like a sour lozenge.

'Tell you what, Connie?'

'Nothing,' she said, dropping her eyes. 'Just when are you going to stop being so distant from us, that's all.'

He pulled her to him then, holding on

fiercely, kissing the top of her head until she grew calmer.

'I trust you,' she whispered against his chest. 'Always. Always, d'you hear me?'

'Connie please — ' His body had stiffened as though in response to a sharp blow. Connie stepped out of his grip, backing away with her eyes fixed on his. Her face burned a feverish scarlet.

'I trust you, Matt.'

'So you keep saying.'

That exchange had occurred about a month previously and since then there had been a series of small improvements noticeable only to Connie. So far as the boys were concerned, except for Benny perhaps, there hadn't been any changes in the run of things in the first place. Tall, loving, endlessly patient Dad was doing what Dad always did. We'll get by, she found herself chanting a dozen times a day. We'll get by, we'll get by, picking up speed like a train. By by by.

It was nearly Christmas and, yes, so far they'd managed. The train was back on track, though there were sections missing. Connie shunted into her coat in the hall and stood by the living-room door watching her family for a minute. A sense of disbelief overwhelmed her at times that their sons existed at all. It was almost a joke that they'd managed to get so far already. Had been fed, clothed, watered up to now, without, or so it seemed, any conscious decision on their parents' part. For God's sake, they were still growing up themselves, how had their sons almost caught up with them?

Red Hot Chili Peppers blasted around the walls; they liked to use every opportunity to let their father know their music, too. Matt's head nodded to the pungent beat as he pulled another streamer from the box, eyebrows up, mouth pulled down at the corners, Robert De Niro-style, that's pretty good, pretty damn good lads. Rays of self-satisfaction beamed off Fred and Joe. Benny was surreptitiously, or so he thought, watching her, watching Matt. There was a sort of testosterone ectoplasm between the four males. Pass that, that thing there, whatever that thing was would be slung over a shoulder to be caught in an elaborate feint. Cheers. Four heads bopping as the drum beat turned tribal. Fingers playing air, faces contorted in what looked like agony. Had Matt and Joe always looked so alike? The tall lean bodies, wide knotty shoulders, both were bare-chested in the fire's glow, perhaps it was due to the weight Matt had dropped. He was laughing at something Joe said, big white teeth gleaming and she experienced a sudden spasm of desire.

'Right everybody. I'll catch you later in Kingston. I'm off to Mary's.'

Matt looked across. For a second their eyes held fast. A slow intimate smile crept over his face and she blew him a kiss. More a soft, plosive puckering of lips but enough to call into memory, that fine invisible line between them that had managed to hold fast through all the ups and downs of married life. It still is, she thought with a stab of joy. It still is. She stepped out on to gritty, soiled snow with a lighter heart.

★   ★   ★

'Really, it's an almost impossible brief you've given us,' Mary said to the woman as she passed a mug of tea. 'You want to remind him of the years you loved one another, show your rage and hurt and contempt for what he's done and somehow wish him a happy fiftieth birthday at the same time.'

Connie turned to the woman whose mouth had twisted in a regretful coil of smile. Carmel Bennett had travelled from Dublin to meet with Connie and Mary. They'd been trying to come up with something for the past month, spending days in different galleries and museums in search of inspiration. Carmel was in the early stages of a particularly nasty break-up and they had come to realize what she was really looking for was a searing cry from the heart, something that would bring him back. There wasn't a card in the world that could do that but she'd seemed so fragile on the phone and in her e-mail messages, they hadn't the heart to tell her they'd privately long since given up. She had latched on to strangers because she was still in denial and talking to friends or family would have allowed a degree of acceptance. In the flesh, she was an attractive woman in her late forties, with a narrow brittle face that looked set for tears at any moment. She had dressed in a sharp, expensive suit which tugged at Connie's heart. The poor woman was hoping to do business. Instinctively, Connie reached across and squeezed Carmel's hand.

'It's very hard,' Connie said.

'It is. I don't know if — ' Carmel broke off. She took a sip of tea to steady the quiver of her mouth. 'I keep — that's what I keep — starting sentences and — '

'Perhaps it would be best if you ignored his birthday,' Mary suggested gently.

'I'm with him twenty years.'

'I know, dear.'

'Twenty years. What was I doing? Cooking him for her?' Carmel's fingers flittered across her face, then settled on pulling her lower lip down like a child who's done wrong but doesn't know yet exactly what.

Mary rubbed her jaw and looked at Connie.

'Carmel, we just do cards, you know, light stuff, sometimes acerbic if that's what somebody wants — a parting shot if you will. It may be childish but it can make a person feel that they've had the last word, closes the book for them. Often they get to play with hidden messages that make them and sometimes us, to be perfectly frank, feel a bit cleverclogs. Nine times out of ten the message is never decoded by the recipient, only for a second the sender gets to feel a bit superior. But it's still a card, doesn't actually change anything.' Mary put a hand on Carmel's shoulder. 'It seems to me that if a person has actually left the family home, if the other relationship is out in the open, if they've already faced the wrath of their children — '

Connie was shaking her head — any more would be too cruel. She imagined herself listening to those words. How easily it happens. The atomizing implosion of betrayal, how could this unfortunate woman be expected to comprehend that what had taken a lifetime to build up could become so much rubble in the utterance of a sentence. Carmel — I have something to tell you.

'It's not all about men and this midlife crisis business, looking for a younger model to keep themselves young,' Carmel ventured.

'You'd be surprised how much of it is,' Mary said dolefully. 'Carmel, would you like a glass of wine instead of that tea?'

'I would. Please.'

'I've only got red.' Mary poured three glasses.

'She was my best friend,' Carmel continued. 'I mean, we had our children together. We walked them to and from school every day. When she had her miscarriage it was me at the hospital, not her husband. We'd fall out sometimes and then it'd be worse than the pain of falling out with your mother or your sister. We wouldn't be able to sleep until we'd made up again. If I was having problems with Niall who would I turn to only Valerie — Val. She'd never give advice, the way you want from your best friend, only listen and say 'the bastard' at the right moment. Then she'd forget about whatever I told her because she knew that's the way it is in a marriage, you say you can't live with somebody another minute, then you go home, you put on the dinner and you take it from there.' Carmel paused for a sip of wine. Connie exploded.

'You must have felt like killing them.'

Carmel looked up, eyes burning.

'You have no idea. I really think you can make yourself sick with rage. You can't have a normal thought. A decent thought — even about your own children and that makes you more angry. Like, how did you take all my everyday thoughts from me? What right did you have to do that? It's one of those candles you can't ever blow out only it's more like a torch inside you. And then you start wondering, analysing every moment — when did it begin? How? It must have started with the odd flirt, maybe he paid her a compliment one night that I didn't notice. Maybe she bumped into him in the kitchen and they both ended up a bit breathless. Or they were both laughing at something and their eyes met of a sudden. You can't imagine how I went over every solitary moment in my head.'

'I think I can,' Connie said in a quiet voice.

'They must have felt guilty,' Carmel continued. 'They couldn't not. Alone they must have felt horrible, but together they had a duvet over them, not the real thing I mean, though yeah, I suppose that too, but I really mean a blanket, them being wrong but sort of feeling it was — Oh I don't know — they were so wrong it had to be right, mad as that sounds. As you can tell, I've thought of every little thing. In a way, I've lived it for them. I'm doing the final edit. The stupid thing is, I thought me and Niall were sound enough. We were getting on better than we had for ages, now I see it was all a cover-up. What I want to know is this — at what point did he choose not to love me? Because he must have. He'd known Val as long as me, how come one day it's head over heels and it wasn't all those years? Was it one moment, like that.' She clicked her fingers. 'Or a million moments finally added up together which could have made a deep solid friendship just as well and left it at that. What's the thing that flips it because don't tell me it's all mad passion and — and — uncontrollable. These were two mature middle-aged people. Two of the people I cared most about in the world, shared sex, births, deaths, friendship — I mean, I *knew* them. They *knew* me. At what point did they make me not human any more so that they could do this?' Tears slid down her cheeks making little plinking sounds as they plopped into the wine. 'That's the one that really gets to me. How could they make me a non-person, a nothing.'

There was a long silence while Carmel cried in a strange, soundless manner. Connie and Mary hardly dared look at one another.

'I've examined every angle,' Carmel was saying. 'Even to the point of wondering, if it is a passion he couldn't — Isn't that what I wanted too? Didn't I long for something like that in my life? And then I'd wonder, how did I let something like that grow right there under my very own eyes? If I'd seen signs even — '

'What would you have done?' Connie asked. Carmel pulled her lower lip down again with three fingers.

'I don't know. In a funny sort of way I think I'd have forced them together more in my presence. That doesn't make any sense, does it?'

'I'm not sure what you — '

'They made me invisible. They had to, can you see that? There had to come a point when they simply didn't see me any longer. If I'd known — at least I could have tried to make them look at me. *Me*.'

Connie's mouth gaped open. Invisible, God how she understood that word as if it were imprinted on her birth certificate. Colour drained from her face leaving her blanched and etiolated. Mary was trying to catch her eye but she turned away.

'I'm so sorry,' Connie said after a long time. She wished she could think of something bigger to say. But what was there really? In the time it took for her husband to utter that first sentence, Carmel I have something to tell you, this woman's life had been taken out of her hands. She had been transformed into another person — single, enraged, confused. Unwillingly part of her husband's cliché — the bitter ex-wife though she hadn't set out to be bitter and she hadn't set out to be ex.

'But, you know,' Carmel pulled a tissue from her bag and blew her nose. 'There *is* a part of me that still loves him. It's taken me a long time to admit that. *He* can say that — I just didn't love her any more — It wasn't right between us for years — ' she broke off, unconsciously mimicking her husband's defensive shrug. 'He can say all of that if it helps him look in the mirror. And, of course, part of me hates him to the point of wishing him dead. Her too. But he's decided so much for me now, this new life I never asked for. I won't let him decide that I can't still love him. Maybe you think that's stupid but it makes me feel true to myself, to the 'us' that once was. I know you think I'm clutching at straws, that if I could find the right words he'd come back. I don't. He used to be an art student.' She gave a bitter laugh. 'I bet he can hardly remember that. But I remember how it used to be such an important part of his life before money and lies and looking over his shoulder took over.' Carmel blew out a great gust of breath. 'Look. It's his fiftieth, a big birthday, I'd like to send him a handpainted card. Really, I suppose, I'd like to take back my dignity and find a way, on my own terms, maybe only recognizable to me — to say goodbye.'

Connie and Mary exchanged glances. They had entirely misread the intention behind Carmel's card. Connie felt that they had dealt her an injustice, she was stronger, braver, certainly more noble than they had given credit. The bitter ex-wife, how slickly they had bought into the picture. How easy to categorize feelings and responses that were complex, unique to each individual, often contradictory. It would be expected that she would be suffused with righteous anger, that overnight they would become her mortal enemies, that she would harbour thoughts and long tortuous dreams of revenge; how easy to ignore the simple little fact that she still loved her husband.

'I'm sure we'll think of something,' Mary said, her voice sounding a little hoarse.

When Carmel had gone, Connie sat on an upturned wooden crate staring down at her hands pressed together between her knees. She was very pale.

'Connie?'

'Invisible.' She looked up, her eyes were cloudy. 'Mary, there's something I've been wanting to tell you — '

'What is it dear? You look wretched, do you want to be sick or something?'

Connie shook her head, she opened her mouth to continue and at that moment her mobile phone trilled. She answered.

'Yeah yeah. Meet you there. No, I'm on my way right now.' She stood to leave. Mary reached for her own coat.

'What did you want to tell me?' she asked.

'I — Nothing. Nothing important. Look, they're waiting for me. I'll meet you at the Tate Modern tomorrow.'

'But hang on a sec, I'll come with you.'

Connie hesitated but it was enough for Mary to pick up. She took a little step backwards.

'Actually, I'm not sure I could face the Christmas crowds. And William said he might drop by so I'll leave you to it.'

'Are you sure?'

'It's bloody cold out there. Don't keep them waiting.'

'You know you're perfectly welcome.' Even as the words were coming out of her mouth, Connie wanted to claw them back. Mary blinked rapidly.

'Hardly needs to be said,' she blustered, twin cherry stings burgeoning high on her cheeks.

★ ★ ★

As Connie ran across Kingston Bridge she could see Matt and the boys at the far end, throwing dirty snowballs with whatever they could glean from the gaps between the bridge's balustrades. Matt was swinging one arm like a cricketer before finding his target dead on. It *will* be a nice family evening, she told herself, arranging a huge smile to greet them. Tomorrow she would explain to Mary that things were still at a delicate and fragile state at home (as if she couldn't see that for herself) there really was no intention of excluding her, they just needed time, yes, perhaps it was a closing in on themselves, but didn't wounds need to do that to heal? Still, she felt guilty.

They all pelted her as she approached and she squealed obligingly. Matt held out the crook of his arm ostentatiously.

'M'Lady?'

She slipped her arm through.

'So where do we dine, Jeeves?' she said in a posh tone.

'We thought we'd let it up to Madam.'

'Oh bloody hell. I thought you'd all have had that argument by now.'

'I want a burger anyway,' Joe said.

'I could eat fishcakes but I'd rather noodles,' Benny offered.

'I could eat stale bread but I'd rather chocolate cake.' Joe took off to perfection Benny's slow deliberate speech pattern.

'What about you?' Connie turned to Matt. 'What do you want?'

'This. All this,' he blew tenderly in her ear, adding in a raised voice, 'I think a big fat juicy steak. Aye. And chips. Man food.'

'Yeah,' Fred pulled his mouth down, then phooted gum into the river. 'That's me too.'

'Listen to yourselves. Just listen to yourselves,' Connie said happily. Matt's finger was circling the collar of her jacket. He leaned down to press his lips against the nape of her neck, his breath was warm and she could smell beer. A dart of desire, of anticipatory pleasure shot through her veins. She felt giddy with relief that she hadn't after all, said what she'd been meaning to say to Mary.

★　★　★

Another large whisky. Though she didn't often drink whisky, when she did, Mary drank with a sense of purpose. She didn't

290

even like the taste but occasionally she did like to get drunk. There was something quite hedonistic about getting drunk on your own. To wilfully set out with that intention. To know that you'd better heap as much abuse on St Anthony's shoulders while the going was good because tomorrow he would pay back with a hangover that would be divinely inspired.

'You have seriously let me down,' she told him now. 'Are you listening? No, you're not. You never listen. Abso-bloody-lutely never. I don't know why I bother with you. Except that I'm loyal.' She considered her own loyalty for a while, sitting on the floor of the studio with her legs splayed out in front.

'Something's not right. Benny can see it. It's all my fault, I made them go to Rome, pestered them until they went. And now Connie doesn't want me around any more, not the way she did before. She gives this kind of a look,' Mary narrowed her eyes, 'when I walk through to the kitchen in the evening. Like she's irritated or something. She didn't even notice that I didn't turn up four times last week. *Four times*. I've never not turned up four times in one week before. I was in the church praying to you as you know full well. And then you still did nothing for me when I sat in my car for all those hours, watching the house. I watched Matt come home and Joe go out with a mate. And Benny at his window looking out. I was keeping them safe from harm by watching. The way I know you do, over me, even if that's all you do. Look how thin Matt is, I think he's possessed! Now, don't tell me, don't tell me, to get a life. Just don't start.' Her lips parted to say something else but it turned into a wail. She hastily clamped a hand to her mouth to stop the eerie sound.

Once she ran away having saved her tuck money for weeks. She made it to the train station where they pretended to print her a ticket and sent her to the waiting room. Miss Smithens, the surly games teacher, came to bring her back. Mary was paraded in front of next morning's assembly as an example of a wilful, recalcitrant child in need of extra discipline. She was letting her parents down, good decent people, such ingratitude — what had they done to deserve such ingratitude. Mary pictured her mother's disappointed eyes, her papa's cold anger, she began to cry though she'd promised herself that she wouldn't. There were sniggers from some of the assembled girls. Mary's weekly phone call home was banned for a month to teach her a lesson. She was nine years old.

'Don't you see?' She looked up to the

ceiling, imagining stars beyond, a place of infinite blue beyond them again. 'You really do have to help us out here. You're our last resort.'

The phone rang. Mary stumbled to her feet looking around for the handset. It was under a crate. William — to say he wouldn't be around later after all. He'd made a mistake with his dates, it was tonight they were going to dinner at a neighbour's. So sorry.

'William?' Mary's tongue felt thick in her mouth. She drew herself up to her full formidable height. 'William dear — it's a matter of sublime indifference to me if you never come around again. As a matter of fact, you left a packet of cigarettes on top of the microwave last time you were here. I shall be flushing them down the toilet tonight. Much as I would like to flush you. Goodbye.'

She took another slug of whisky rolling it around her tongue. St Anthony chuckled.

'Oh piss off,' Mary barked at the ceiling. Her burst of bravado was short-lived, deep in her abdomen the dropped stone of loneliness rippled out in widening circles. Her insides felt hollow and scooped out. How she missed the clamour of young males, heave of bodies around a table, Mary's chair saved always just for her, dim light sticking them ever closer together, dense frown of pretend concentration on Connie's face — ladling, scooping, splatting — food conjured out of nowhere or so it seemed. She made it look *that* easy. The heels of Mary's hands flew to her eyes.

Connie, there's nothing I wouldn't do to make you happy. Dear Lord, I'd stab St Anthony himself.

★ ★ ★

They lay in the darkness mulling over the evening, enjoying a peace that felt like the return of something after months. A quiet, unquestioning kind of peace. Matt's arms were wrapped around Connie, she could feel his erection against the back of her thigh. There was no rush, they could doze, wake in a half-dream, make love then or make love now. She shifted a little to gauge his response. He was on her in a flash.

'Shh,' she whispered, smiling, the brass bed creaked with an urgency she found thrilling. Matt's hands were all over her, squeezing, kneading, she felt — reclaiming. He kissed her face, her neck and breasts as though rediscovering previously charted territory. For the first time since his return, she knew unequivocally that he was with her, inside her flesh, there wasn't that niggling doubt in her mind that he was thinking of someone else. She caught his head between her hands, latching on to his mouth with open lips, thrusting her tongue in as far as she could. He moaned, she could feel a little shiver of pleasure run up his body. She had power again. What had always gratified her most about sex with Matt was making him lose control. It didn't always happen but when it did, he surrendered to instincts completely. He forgot to be calm and allowed his inner anger to propel the thrusts of his body.

They were back in the old familiar rhythm, legs moving with the synchronicity of a clock, his thigh outside hers, a gentle press and she knew instinctively what time to make it, two o'clock, or one tight body, leg on leg — six o'clock. There was the triangle of ceiling over his shoulder, the cool marble feel of that shoulder against her mouth. The patina of sweat joining their bodies on the outside as they were joined within. Tiny gusty sighs in her ear as he lost himself inside her. It all came back and she could have wept with relief. They were their own island again, safe in the darkness, protected from all harm. She choked back a sob.

'Connie, what is it, are you all right?'

'I'm fine.'

'D'you want me to stop?' He hesitated and

she pulled his buttocks tighter.

'I don't ever want you to stop.'

But at the very end — as his breaths burst out in little pants — she knew she'd lost him again. He had tried and she'd understood how hard he'd tried, but the part of him that had gone missing was still absent. Perhaps he would never fully return.

Afterwards, they lay entwined until he turned on his side, breaths decelerating until he was asleep. She thought about a world of people who had just made love as they had done. Fates already hurtling towards them even as legs twisted and mouths sought mouths; that jack-knifed lorry on the motorway, a clutch of hand to a seized chest, a rogue wave on an otherwise calm sea, the sombre policeman at the door — a lunatic with a hammer had just struck again; for some, it would be the last of love and they would not know.

She could hear Benny rumbling about, pad of his feet to the bathroom, back again. He was rambling practically every other night now, several times she'd found him downstairs in the kitchen, just sitting in the cold and dark. At first she'd thought he was sleepwalking but he responded to her questions perfectly wide awake. No, there was nothing wrong. Yes, he couldn't sleep. No reason for the kitchen really, just maybe he might have a glass of milk and the fridge was in the kitchen with the milk. She'd walked him back up to bed knowing that he would lie there, sleepless, for hours yet. When she'd mentioned this increased nocturnal activity to Matt, he looked worried but didn't offer any explanation, it didn't have to be said that he was concerned, as she was, that it had something to do with them. Benny lived on his senses the way other people lived on their wits. He couldn't say what was the matter but he could feel that something was. The relief she'd felt just moments ago continued to ebb away. Her youngest son was like a small supernatural beast constantly prowling around inside her head. Sometimes she thought he was the embodiment of her own conscience.

13

It was definitely Greta, that slender figure she'd seen wrapped in a beige trench coat, swishing out through the side entrance of the Tate Modern. Connie grabbed Mary's arm, stood for a moment with her mouth open before breaking into a run.

'Connie! Connie!' Mary called after her.

Connie brushed past a line of people on the down escalator, swooping forward nearly losing her footing as she jumped the last few treads. She thought how demented she must look tearing up the long lower level with her open coat swinging in the air behind. When she got outside she was already winded. She reached the river's tow path, leaning forward hands on her knees to catch her breath. Which direction? Right, to the Millennium Bridge, or left towards the South Bank. She strained for signs of a trench coat on the bridge but if there was it would doubtless be obscured by the passing throngs. Left, she thought, going on instinct. She began to run again.

It was almost impossible to pick up a decent pace along the narrow path with joggers and strollers having to stop in their tracks to avoid slamming into her. She had to stop again to catch her breath, peering into the distance just as a beige coat rounded a corner. She was seriously winded by now with the beginning of a painful stitch on her left side but she forced herself on, cheeks glowing like blood-red apples. She managed to make the Royal Festival Hall without stopping again. Another glance around, turning in full circles with her arms spread out. She thought she might faint. A few people eyed her oddly but they moved along at a smartish clip, heaven only knew what kind of nutter she was.

Greta could have been anywhere. In a café, in the Festival Hall or the National Film Theatre, or slipped down steps heading through back streets towards Waterloo station. There was no sign of the trench coat and shiny auburn hair.

'Greta?' Connie called at the top of her lungs. Now people really were stopping to look. 'Gret-aaa?' But no one answered to that name. Her pounding heart was thrumming in her ears. She didn't care how mad or ridiculous she looked. Greta was gone.

Connie found a vacant bench and sat with her elbows on her lap, hands holding her feverish head. A few drops of rain bulleted across the dull brown surface of the Thames. A moment later the sky belched open releasing rods of water. They beat across her head, trickling into her ears. At least her cheeks were cooling. Umbrellas were up all around, bodies darting for shelter. The river bank rapidly cleared of strollers. Connie sat for a good fifteen minutes until every inch of her body was soaked. A tall figure came and sat beside her. Mary.

'You thought you saw her last week, too.' Mary licked rain from her lips. 'At the National Gallery. I was watching when you followed a woman with hair. It wasn't her then and it wasn't her today either, Connie.'

'It was. I'm sure of it.'

'She's in Rome. Forget about her.'

Connie stared ahead at the river forming concentric swirls with the rain.

'She's not. In Rome, I mean.'

'How can you be so sure?'

'Because I've phoned. She used to answer, then I'd hang up. She's not answering any more. And her sister said she was coming to London.'

'You *phoned?* Well, she could be anywhere for heaven's — '

'She's here,' Connie said in a flat voice. 'C'mon. Now we're both drenched.'

They headed towards Waterloo, Mary

300

sending Connie sideways glances as though she were afraid that Connie would dissolve in rain never to be seen again.

'Please stop looking at me that way,' Connie said after a while. 'I'm not cracking up if that's what you think.'

'If you don't mind, I'll be the judge of that,' Mary said. They both smiled. 'I was thinking Rodin's *The Kiss*,' Mary continued in a lighter tone. 'For Carmel's card? If her husband studied art then he'll know the background story, that it's not what it appears — two lovers in a passionate clinch.'

'What then?'

'Look at the version in the Tate Modern next time we visit. There's more of a bump in the man's groin area certainly than the one in Paris but it's still a pretty flaccid affair. Look at his back, knotted with tension. His toes are curled. She's doing all the work, pulling his head down to meet her mouth. His hand just rests on her thigh, no real oomph there. You see, originally it's meant to be Paolo and Francesca of Dante's *Divine Comedy*. Francesca's husband caught the couple kissing and killed them both. They were eternally damned for having fallen in love while married to others. The couple originally appeared in his portrait of damnation called *The Gates of Hell*. Really *The Kiss* isn't a prelude to bliss, it's the prelude to tragedy.'

'I think she'll like that,' Connie responded after a while. 'Yes. I would. And there's that Judas thing as well. A kiss is just a kiss — ' She broke off deep in thought. 'Time goes by will be the caption. Time goes by she'll get over him, time gone by — his birthday — the years they spent together. Okay. Carmel gets to say her goodbye, her way.'

'Connie — ?'

'I'm fine, Mary. Really.'

'I wish I could *really* believe you.'

★ ★ ★

In his heart Matt believed that people were born with a capacity for happiness, or, like his own mother, it simply did not come easily to them, if at all. For her it remained something at a distance, a brightness waiting at the end of dark tunnels. No matter how hard she tried she could not extricate herself from the labyrinth of darkness to reach that light. He had made a conscious effort throughout his life to be as happy in each moment as was possible in any given set of circumstances. He had worked hard, savoured varying degrees of success, enjoyed his family and home. It would have struck him as obscene to want for anything else, to admit to dissatisfaction.

Now, all that seemed a naively uncomplicated view. What was present did not necessarily compensate for what was absent.

There was nothing to do but hope that in time he might wake up one morning and Greta's face wouldn't be there waiting for him, the first thought, the last thought, a constant icon hovering on the periphery of his vision throughout every conversation. He had tried to convince himself that his attachment was a form of sickness. An obsession masking some other deep flaw in his character. He didn't love Connie any less, if anything, she had swelled in his admiration for the way she had handled his homecoming. She had left the door open for tenderness from the beginning and he often wondered if he would be able to do the same for her. He was in fact, surprised by her unstinting goodness. There was genuine sympathy in her voice when she spoke about Greta's loss. How could she have known in the carefree days of the farm that there would be so much pain ahead? If a person could know, really know, would they still make the same choices? She'd turned to face Matt. She would still have wanted Fred and Joe and Benny, just as they were, for however long she might have with them. She was certain it would be the same for Greta.

Jennifer stepped in to tell him Mr Holden was waiting in reception. She rolled her eyes sympathetically. Mr Holden was that bane of dental practice, the elderly denture patient who refuses to be satisfied. There was an innate reluctance to accept that false teeth were not a replacement for the real thing, they were a replacement for *no* teeth. This was the fifth return to the surgery in as many weeks.

'Show him in,' Matt groaned.

The man came through, silver-tipped cane quivering with indignation. He was wearing his old teeth again and slapped the new set on a counter top.

'More problems?' Matt asked.

'These,' Mr Holden stabbed the offending items with a crooked finger, 'are not what we agreed.'

'I think you'll find they are exactly what we agreed.' Matt suppressed his sigh before launching the counter-attack. Really, sometimes it wasn't so much the will to live he lost as the will to breathe through the next already-set-in-stone moments. 'We've changed colour, size, shape — at least six times now. If you'll remember, each time I got the technician to set them in wax so you could get used to them at home, see what your family thinks. You didn't feel comfortable with the first set, your wife didn't like the second, your sons felt a bit funny about the third, so you said. We were all finally in agreement and you gave the go ahead for the real plate to be made. There's really nothing left to change.'

Mr Holden sucked his old dentures. The problem was they had become as familiar to him as his own tongue. Matt could sympathize to a point, they were replacing something in shocking condition, the plate worn paper thin in some gum areas, with poor quality teeth that had never met in a good bite. They were also crooked forcing his jaw to overcompensate through the years. Nevertheless, like a much worn cherished shoe, the dentures had yielded to accommodate and the shock of the new in his mouth after close on a lifetime was too much for the elderly man. Matt understood only too well that nothing was right in a person's life when things weren't right in his mouth.

'The colour isn't what I picked,' Mr Holden sniffed.

Matt showed him the porcelain colour chart.

'D2 — what you asked for.'

'Well, it's different. My wife agrees. And they're too straight.'

'You asked me to straighten the last set.'

'Not this much!'

'But you wore the mock-ups. You were quite happy. What's happened to change your mind?' Matt curled his fists to suppress his temper, concentrating on fingernails digging into pads of flesh.

'I haven't changed I tell you.' Mr Holden's voice rose in a querulous whine. 'It's the damn teeth that have changed.'

At that point Matt's associate, Martin, stepped in, doubtless sent by Jennifer who was well used to these pointless arguments. Matt had often had to rescue Martin from similar encounters. The psychology working along the lines of whoever was new to the scene automatically adopted the role of referee, giving the patient somewhere to go with their complaint at the very least.

'Martin.' Matt adopted his most professional voice. 'Could you take a look at Mr Holden's records please?' Martin obliged, frowning with concentration. 'Now, can you please look through size, shape, colour of what we finally agreed? Yes? Here is the end result.' Matt held up the new dentures. Martin frowned harder, examining with engineer-like precision. He tapped, held under the light, rubbed with cleaning fluid. Mr Holden looked as though he were holding his breath.

'Well?' He couldn't hold back a moment longer.

Martin turned his head this way and that. 'There's no doubt in my mind that they're *absolutely* what was agreed.' Mr Holden flared red with temper but Martin was continuing: 'However, I think the answer to the problem could be in just a touch of benching. What do you think Matt?'

Matt thought very hard, then inclined his head.

'You're perfectly right. I don't know why I didn't see it myself.' He took the dentures, wrapping them in gauze with great care before turning to Mr Holden. 'It's just a refining process we sometimes deploy at the very end. The technician will do a final bench and your teeth will be right as rain, Mr Holden. Make an appointment for, say, two weeks?'

'I don't know why you didn't just do that in the first place,' the elderly man humphed but there was a satisfied gleam in his eye. He shared a superior look with Martin as he left. Matt tossed the dentures to Martin.

'Tell Jennifer — two weeks — put 'em on the bench. Thanks.'

Martin chuckled, stopping at the door. He was a thin restless man with sensual lips on an otherwise pointy face, younger by ten years. If he ever thought about it, he was, Matt supposed, his one true male friend down south. He wasn't a man for forming close bonds with other men. His brother, Stanley, and old school mates were still his idea of friends, bonds forged in childhood, nothing he could ever explain, just something accustomed like the smell of a familiar kitchen. Now all he wanted from another man was to share a pint, talk of football or rugby, maybe something big on the news. Martin understood the unspoken rules, being a reserved man himself. Matt could enjoy a long evening in the pub with him and never have to worry that the younger man would end up crying on his shoulder. As he hadn't had to worry that his colleague would feel compelled by a prurient sense of curiosity to ask about what the stay in Rome was *really* about. Matt hadn't offered an explanation so Martin didn't expect one.

'Have you thought any more about the partnership?' he was saying now. 'I don't mean to push you, mate.'

'It's a lot of money for you to come up with,' Matt said. 'I want to be sure in my own mind before I talk it over with Connie. Nothing to do with how I feel about you as a partner, you understand.' Even allowing for Matt giving Martin a good deal, it was still a couple of hundred grand the younger man had to come up with, and he had a young family to consider. Matt felt a responsibility towards him, he knew what it was like to overcommit in the early days. Connie wouldn't have the same level of obligation towards Martin and quite understandably would jump at a great pot of cash. Matt had to consider the long view, what if Martin got into difficulties with the bank, how it might affect his professional capacity.

'Listen, a few pints tonight, yeah?' Martin grinned. 'See if I can't lighten your conscience.'

It was unlikely that anything would ever be able to do that but Matt smiled his assent.

★   ★   ★

Even in his slightly inebriated state Matt could see that Connie had long since past the point of reasonable curiosity. With Martin? Which pub? Was it busy? She placed their warmed plates of dinner on the table and sat with her head bent, not touching a bite.

'Aren't you hungry?' Matt asked.

'Not much.'

He reached across to touch her arm.

'Do you want to tell me?'

Her head shot back, he noticed her eyes were over-bright.

'Tell you what?' she said.

'I don't know. Whatever's bothering you.'

'Nothing's bothering me.' She craned around as if looking for something to bother her. 'I'm just not feeling very — Anything you want to tell me?'

'Me?' Matt pulled his mouth down. 'No. Just an ordinary day really. That Holden man I told you about was playing up again.' He paused, deliberating. 'And Martin wants to buy a partnership. A lot of money. Is he ready, what d'you think?'

Connie pushed her dinner away. She looked flushed enough to have a temperature. He had thought she'd be pleased.

'I think I'll have a bath. Go to bed early.' She got up from the table, standing for a while leaning on two fists pressed down on to the pine surface. 'The colour of us has gone all wrong. This is not easy, is it?'

He didn't know how best to respond without causing hurt. His cooling dinner congealed on the plate like an accusation. When he looked up, Connie was already by the door.

★ ★ ★

310

'What're you up to Bunny boy?' Connie asked with her head to the side studying him. He was sitting very properly on the edge of their big brass bed, legs dangling over the side, one of her old photo albums on his lap. In his unwitting though unerring fashion he had managed to get to the core of the problem without so much as realizing what he was doing. His ramblings often ended up in their bedroom, sensing, seeking — what though? What was he looking for or hoping to find? The invisible umbilical cord that bound his parents before something changed it all, changed the colour of them?

'Just looking,' he shrugged. Connie sat beside him pressing her palms together, prayer-like. She remembered to chuckle lightly as he turned a page.

'That's your dad with Uncle Stanley. Look at the sticky out ears on the pair of them and the big teeth.'

'There's a lot of Dad with Greta.'

She was startled by the matter-of-fact way he dropped the name of a complete stranger.

'How do you know about Greta?' She couldn't disguise her shock.

'You told us. We were outside her house, remember?'

'Yes but — I never *showed* you — how can

you be so sure that it's her in the photographs? Benny?'

'I just knew is all.' He shrugged but his eyes had widened, staring down, sensing that he had said something wrong. Connie forced herself to sound light and breezy.

'Well, you're quite the detective, aren't you pet? Yep, you're dead right. That's her. A long long time ago. We used to be inseparable us lot. Way back in the time of the dinosaurs.'

He didn't say anything for a long time, while she bit her lip to make a silence to match his own.

'Who took all of these?' he ventured, nodding at the album.

'Why me, pet. It's my album after all.'

He craned and gave her a hasty sideways glance before his eyelids dropped again.

'You should've got somebody to put you in there, too.'

'How d'you mean?'

He flipped back and pointed.

'There's only one of you with them.'

She peered over his shoulder. Smiling up at her was Matt with an arm wrapped around Greta's waist, while Connie stood at a slight gap staring away from the lens. It was as though she had no interest in the picture if she wasn't taking it. A hand fluttered up to her throat. 'D'you know — I've never really noticed that before. How odd. Okay Benny, enough history for one night. Time for bed, I think.'

He closed the album and handed it to her in a solemn gesture. For once he waited for the night-time kiss on his cheek and didn't flinch involuntarily or narrow his eyes. He smelled of milk and fresh vegetables, so good, she stole another kiss and nuzzled her nose into the velvety crevice of his neck. She pulled back and he hopped off the bed at the same time.

'Try not to prowl around tonight, Benny, huh?'

'I'll try.'

She waited until she heard the click of his bedroom door. Downstairs, Joe hooted at something on the telly. Fred was still out for the night. She peered on to the landing and, satisfied that Matt was in the kitchen, she closed the door again, very quietly, and stepped across to the far side of the room to use her mobile phone.

★ ★ ★

Connie had just placed the milk bottles inside the front door, withdrawn her key from the top lock when a hand tapped her shoulder. She jumped and turned, Mary was standing there with a toothy if somewhat sheepish grin.

'Mary! And so early too.' There was an unavoidable grain of irritation in her voice.

'Just caught you,' Mary panted with a hand to her chest as though she'd been running, though it was obvious that she hadn't. 'I thought we might go into town, get some postcards of *The Kiss*, stuff like that. Have you made plans already?'

Connie's eyes swept back and forth across Mary's huge feet, looking for a quick lie, something that wouldn't hurt her friend's feelings but something that would also get rid of her. Anything that came to mind was something that they would have done together in the past without so much as a thought. It struck her with force how much distance she had placed between them since Matt's return and how painful Mary's exclusion from the family must be to a woman who had once practically lived with them.

'I have to get something for Matt,' she said in a softer tone. 'Just boring stuff like that. You hate the Christmas crowds as much as me so I didn't bother to say. I'm not going to stop for lunch or anything. So — I didn't bother to say.' Her voice trailed off at the repetition. Connie knew her cheeks were blazing and she couldn't meet Mary's eyes. She slapped her bag, frowning and staring ahead as if distracted by the many other things she had to do. How uncanny that she should turn up right at this very instant, a couple of minutes along and Connie would have been alone, on her train to town. For all the world it was as though Mary had evolved some preternatural sense of the comings and goings of this house.

'I'm going in anyway,' Mary was saying, 'we might as well — ' She broke off with a shrug but there was a nervous quality to her voice that tamped down the rising mini cyclone of irritation in Connie's chest. She nodded and linked her arm through Mary's but it felt odd.

They were on the train, mutually staring out of the same window in a new strained silence, before Connie said that really she would only spend a few moments at the Tate Modern, then she would head off to the shops — on her own — because, well because, it would be quicker that way. Mary opened her mouth to say something then hastily clamped it shut again at a sharpish glance.

The Rodin managed to distract them both for a brief period. They marvelled at the smooth marble contours and simplicity of line. Knowing the true history of the sculpture lent the entwined couple a bitter-sweet, doomed resonance. There was a lassitude, a sense of resignation in the embrace, an almost desperate clinging on of the woman that brought hot stinging tears to Connie's eyes. She rubbed at an imaginary speck of dust and turned her back to Mary.

'I have to go,' she said, already walking away. Mary watched as Connie proceeded along the concourse, head down, hands thrust deep in her coat pockets. Her friend cut a slight figure, frail and somehow diminished, forced to turn sideways to let a boisterous school group walk past. It seemed to Mary at that moment that the shapes of their lives had, indeed, changed inalterably and that nothing could ever be the same again.

The rare times when she sat with Connie and Matt now, eating, playing their customary Scrabble in the evenings, she had tried her best to ignore the disquieting vibe between them. She knew she was being over-cheerful, annoyingly so at times, in the breathless way a child draws attention to himself when there is a persistent cloud hovering between the parents. For their part, it was clear that the strain of trying to ignore the cloud, too, was taking its toll. And for them, the strain lasted all day and into the night. One evening, in particular, they had both looked a little frightened and very exhausted. Dark circles brooded under Matt's eyes, he had been quiet throughout supper, distractedly tapping a hand against his forehead as though trying to rid his head of unwanted thoughts. Mary had caught Connie's quick glance in his direction and saw the flicker of something she couldn't quite put her finger on at the time. She had caught Matt's reciprocal glance and a similar flicker before they sent one another a fleeting smile. Back then, Mary put it down to the strain, just a touch of fear, she had thought, bound to be the case, how much might have been lost and how swiftly, ruthlessly. A chance unpredictable meeting in Rome leading to chaos. It was inevitable that an element of shellshock would carry over for a while. But now as she picked out Connie's copper hair bobbing across the ground level, it struck Mary with a certainty that forced a little cry from her lips what it really was that she had sensed between them that evening. Not fear, but grief. Even in one another's presence — they were grieving each the other.

Her eyes cast a last lingering sweep over the Rodin before she moved to follow.

Mary watched as Connie managed a desultory peck at shopping in an uncomfortably crowded Selfridges. Out on Oxford Street the police guided the heaving throngs along by megaphone. Usually, Connie went to great pains to avoid the centre of town the weeks leading up to Christmas. It made a chore of shopping, she'd said, it made you hate yourself and the people you were buying for. What was the point of a gift purchased under such duress?

The scent of randomly sprayed perfumes in the cosmetics hall cloyed at the back of Mary's throat after a while. Besides, it wasn't exactly the easiest feat in the world to maintain a reasonably close vigil considering her great height. She found herself bent at the knee, hiding behind fat women who turned to give her curious glances from time to time. Then Mary would cough and bend over further as if to catch her breath. After one particularly beady glare when she doubled up so much her hands were nearly clutching her ankles, she told herself she was being ridiculous. It was just a further manifestation of watching the house. Connie was Christmas shopping for heaven's sake. The most natural thing in the world for the time of year. She told herself that she was growing sick in the head, perhaps fear of losing her friend, perhaps the accumulated years of loneliness had finally unhinged her sanity. She watched Connie pay for her purchases, a leather notebook, a tie, gloves — ladies' extra large, no doubt for herself — and leave by a side exit. Mary dithered for a brief moment then cut a swathe through a cornfield of shoppers to catch a glimpse of Connie's coat flipping around a corner.

★　★　★

It was a small, rather rundown hotel off Tottenham Court Road. Tucked between wholesale outlets with multicoloured saris and floaty, transparent fabrics in their windows. The curtains of the hotel windows were dingy nets, twisted into one central knot in certain places. The front entrance looked gloomy and uninviting. Connie wouldn't have been in the least surprised if the blackened brick façade housed a knocking shop of some description. She walked up and down the narrow street for a while, gazing at fabrics, listening to the drone of industrial sewing machines slough back and forth from the upper storeys. She checked her watch and headed for a dimly lit café directly across from the hotel.

Inside, she ordered coffee which would have been pallid and undrinkable in another life but today she drank it anyway, forcing the murky liquid back in small sips. Her hands were trembling and she had to use both to get the mug to her lips. A couple argued in a far corner. She wanted them to shut up so she could concentrate on her thoughts, perhaps even dissuade herself from this crazy exercise as she had tried all morning without success. Just as she was draining the last drops of the foul coffee, wondering what she could possibly stomach next in this dive of a place, Greta stepped through the hotel's portal practically to the minute that her sister, Rita, had hazarded a guess on the phone last night. Connie jumped to her feet throwing pound coins on the table. She ran outside and across the street.

'Greta!'

She turned, startled to hear her name in such unfamiliar surroundings. When she saw Connie running towards her, flapping one arm up and down like someone trying to stop traffic, she looked terrified at first then blanched a pearly egg-white on realizing who it was.

'Constance? What — I mean — ' Grey eyes skimmed the street as though expecting a full brass band, or the bulls of Pamplona at the very least, to come rappelling through in Connie's wake.

'I called Rita.' With one hand Connie clutched at Greta's arm while the other squeezed tightly around the bags of shopping to stop the trembling. She was breathless but smiling broadly. 'Didn't she tell you?'

Greta looked completely fazed. 'Rita? Well, she left a message but I haven't got back to her yet. What're you — I mean, I'm sorry — you, here — ' Her voice trailed away. There was an awkward silence. Connie cleared her throat, stared at the pavement then lifted her head. The fixed smile on her lips grew even broader.

'I've come to bring you home with me.' She shrugged.

'*What?*'

'I wanted to see if you were staying in a decent place. But this is a shithole. You're our friend, we can't let you — Matt's told me everything.'

Greta's lips parted slightly letting out a puff of breath. She looked at Connie then turned away.

'I don't understand,' she said after a while. A deep frown creased her forehead. Connie was still clutching her arm.

'He told me about your son. The way you

live now. How he tried to help. But it's cutting him up thinking he's abandoned — '

'Do you know what you're saying?' Greta cut across. Wind whipped across her oval face, her grey eyes were fogged with shock and puzzlement. There wasn't a trace of make-up, not even a smudge of lipstick, she was even more slender than the day they'd come across her in that bar in Rome, and Connie found herself reeling from the needle-sharp pierce of her beauty. There had never been anything other to do but to surrender to it.

'I know exactly what I'm saying,' Connie responded. 'I won't take no for an answer. I'll come back to collect you later today.'

'I can't stay at your house, Constance.' Greta's hands flew into the air in a tortured sign language known only to her.

'It's Connie now, please.'

'Sorry, Connie, but you know I can't.'

'Why would I know that?' The smile brightened further, stretching lips into two taut elastic bands though that was the opposite of the effect she intended, her head cocked to one side to try to compensate. Greta was struggling, trying to get a handle on things. She looked desperate to flee. A pear-drop tear perched at the lower rim of one grey eye.

'Please,' she whispered, making direct eye contact for the first time though her body was visibly recoiling. 'Don't do this.'

'What?' Connie was saying. 'What terrible thing am I doing? Look, let me try and explain. We used to be, well, it was all for one, one for all, wasn't it? We were so close us three.'

'We?'

'Yes. Matt, you and me. Don't you remember?'

'Well I — '

'He's part of me now, Greta. Yes, I admit for a while there when he stayed on in Rome, I was, yes, a bit shaken. But he's a good man, an honourable man, I believe that, don't you?' Greta hung her head in limp agreement. Connie continued: 'So, of course, I trust him. Completely. As, of course, I trust you. And I just feel it would be good for you to — to not be here, all alone in London when we're just a few stops away on a train for goodness sake — '

'Connie — '

'Just hear me out. Please?'

Greta nodded but her already blanched face had grown transparent so that blue veins stood out on both temples. Her slender frame had taken up a violent quaking. Connie applied pressure to the arm she was holding to steady the fragile creature.

'It's not just Matt,' Connie continued. 'I want to help. To be part of things. I watch him wondering about you. Wondering if you're all right. And I — Please — it's tearing us apart. Just come, look at us, look at us all together. Show him that you can do that, that you can visit then go away and maybe come back again. Let him know that you're going to be okay. Greta, I know, I do know, how selfish this must sound. You've been living in hell, I understand that. But this is something you can do, for Matt, for me, for the friends we once were.'

'Forgive me, but I don't remember — I mean, you, me — I was unkind to you at times, I remember that, but this closeness you speak of — ' Greta broke off, lifting her shoulders in incomprehension.

'It didn't matter,' Connie insisted. 'We were still best friends.'

There was a slight recoiling movement like the flick of a snake's head uncertain whether to attack or defend. 'But you didn't even know me.'

Connie reached up to gently thumb a stray tear rolling down the other woman's stricken face.

'Matt knew you. That was enough for me. We have to look out for one another.'

'Does he know you've come here?'

Connie's hand fell away. 'No. I don't think he'd understand. But you do, don't you?'

The pale face looked close to being physically sick but she nodded.

'Can you do this for me? For us?' Connie's voice was a whisper. She held her breath.

'It's impossible. You know I can't. What you're asking is impossible.' Greta tore her hand away from Connie's grip. She fumbled in her bag for a pack of cigarettes. It took several attempts to light one.

'Think about it — why should it be impossible? If Matt can stay with you in Rome, why can't you stay in London with us?'

A hand flew to Greta's mouth trying to stop a tiny moan escaping but it hovered there between them, a bleak sound, reminding Connie of a caged bird. A flood of sympathy coursed through her veins for this wretched, broken woman who had finally succumbed to her own powers of destruction. She couldn't help but remember the dancing girl with a halo of sunlight picking out dozens of sparking shades in flying auburn hair. So much life and energy — extinguished now, emptied, a beautiful carapace still, holding nothing. While her gaze flickered across the white chiselled planes of the oval face, it occurred to Connie that this moment had always been inevitable. Somewhere deep inside, in a place she hadn't dared to examine, she had understood that the complex triangle of the three relationships had continued to exist.

She had to bring this woman back into the photographic catalogue of their lives but this time she would be the intruder, the one taking the pictures. Of course the risks were huge but any risk was worth taking if she could turn dazzling sunlight into safe shade, if she could make of Greta — a visitor.

'I'm so sorry about your son,' she said. 'We can't imagine . . .'

'Did Matt — did he tell you — '

'Yes.' A tongue flickered across Connie's dry lips. She wanted to be honest but not wantonly cruel. Any attempt at dissembling came to an end at the death of a child. 'He told me you blame yourself.'

'I do. With very good reason.'

'I would if it were me in similar circumstances.'

Greta's eyes widened slightly then a sketch of a crooked smile played at one corner of her mouth.

'Thank you. You're the first person to say that, baldly, out in the open. It almost feels good to hear it. Of course, you would blame yourself but from the things Matt told me about you — it would never happen. You would never be so selfish or irresponsible.'

Connie took a step back. Their eyes were locked in a silent, anguished battle. Greta resisting, understanding completely what was being asked of her. Understanding what was being placed into her reluctant hands — a family, their future, the story of Matt and Connie; the excision of her presence by, conversely, the addition of it if only for a brief period of time. She stood there transfixed, staring into Connie's eyes. 'I want to be good.' Her head dropped.

'I know you do. Matt told me. So you can do this.'

'I can't, really I can't.'

'If you don't,' Connie persisted in a gentle voice, 'then where does that leave me, Greta? What am I to think?'

'I don't understand.'

'I think you do.' She took a deep gulp of air. They were stuck in mid-manoeuvre in such dangerous airspace, a wrong move and down they both would spiral.

'Rome, you mean,' Greta uttered quietly. Connie nodded then quickly raised a hand before any more might be said.

'I don't want lies. Please don't. Not the truth either. Help me believe what I want to

327

believe. Come to my house. Be a guest. And then go. You need to turn at the front door, say goodbye and leave. I'll watch you. Matt will watch you. I'll close the door once you've disappeared from sight. Maybe then we all can go back to some sort of normality.'

'But how do I explain — '

'What's to explain? You're an old friend visiting old friends in London. You phoned, I came into town to meet you. What could be more simple than that? Just showing up as friends do.'

'I could leave today. Just go away. You'd never have to see me again.'

'Why shouldn't I want to see you?'

'Now. I'll go now. Pack my bags — I won't even go up North.'

'It's the staying away that makes things complex. Don't you see?'

'Are you — Are you sure you know what you're asking?'

Connie had to consider for a moment.

'You'll have to trust me on that,' she responded with a shaky smile. 'As I'll trust you. Please. I need you to do this.'

'Oh Jesus.' Greta's jaw thrust out, she stared up at the soiled linen sky. 'Give me a couple of hours. I'll meet you by the door to the hotel.' She backed away then turned and broke into a run. Connie stared after her, drawing her hands down either side of her face. Pinprick flashes of white light exploded at the edge of her vision. She had to lean forward, palms resting on her knees, to quell an attack of hyperventilation. If it all blew up in her face, so be it. Anything was better than enduring this demi-life with a man who remained abroad though he had come home.

At some distance, hunkered down behind a white van with a pitched-back snoring driver, Mary gave up on St Anthony and turned instead to St Jude, patron of hopeless causes.

She could not for the life of her imagine any good coming from a meeting between two women so locked together in their own strange time capsule. It was there, visible for anyone with a will to see, the hank of rope binding one to the other. Years, distance, marriages, children, changes of circumstance, nothing had managed to sever the tie. It had everything and nothing at all to do with Matt. It had to do with birthplace, shared air, shared childhoods, the same formative experiences, all the places that Connie had put into verbal pictures for Mary so that they might reach into the past and be together there, too. While Connie spoke and sometimes Matt, Mary had closed her eyes, imagining what was then a red dying town, table mountain slag heaps with rivers of pitch marbling down through grey sludge, pink paste on wet car windscreens slapping left and right, impelled by worn-out wipers, patient stack of copper coins for Friday night out.

She had tried to inveigle herself into their history, tried to see what she might have looked like on the farm, on the dusty streets of Consett, always with Connie by her side. Had gone so far as to imagine their childish conversations together while picking blackberries or eating Brenda Bradley's soup. They had made it sound impossibly romantic, close-knit and warm so that it hadn't taken a huge leap to move from inventing a whole other childhood to actually believing in it. She wanted to laugh bitterly now at her own fancifulness — what had her friend, her very best friend, yes — only — if the absolute harsh truth be told, ever seen in an oversized scuttling crab, when all along she had Greta.

Though she had not been able to hear what was being said between the women, for moments, as laden, silent glances passed back and forth, it had seemed to Mary that what she was really observing was the pregnant exchange between two people forced as if by a chance, shock encounter to confront all the long-forgotten things that had bound them in the past. In the manner of once-close school chums, the rivalries, the arguments, the laughter, all flooding back in an instant, in the time it takes to turn a street corner. Of a sudden she felt overcome with a rising surge of panic. There really was no place for her in their world.

14

A white noise crackled in Mary's eardrums. It fizzed and hissed like a television left on throughout the night. She had to plunge her fingers in and give her head a good shake. No matter how many times her eyes swivelled she still could not absorb the vision confronting her at Connie's.

Mary had pitched up at her usual time, or more to the point, what had always been her usual time, determined not to mention a thing about seeing that strange encounter earlier. For one thing she would have had to confess to spying and for another she just wanted to consign Greta to some far, icy region in the back of her head. Antarctica, no less. Yet, here was that self-same woman sat in the middle of Connie's kitchen, pale-skinned, smoky-eyed, more ethereal than she had imagined at a distance. Sipping tea from a mug, the one that Mary always used, while seated on the chair Mary always sat on. And smoking for heaven's sake.

She could barely manage to mumble a greeting to Connie who was chattering lightly with her back to them, waving a spatula in the air, as if Greta in her house was an everyday occurrence. Mary looked around open-mouthed for Matt who couldn't be home yet or could he? There didn't seem to be any outer limits to this surreal tableau.

'Hello hello?' Mary said to Greta, her voice sounding garbled to her own ears as though it were treading water.

'Pull up a pew, Mary,' Connie said cheerily, turning so that Mary nearly gasped at the spades of make-up she'd applied to her face. All the more startling because she hardly ever wore the stuff and then only a light frosting, a touch of sheer lipgloss, mascara maybe. This evening she could very well be in drag. Forest-green eyeshadow made her eyes look tight and small, the matt red lipstick was like something out of the forties, couldn't she see that it made her teeth look yellow like the yellow flesh inside dark red glossy apples. And that strange falsetto voice. 'Meet Greta, an old friend from Consett days. I may have mentioned her? Rome?' With a shrug, what did it matter one way or the other, Connie continued frying three sirloin steaks.

'Pleased to meet you.' Greta extended a hand. Shiny scarlet fingernails as if Mary couldn't have guessed, she grabbed and shook so hard it took her a while to notice the other woman's pained wince.

'What are you doing here?' Mary blurted then gathered herself at a narrow-eyed glance from Connie. 'I mean, in London. Business or pleasure?'

'I used to live here.' Greta took a sip of tea. She wore the startled expression of a newly trapped animal, Mary thought, with a spurt of gratification. At least that made sense. What Connie was playing at, the world and his wife couldn't figure.

Mary sat, buttocks grinding over the unfamiliar grooves of an unfamiliar chair. It took her some time to realize that Connie was talking again, telling Greta about her sons, each child receiving about a minute and a half each. They bore little resemblance to the boys Mary had known and loved since infancy. Easy-going, borderline lazy Fred had metamorphosed into a prodigious academic, Joe was highly strung certainly but that was down to his creativity, which was a burden he was going to have to bear all his life. What creativity? There was none, zip, they'd all gone looking but it had failed to show. Mary's eyes bored holes in Connie's back, what was she going to advance about Benny? Clearly it was a shared thought because there was a small pause before the youngest turned into a deep, serious thinker who inspired his many friends without the slightest idea that he had that sort of effect on people. No idea at all, imagine? Mary had to choke back a cough.

'Wait until you see Joe,' Connie was chuckling over her shoulder. 'You'll think it's Matt standing there. Well, the way he used to look, of course. And here's Benny now. Say hi to Greta, Benny. Remember — in the photo?' She was pointing at something. Mary and Benny turned at the same time. On the dresser stood a framed photograph of a young Matt, Connie and Greta together. When had that been put up?

Benny looked ill at ease; he sat beside Mary while they both stared at Greta drinking her tea in what appeared to be great discomfort, knees jittering up and down making the table shake. Through the constant hiss in her own ears, Mary could just pick up snatches of the rest of Connie's meandering chatter. This house, how it had seemed sheer folly at the time and then she found out she was pregnant° with Benny and the decorating schedule had to be brought forward. The hours Matt worked in those years. Jesus! The garden was entirely her territory though, a jungle when they moved in first but section by section she had managed to tame it into shape. Come see!

Connie flung open the back door. Greta didn't seem to understand what was expected of her at first. Perhaps, like Mary, she was trying to make sense of where she was, what was happening. Failing miserably by the look of it. Mary could see her own stunned expression in the woman's pebble-grey eyes.

'She wants you to look at the garden,' Benny mouthed, leaning across the table.

'Oh.' Greta stood so suddenly, her tea slopped over the rim. 'Beautiful, really well put together,' she murmured, standing beside Connie as they both peered out. Unconsciously, in perhaps a self-comforting gesture, Greta was rubbing the back of her head. Hair parted and Mary could see the ropy scar tissue that Connie had spoken of, it bisected the entire scalp. She must have taken a hell of a tumble, Mary had to draw on every ounce of inner strength not to add a coda to that thought. It had been one thing to wish this unfortunate woman dead when she'd never met her, quite another to wish the same once you'd shaken someone's hand.

'I'm quite proud of it,' Connie said of the garden. 'D'you want to see upstairs?' Before the other woman could respond, her hand was clutched and she was being led from the room as a person unsteady on their feet might be led. Or a person who might be on the verge of bolting.

Benny's eyes fixed on Mary, rounding like

twin space ships. She had to make a monumental effort to force what she hoped was some semblance of an easy grin but which she knew looked like someone in mid-sneeze. How much or how little he might have heard about this Greta person in the house, she had no idea. Enough to put that little pleat of concern on his forehead, she could only surmise.

'An old friend,' she said in this new watery voice that seemed set to stay. An o-o-l-d fri-e-n-n-d.

'I know,' he said.

'Nice. A visit.'

'She's pretty.'

'Yes! Yes, she is. Ve-rr-yy.'

The forgotten steaks sent up black fumes from the pan. Mary leaped up to salvage what she could but they'd turned into lumps of charcoal. She slanted Benny a glance, his mouth turned down, sling 'em, in complete agreement she tossed them into the bin just as Connie and Greta returned. How lovely it all was, Greta was saying. Really lovely. She sounded, and even moved, like a robot with parts missing. For a split second Mary experienced a shiver of sympathy.

'Oh no!' Connie cried. 'What've you done with my steaks?'

'They were — ask Benny.'

'Cremated,' Benny said.

'But Greta always liked her meat that way.' Connie looked into the bin, there was too much rubbish clinging to the blackened steaks to save them. 'I was deliberately burning them, Mary.'

'Well, you might have said. Besides, why burn all three?'

'You're right. Sorry. I'll — ' Connie stopped, she looked around as though unsure where she was for a moment. Mary realized they were all in the same adrift boat. She wanted to seize Connie by the shoulders, drag her into the garden, give her a good shake and demand to know what she thought she was doing. You didn't invite the enemy over the threshold. For God's sake, you didn't invite them into your *home*. Feed them cremated steak, put up pictures when they're were no pictures before. Introduce them to your nearest and dearest. What was she hoping to achieve? That Greta would raise two arms in surrender, back away pleading for mercy — *enough*, enough happiness, enough domestic bliss — I can't take any more!

She wanted the old Connie back. The sweet-natured friend who had it all sussed, the quirky mother with everything that Mary had ever dreamed of, the friend who shared moderate moments of discontent but generously shared moments of contentment as well. It was all disappearing even as Mary tried to focus and the very worst thing was, she could quite clearly see that Greta was trying to help Connie out in a way that Mary couldn't possibly. She wanted to bellow, 'Can't you see? What's the matter with you? She's not who she was! She's just a shadow. A figment from your past. She's just become larger than life in your head like she has with Matt. She's really very, very small. Nothing in fact. No one.'

A runnel of sweat trickled down Mary's nose. Silently, she prayed to St Jude but his stall was closed for the day. St Anthony was still dealing with rejection, he was small and petty that way. She looked to Benny. He was studiously avoiding her concentration. The buzzing in her ears had reached a level she thought they all must surely hear. Strangely, absurdly, it was Greta who was stretching an arm toward her.

'Are you all right? You seem a little — '

'I'm fine.' Without meaning to, Mary swiped the concerned hand away. She thought but couldn't be entirely certain that Connie was openly glaring at her now. 'I think — I think I ate something funny for lunch.' To distract attention, Mary practically rocketed from her chair to pluck the photograph from the dresser.

'You've hardly aged a day,' she said to Greta, meaning to be friendly to put Connie at ease. For some reason it came out like a rank insult.

'Thank you but — ' Greta responded with a rueful smile. She extended a hand for the picture, a touch too regally for Mary's liking, making her press the frame against her chest for a moment before reluctantly relinquishing it.

'Did you keep all those photos you were always taking?'

Connie nodded but she looked slightly uncomfortable. Mary realized with a plunge of heart that she had done the wrong thing again, drawing attention to it.

'They're in the house somewhere,' Connie waved a hand airily.

'The photo album's in your room,' Benny interjected with a confused expression.

'Oh yes.'

'They've always been in your room.' Benny's frown deepened, eyes darting across his mother's steadily flushing face. Greta handed the frame back to Mary, everyone aware that whatever they were doing was the wrong thing but there didn't seem to be a right thing. Mary let out what she intended as a hearty laugh.

'I've only just noticed,' she said as though she looked at this picture every day. 'The jeans.' She tilted so they could all look. 'Those are the faded, slashed jeans you got from cousins in America, Greta?' The instant the sentence was out of her mouth she realized she had just committed her greatest faux pas yet. She was telling Greta that she was the subject of many an intense conversation in this household, that even what she used to wear had come under scrutiny. That she had been a presence long before this happy-go-lucky visit. Mary wanted to crawl into any crack in the floorboards, she turned to replace the frame pretending to look still so that she didn't have to face what had to be her friend's certain wrath. It was Greta who rescued the situation.

'The American jeans! That sister of mine, Rita, she always denied nicking them but I knew. She was always taking my stuff. Mind you, four sisters in one house — Funny how you remember simple, insignificant things from youth when the big things are often — You had a blue dress, Constan — Connie, d'you remember — I bet you don't, with tiny white flowers? A sweetheart neckline with three little buttons just here,' she made a stabbing motion down her chest. Connie's inflamed face grew less red though Mary felt sure that she was emitting a clear if unspoken directive to get the hell out of there before she caused any further damage. Connie had to be looking from one friend to the other, wondering what she had ever seen in Mary compared to this subtle, intuitive, and yes, yes, luminous woman sitting in her kitchen with slender ankles wrapped around one leg of her chair. She even knew how to sit right.

'I'd better be going,' Mary said.

'There's no need to rush off, is there?' Connie made to reach out but Mary recoiled afraid that kindness would surely make her burst into tears and if that happened she could never come here again.

'I — I've prep work to get on with — Carmel's card?'

'Oh yes.' Connie smiled, eyes flicking back and forth across her friend's face. She looked concerned but Mary figured it was probably more to do with what Greta must be thinking of this stupid crab than anything else. Connie continued: 'We'll get a takeaway. Why don't you at least stay for that?'

'No, no. I can't.' Mary took a forceful step back hitting the dresser with the tops of her thighs. There was the ominous sound of wobbling china and glass hitting wood then sliding until the splintery sound of glass hitting the kitchen floor. The photograph lay smashed by Mary's feet. She let out a long moan.

'For God's sake what's the matter? It's only glass, no big deal,' Connie's voice sounded through the deafening white noise.

Mary's eyes flickered to the door anxious to make her escape. Matt was standing there, shock giving his drained face a spectral quality as though he were the ghost surprised by a mortal. No one else had noticed him as yet, all eyes were still trained on Mary backed up against the dresser, rigid with shame. She must be acting even stranger than she'd figured, the way they were looking at her. Matt stepped into the kitchen.

'Greta? *Greta?*'

'Isn't this a nice surprise.' Connie whirled around, beaming. 'Greta called and I *insisted* she come and stay with us for a few days. We've spent a lovely time talking about the old days and what have you. She's very well.' She focused on the sitting woman. 'You do look well, I'm pleased to say. We've been so worried about you. Haven't we, Matt?'

He can't move, Mary thought, he should be moving, air kissing Greta's cheeks in welcome. She should be moving, too, scraping back her chair to meet him halfway, saying something light about meeting twice in one year having never met for decades. There should be banter, how are yous, how are you finding London, what a wonderful home — how nice to meet your family at last. Damn it, if this was the show that Connie had chosen, the least they could do was play by the rules. But they were frozen, eyes locked, a pull of intimacy stretched so tautly between them that Mary was certain if she reached out her fingers she would feel something hot and visceral issuing across the room. Benny was shifting uncomfortably on his chair equally aware in his childish way that there were things they should be saying, grown-ups didn't greet one another in silence. Greta cleared her throat to speak but it must have constricted into a sealed dryness because nothing came out. Mary could sense Connie's growing agitation, she'd given them their cue and they hadn't picked up.

'Matt,' Greta finally managed, half stumbling out of her seat to reach him so that he instinctively surged forward to steady her footsteps. They ended up midway across the room in an awkward fumbling embrace before both stepped back at the same time.

'You called?' Matt asked in a tone of bewilderment. 'You called here?'

Greta turned to look at Connie as if seeking direction.

344

'Well, don't look so surprised,' she exclaimed. 'Why not? Of course she'd call us if she's in London.'

Mary slipped to the door in a sideways motion, entering the hall with an exhalation of relief. Behind her came the quick scuffle of small feet, Benny, as he raced past her without a word to run upstairs. At the front door she turned to look back into the kitchen one last time. Matt was saying something to Greta's upturned face, an involuntary smile splitting his own cheeks, at a little distance stood Connie half-turned away though her eyes were fixed on both of them. Almost exactly as it had been in the photograph that Mary had just broken.

She closed the door quietly behind her.

★ ★ ★

It was nearly midnight already and still Matt hadn't had a chance to speak with either Connie or Greta alone. He wasn't entirely sure for that matter if he was capable of coherent speech, the shock of seeing Greta was percolating through his nervous system like a slow, sweet poison — dangerous but headily so. Within minutes of hearing her voice he had, on the one hand, entered a bizarre parallel reality while, on the other, he had been jolted back into a sense of reality that he only now saw fully had been missing for the past few months. It was as though he had been living within a cobweb, not intentionally, more despite his best intentions.

Connie had chattered throughout the takeaway Indian with a fervour bordering on zealous, taking care not to meet his eyes except to crinkle a reassuring smile as she passed the aloo sag or the prawn biryani. *We can do this. We can,* she seemed to be saying, even as Matt had had to detach his retinas from the vision of Greta picking politely at her plate, tucking a skein of hair behind one ear in a gesture that made his heart contract. She did look better, more alert, less spacey; she had promised faithfully to continue cutting back on the pills the day he'd bit down on his lower lip, nearly drawing blood, as he'd turned to walk away from her at Fiumicino airport, resolved not to glance over his shoulder even one time. It was only at the top step, just before he boarded the aircraft that he had allowed himself a backward sweeping look but there was nothing there, of course, except tarmac and other people's planes. He had been half expecting something of her, a spirit, an essence, to have followed.

Fred had eyed her throughout the meal with polite suspicion, asking questions about life in Rome, chewing ruminatively as Greta responded with plastic enthusiasm. Needless to say, it was Joe who added his own brand of mayhem to the strange gathering by flirting like a peacock with all feathers on show. Chatting intimately as if he'd known her all his life, ironic downward pull on the last vowel of her name, Gret-ah, the blatant hair ruffling and booming voice shouting down everyone else. Matt didn't know if he was feeling amused or jealous. A curious thing watching your teenage son square up to you, watching his instinctive attraction to the same person. He envied his youth but felt sorry for him, too, for all the years stretching ahead when the swagger and cockiness might be driven out of him to end up just another mixed-up and confused old bloke like his father.

As usual Joe went too far, pulling off his sweatshirt at one point to reveal his lean torso, something he'd never done at the table before. Matt was about to correct him when Connie had leaned forward with her eyes issuing a clear warning. She'd tossed the sweatshirt back at Joe, telling him with a nod of her head to get it on double quick or else.

'*Chill*,' Joe countered. 'I'm eating vindaloo for Christ's sake. It's hot.' He turned to Greta. 'It's this country innit. I bet you don't miss that in Rome. Like it's just flesh man. Like we don't all have bodies.'

'Not at the table, Joe,' Connie remonstrated with a tight smile. How middle-aged, how staid they must appear, Matt thought. Joe continued shovelling small mountains of chicken sagwaloo down his throat. Matt counted to ten under his breath, wanting to give the boy a chance to save himself in his own time but it wasn't going to happen. He didn't mean to make them all jump out of their skins by slashing his cutlery on to the plate.

'Joe! Shirt on NOW.'

There was a brief moment when he thought that Joe might challenge him. Blue eyes swivelled insolently in his direction while his son continued chewing. What was that throbbing silent stare about? Was Joe letting him know that he understood perfectly well about this stranger in their midst? Was he measuring his father, finding him wanting, finding him a poor and diminished rival? Or perhaps in his own way he was trying to stick up for his mother. A flickering shadow of confusion entered the blue stare and Matt was pierced for his middle child. The difficult awkward one, the boy with words that his father never had, reduced to taking his top off at the table to make a statement.

348

'C'mon son,' Matt urged in a quiet voice. 'Don't let yourself down now.'

Joe pushed his plate away, letting out a long sigh. He got up dragging the sweatshirt along the floor in his wake.

'I'm done anyway,' he said. The door was about to slam shut but he'd caught it outside just in time. It closed with a soft click instead. Fred shot his father a look of cold steel.

Connie kept hopping up and down from the table, taking tiny mincing steps to the oven to draw out new warmed dishes. Matt couldn't help but think of those Chinese women with bound feet; he wanted her to stop but understood that she had no choice but to keep in constant motion. It was all he could do to keep his own body glued to his chair. He would find himself starting to say something to Greta, anything, how was work, how long was she intending to stay, but his throat sealed so he tried small watery smiles instead, which was worse because then he had to look at her. Out of the corner of his eye he could see that Benny had taken to lining up chickpeas in narrow rectangles along his plate. Connie was doing her best not to comment, not to draw attention but a film of perspiration gleamed across her forehead. While she managed to keep up what could only be described as a barrage of idle chatter to Greta, her gaze was constantly drawn to her 9-year-old's fingers making shapes, the way his tongue peeped from the corner of his mouth in studied concentration. He was not presenting in best light it had to be said. The rectangles turned into squares within squares. Connie's hand snaked out, gently restraining his wrist.

'Enough lining, Benny,' she said almost in a whisper.

The crooked smile breaking on Greta's face nearly made Matt choke on a prawn.

'My son used to do that,' she said. There was a tremulous silence until Connie, Connie with her great big floppy heart, Matt had never truly understood how big it really was until that precise moment, stretched across the table to squeeze her guest's hand with tears glittering in her eyes.

'Oh Greta,' she said.

'I used to try and stop him too.'

'I'll grow out of it,' Benny interjected, startled by the new layers of things he couldn't understand crisscrossing the room.

'Of course you will,' Greta said. 'And it doesn't really matter if you don't. Don't tell anyone but I've been known to suck my thumb, even now.' She bit her lip and quickly glanced around as though immediately understanding that this introduced a level of intimacy they were not quite prepared for. Connie's hand withdrew as she took up her incessant stream of small talk once more. Matt was torn between wanting to shout at her to shut the hell up for one second, just one second to let him try and think straight, and a sense of gratitude that he was not having to negotiate any jarring silences himself.

Somehow the evening passed in a series of fits and starts, awkward subjects were rapidly changed, mostly they stuck to the past and mutual acquaintances though there were minefields there, too. Greta appeared limp and unresisting to whatever Connie suggested and when she offered to run her a nice warm bath, the cold after Rome must be such a shock to the system, Greta assented with a 'yes please' that was meek and childlike. He desperately wanted to speak with her alone, it just didn't ring true that she would randomly call like that then show up, even if Connie did insist. A dozen different explanations ran through his mind. And through them all though he tried his hardest to push the thought out, the same note kept repeating — perhaps she's come for me. Perhaps in the end it will be as simple as that.

There had been moments during the past few months, frightening in their intensity, leaving him shaken and breathless, when he had felt that he was capable of leaving everything behind to simply go to her. Just that, walk out of the front door and not walk back in. He had gone so far as to fantasize about the stratospheric levels of guilt to the point where even thinking about it became an exquisite form of torture. It was a strange inkling into Greta's mind, what she experienced, though in her case, compounded a thousandfold, every day of this nether existence she was enduring.

The boys were still around flitting in and out of the living room while Connie ran the bath, so the most he could actually manage was a terse, 'Are you okay?' Greta nodded but she turned beseeching eyes on him, she hadn't asked for this he understood in an instant, she wanted to be rescued. He blinked that he understood.

Connie returned carrying fresh towels which she placed in a pile on Greta's lap.

'I've put your bag in the guest room,' she said, 'and I've switched on the electric blanket, if you find it too warm just turn it down to one, that should see you through the night.'

'Thank you.'

'Not at all. Bath's all ready if you are?' Unwittingly she had adopted the same tone she would use to a child. Matt experienced a flash of anger which he couldn't fathom. This was a huge thing his wife was doing, he couldn't imagine many other women drawing on the same reserves of simple goodness in similar circumstances, she didn't know how not to be kind. He should be down on his knees with admiration instead of harbouring what was a steadily rising resentment against her. Nevertheless, it burned like a hot unquenchable coal throughout the rest of the evening.

Every time he tried to catch her alone in the kitchen, or once in their bedroom, he was called to the phone or she was, or one of the boys walked in. He had never realized before quite how unprivate this house really was. They all seemed to drift apart then together in one amorphous blob like the coloured wax in a lava lamp. Finally, some time after midnight even Fred had had enough of whatever crap was on the telly and uttered the magic goodnight word. The door to the guest room had sealed shut hours ago. Matt could only imagine Greta lying there, the electric blanket, open eyes fixed on the strange ceiling above her head, sweating in the sauna of Connie's kindness.

He poured a brandy, signalling with his brows if she wanted one, she nodded. They settled on the sofa, Connie with her legs tucked under her body, both staring into the dying embers of the fire. A last lick of flame danced up from one blackened log before subsiding into a series of sparks. Matt took a long pull on his brandy before swivelling to meet her eyes.

'What's going on, Connie? What's all this about? Don't say 'all what'.'

She deliberated for a while before responding.

'It's my way of coping with this — this — her, you.'

'There isn't a her, me.'

A look of derision twisted across her face, one hand impatiently chopped air.

'The funny thing is, she understands why she's here. *She* knows. I had to invite her. Why not? You were her guest in Rome, now she's ours. I'm not putting on an act if that's what you think. Someone in her situation, you'd need to be made of stone not to feel for them. I should hate her but I don't. Believe me, I've tried to hate you.' She paused to take a sip of brandy, she might have been speaking about the weather. 'But it seems I can't.'

'Connie — '

'She's changed, hasn't she? There's something almost lifeless about her.'

'Almost.'

They sipped in silence for a while.

'I'd like her to stay for a couple of days,' Connie said. 'I'll be kind to her. She'll see us as a family, see you as part of that family. She'll simply be a guest and then she'll leave.' She turned and their eyes locked. 'It was a long time — such a long time ago, Matt. You have to let it — We've all changed in different ways. She'll never come back, not the way she was, not after losing a child.'

'I wish you hadn't done this.'

'I wish I didn't have to.' A rueful smile played fleetingly on her lips, she drained the brandy glass, uncurled her legs and left the room without a backward glance.

Matt continued to stare into the glowing hearth. A screech of high wind whipped across the roof over their heads. It spiralled down the chimney inflaming little eruptions of sparks. Looking into a dying fire late at night — there was always that other life you might have lived. The one that had slipped away when you weren't looking. The one that continued to unravel along a barely visible lick of flame in the furthermost corner of your eye.

15

There was wet, melting sleet on the ground the following morning when Connie finally managed to drag her body out of bed. She rubbed her eyes, for a split second it looked like Mary's car rounding a corner at the top of the street but it had to be her imagination. By the pavement outside, Matt was getting into his car, an old overcoat slung over his shoulders. He looked up and caught her by the bedroom window. They both raised a hand, Connie's remaining up in a limp curl long after he'd driven off. For most of the night they'd lain together listening to the wind, both pretending to be fast asleep. Both pretending it was just another ordinary night while Benny prowled around downstairs, tinkling baubles on the Christmas tree, rustling wrapped presents, while Connie could almost feel the list of her husband's body towards another room.

She showered, moisturized, contemplated make-up then decided against, the look of horror on Mary's face yesterday was enough to put her off eyeshadow for life. She went downstairs still in her dressing gown.

Normal family life, wasn't it? Smell of coffee, porridge in the microwave. Faint, rank odour of sweat from trainers lined up in the hall. Milk bottles in a row brought in earlier by Matt. Pungent Indian takeaway drifting through the house: foreign, tangy, infinitely more exotic than the scent of meat and two veg. And something new, the lingering scent of another woman's perfume and stale cigarette smoke.

She tried a few mouthfuls of sugary porridge but couldn't face it. Instead, she sipped a mug of coffee, nursing it with both hands, elbows on the table. Usually this was her favourite time, before the day would start racing so fast leaving her flying along in its wake, clutching on for dear life. A head peeped tentatively around the door.

'Come in, Greta. Did you sleep okay?'

'Very well, thank you.' She was fully dressed, lack of sleep gouging dark circles under the grey eyes. 'It's a lovely room.'

'Coffee?'

'Yes please. No, no, don't get up. I can — '

But Connie was already on her feet, pulling out a chair, pouring another mug.

'There.'

'Thank you.' Greta added a drop of milk then sipped. 'Good coffee.'

'I get it in Sainsbury's. Italian would you

believe?' They both smiled before lapsing into a long silence.

'I thought we might go shopping today,' Connie began hesitantly. 'You know, last minute presents? It's nearly always last minute with me I'm afraid.' *Jesus, Connie, who's she got to buy for? Where's your head?* 'Rita maybe?' she added quickly.

'I'm hopeless at choosing presents,' Greta said. 'Though I always liked getting them. Very much.' There was another long silence while they blew on their coffees and sipped alternately.

'I'll head up north this afternoon if it's all the same to you.' Greta tucked a tendril of hair behind her ear. Such a simple gesture but it immediately transported Connie to another place, another time, she could almost believe that she was pre-adolescent again, there was none of this, this house, this family, the years melted away before her eyes. She nearly choked. 'It's been so nice being here,' Greta was continuing, she raised her gaze pointedly. 'Seeing you and your family and — everything. You've done very well, Connie. You should be proud of yourself.'

'Thank you but please stay a couple more days at least.'

'It's Christmas. Family time, I have no business intruding.'

'You're not intruding. I've invited you.' It came out sounding like a punishment. Connie softened her tone, 'I've invited you, Greta.'

'Please I — '

'You can't just leave without talking to Matt. He'll want to know what's happening in your life since he left.'

'There's not a lot to tell, to be honest.'

'Even so.'

'There's a train to Durham at quarter past three.'

'He told me about the ancient port. Maybe you could show me if we get to Rome sometime soon again.'

'Antica Ostia. You hardly need me to show you around. It shows itself really.'

'Have you been lately?'

'The port? Yes, actually I have. Practically every weekend since — '

'Since?'

'Since the summer. I could probably catch an earlier train.'

'It's a lousy day for travelling.'

'I don't mind. Read a book, sleep, you know, it passes.'

'You've turned our lives upside down, inside out, d'you know that?'

'I'm sorry. I never meant to. It's better if I go today.'

'It doesn't matter if you're there or here or nowhere. It doesn't seem to matter. Like we're all stuck. I've had terrible thoughts about you, wished things that make me feel ashamed. You don't want to be the old Greta and I don't want to be the old — ' She broke off with a sigh. Pale fingers were sliding across the table top, Greta, preparing to withdraw. She was trembling.

Connie's lips compressed, her face was burning up. She took a deep breath reaching across to grab one of the sliding hands. She squeezed and stared into the grey eyes as though her life depended on it.

'Listen, you can do this. If I can, you can. You owe it to me and you damn well know you do. It's been making us ill, him remembering — me, imagining him lying there next to you. Imagining him on top of you. Jesus!' She put a hand to her mouth for a second thinking she might be sick. With the other hand she flapped not wanting to be interrupted, not wanting the lies the other woman would surely feel she should be offering. When the bile subsided down her throat again, she resumed eye contact.

'I've been with him since I was fifteen years of age. And long long before that if the truth be told, even if he didn't know it. You walked away. You left. Now you have to leave again.

But not like that, not with him always wondering. You have to say goodbye. Look him in the eyes and say it. Tell him you've met someone else. Tell him you're well again, I don't know, say anything you like but get the job done. I am truly sorry about your little boy, Greta. But I have my own sons to think about, you understand that, don't you?'

Greta hung her head. Connie loosened the grip on her hand. She wiped away hot tears bubbling down her cheeks, salty liquid seeped between her clenched lips. 'This is the way to be good. Not just you but me too. This is the way.'

Benny had slipped into the kitchen unnoticed. Connie couldn't be sure how much he'd heard. The shiny troubled face told its own story, though as usual he said nothing, just let it all filter in to add to the rest of the incomprehensible clutter that accumulated daily in his mind.

'Bunny boy!'

'They're collecting glass today. I have to sort out the different colours.'

He was carrying a brush and pan and made immediately for the broken photograph frame forgotten by everyone the evening before, he must have had to sit on his hands all through the night in order to ignore it. A little thing like that could disturb his equilibrium for days on end. It might have disturbed his already restive sleep. He brushed the glass into the pan, raising it to show them.

'Clear glass tub,' he pronounced as if they mightn't know. The photograph had come loose when he lifted the back of the frame. Carefully, he turned it over. A little frown stood out on his forehead. He was giving something insignificant the full weight of his concentration in the way he did which at once irritated his mother while tugging at her heart.

'Something wrong, pet?'

He looked at her, a touch strangely, she thought, but then things were often a touch strange with her youngest.

'Benny?'

'Nothing.' He shrugged, placing the photograph on the dresser.

'He's very conscious of the environment,' Connie said, wanting to blub again.

'That's — well, great. Commendable.'

'He cares about things. Stuff the rest of us don't notice half the time.'

'A lovely lad.'

'So you'll stay for a bit?'

Greta stared at Benny hauling plastic tubs for sorting glass into the middle of the room. She nodded miserably.

★ ★ ★

Mr Holden was back with a vengeance. Somehow that made sense to Matt, it had been one of those crazy kind of days in any case. A screaming child with a broken tooth and a really nasty root canal job. No less than three extractions, two of them children which still affected him — that instant pearly flush, eyes widening, filling with tears at the shock of the pull deep in their jawline. It wasn't pain they experienced, although understandably they confused it with pain, more a sense of pressure and the horrible psychological factor of this giant of a man, blocking out light, wielding the kind of steely instrument their daddies fixed the car with.

Nevertheless, the hectic hours meant there was no time to be worrying about what was going on at home. He had no idea if Greta would be there or not this evening. No idea what his own response might be either way. He was about to wrap up when Mr Holden dodged the capable Jennifer to crash straight into his room.

'I don't want those teeth benched!'

'Okay. It's not too late to stop the process. Mr Holden, it would be useful if you would make an appointment in the future.'

'I don't want those damn teeth at all.'

363

Matt let out a low whistle and started counting to ten.

'Fine,' he gritted. 'Take them, leave them, whatever you want. They're yours bought and paid for. Throw them in the river if you like.'

'I want my money back and I want you to start all over again. I want a different shape and the *right* colour this time.'

'Mr Holden — '

'It's my mouth! I know what I want.'

'What you want.' Matt edged closer, he could see Martin shoot him a warning glance from reception. 'What you want — is real teeth. You can't have those. What you *can* have is the set of dentures made to your specific, most specific and endless requirements. You will get used to them in time but it will take time. Or you can continue to wear your old, broken, uneven set until the day you — '

'I might be old but I served my country. I could hit you with this cane!' He shook the silver tip in Matt's face. It was the final straw. Matt swept past him to reception. He vaulted over the circular desk, making Jennifer jump back with a hand to her chest in shock.

'Matt — ' Martin began then bit his lip at the damp fury in Matt's eyes.

He was looking for the offensive dentures. Papers, pens, the credit card machine all went flying to the floor with one sweep of hand. He held them up.

'Here we go.' Mr Holden had stepped through. Matt reached over the desk and slammed the teeth into the old man's coat pocket. 'Take them. Jennifer, how much did he pay? Write him a cheque. Now now, give it to him.'

'I'd have to check the records.' She hesitated. Matt slammed the cheque book open by her hands.

'Think of a figure, loose is fine, double it. Give him the cheque.'

'But I don't want a cheque,' Mr Holden whined plaintively.

'Here it is. Take it. Take it! Happy Christmas. Now get out!'

The elderly man wavered for a moment cheque in hand. He appeared to crumple into himself. With the teeth and double-the-cost refund he had nothing left to complain about. A whole chunk of his life was suddenly missing. He turned and hobbled out mumbling to himself. Jennifer and Martin stood like shop mannequins staring at Matt. Martin rolled his eyes and let out a whoaa sound.

'I'm fine,' Matt muttered before they could say anything. He grabbed his coat. Jennifer scuttled to the toilet, possibly in tears.

'What's happening mate?' Martin ventured.

'Nothing. Just don't — ' Matt raised both hands warning him off. There were beads of sweat on his forehead. He managed to get to the door before Martin spoke again.

'Look Matt, your business is your own but it has to be said, ever since you got back from Rome — '

Matt stretched forward, head down, both arms leaning into the glass door.

'Finish that sentence and I'll deck you. We've worked together a long time, Martin. This is a time to keep your mouth shut. Got that?'

'Loud and clear.'

'Okay.' Matt exhaled a deep breath, straightening his spine vertebra by vertebra. 'Okay,' he repeated, stepping out into the slushy evening air.

★   ★   ★

Mary's teeth were chattering. She turned the car's ignition again to let a blast of hot air warm the interior. There was only a mouthful of soup left in the thermos when she gave it a shake. A sweep of wipers cleared speckles of clinging sleet from the windscreen. She was parked a reasonable distance from the house but if anyone should happen to spot her then she would get out, pretending to have just arrived. She'd been there almost three hours already. Sitting in the dark, wrapped in her thickest coat with a woollen scarf twisted tightly around her neck.

That this was absurd, compulsive behaviour she was perfectly aware. What it was she was expecting to see she couldn't for the life of her fathom. It didn't make a lick of sense but if she couldn't be in Connie's house then, for some entirely inexplicable reason, she had to be watching it. As though all the ley lines of her existence were inexorably drawn towards that one particular spot. She had tried pacing up and down her cluttered studio, tried the church, lighting every candle on the stand until Fr Alexander had crept up behind to ask if everything was all right, was there anything he could do. Go boil his head came to mind but she didn't say, instead she told him that she was praying for something, very hard, for somebody other than herself, he might try adding a prayer without knowing what for, later in the privacy of his home. He'd chuckled that generally he liked to know why he was praying. Wouldn't we all, she'd retorted, walking away.

She'd tried drinking cup after cup of endless tea, anything to stop giving in to this obsessive urge to keep up a vigil which had nothing that she could conceive at any rate to yield. Yet, somewhere in the back of her mind, it felt like a strangely soothing form of prayer. That was it, there was a sense of relief after a period of watch that reminded her of the washed-out, limpid feeling she experienced after a long praying jag. A sense of purification.

Up ahead at a safe distance, Greta was coming out of the house, pulling on gloves, holding the neck of her coat against a blast of icy wind. Mary slid as low as she could on the driver's seat but there was only the slimmest of chances that she would be detected. The other woman was stooped against a gale that whipped her hair around her face. Across the street she passed with rapid footsteps and Mary's head swivelled following her progress. At the top by a corner junction a set of car lights had come to a halt. She had to strain her eyes to see through swirling sleet. A streetlamp picked out the tall figure of Matt getting out of his car. The meeting could have been planned or entirely accidental, it was impossible to tell. She decided to take the chance of craning her head out of the window.

Greta was speaking animatedly, hands waving like frantic birds in the air. Matt placed a hand on one shoulder, possibly to calm her. She walked away, then retraced her

368

steps shaking her head, hands in constant motion all the while. To a casual observer it might have appeared that they were arguing but in her bones Mary understood that that was not the case. Of a sudden, Matt gripped her by both shoulders, his head pressing down to meet hers. The fluttering arms flew up to rest around his neck. Mary watched for what seemed like an eternity until the couple pulled apart again, Greta stumbling into far darkness, Matt approaching slowly in his car. He passed without seeing her parked there, one hand pressed across her open mouth.

How could they? A full frontal movie kiss on the street for Christ's sake. On the street where Connie lived, the street where her sons played football, clattered skateboards off the pavement, where Joe stubbed cigarette butts before going inside. How could Matt betray his wife like that? Her dear, dear friend. For that matter, Mary herself? She thought of Carmel's words, *They made me invisible, they had to, can you see that?* And Connie crying into her mobile phone, *Could you do this to me, Matt? Could you do this?* All the stunned women who had passed through Mary's studio when she in her innocence, in her blind stupidity, had believed that all they needed was time. Time to close over their wounds, to pick themselves up, a little dusting, a little straightening and onwards they would go. It wasn't anything like that simple. It wasn't just the betrayal of flesh, one body chosen over another, which was in itself painful enough, it was the betrayal of night-time secrets spilled on a pillow, of the deepest fears and wildest hopes shared alone with this one other person in the whole wide world. It was the moments of despair, the sick child, the mortgage arrears, the wrong turn taken before the path straightened again. The secret smiles over breakfast after good sex, two heads lightly touching bent over the new crib in the nursery room.

These moments flashed through Mary's mind as clearly as if she'd lived them herself. In the way she always supposed she had, vicariously through Connie. She could hardly feel his betrayal more intensely if she were actually married to Matt. A black rage shuddered to the depths of her soul. A fist beat down on the steering wheel then on the dashboard, it rained slanting blows at the side window before coming to an abrupt halt as Greta passed by on her return to the house. Mary waited until her smouldering cheeks had cooled. She took deep breaths, checking her face in the rear view mirror. It took a good fifteen minutes before she felt sufficiently in control to be able to face whatever new betrayal was waiting in Connie's house.

The sound of Joe's hooting laugh greeted her in the hall. It came from the kitchen, the door was closed.

'Mary? Is that you?' Connie called out.

The family, *her* family was seated to dinner. Greta was sitting in Mary's chair in her usual place. She looked pale and uncomfortable and it was clear in an instant that Joe was preening and flirting so hard, he didn't even bother to register Mary's arrival as he normally would with teasing comments, suggesting closeness. Connie was anxiously skimming the table trying to ascertain if she had enough food to stretch to another mouth.

'I'm sure we can — '

'Don't mind me,' Mary interrupted. 'I've eaten already. Just popping in to say hi really.'

'I meant to phone. Tell you a time for dinner,' Connie said with a guilty rictus of smile. Her cheeks were highly flushed, eyes gleaming with the overbright glare of a fever victim. 'Here, pull up a chair, come and speak with us at least. Push up a bit, Benny. Make some room for Mary.'

She couldn't be sure if Matt had caught her frosty glare as she drew her long legs under the table. He was white-faced, chewing in a mechanical grinding motion taking sips of red wine to make the food go down. She turned her glare on Greta instead and saw the other woman hastily drop her eyes. Good.

'You're our Rome expert,' Connie was saying. 'Greta was just telling us about — '

'I finished the prep work on the card for Carmel,' Mary bluntly cut across. 'Has Connie told you what she's working on, Matt?'

'What? No. No, she hasn't.' He appeared to be too distracted to even attempt small talk.

'Emm — I think we were talking about Rome, Mary.'

She realized too late that she had forgotten to conceal the black glowering stare she was casting in Greta's direction. Benny was lining broad beans on his plate with a vengeance that for once his mother was choosing to ignore.

'Rodin's *The Kiss*,' Mary grated, moving her attention to Matt. 'That's what we've chosen. Works on so many levels — '

'You know, if you still feel a little peckish I'm sure there's plenty — ' Connie was trying to interject.

'Betrayal mostly,' Mary continued. 'We think we're looking at — oh, the sublime heights of passion — when what we're really seeing is a grubby little pair not even enjoying the fruits of their own deceit — '

'Mum, why is she talking like — '

'They don't deserve to be happy.' Mary went on. 'Why should they? They're eaten up with fear and guilt because they know what they're doing is — '

'Mary!' Connie shrieked then contorted her features into something resembling a smile. 'Could you come with me for a sec? I just want to — I want to show you something.'

She tripped to the door holding it open for Mary to follow. Matt looked around the table at the sets of eyes pulsing in his direction, moving to Greta then back to him again. 'Jesus,' he said quietly. 'Jesus.'

'Mary?'

'I'm coming.'

In the hall, Connie gripped her hand, digging fingernails into flesh as she dragged Mary into the living room, slamming the door shut behind them.

'What d'you think you're playing at?'

'I might ask you the same question,' Mary hissed back.

'This is *my* house if I have to remind you. I won't have that kind of — '

'What kind of? Plain speaking?'

'You were not speaking plainly. You were being deliberately obtuse and extremely rude. I don't know what the boys will think.'

'No? You know damn well what they'll think. And it's the truth. For Christ's sake Connie — shoot the messenger if you must, but darling, you can't not see it — the way he looks at her — '

'Stop right there.'

'The way she looks at him.'

'Those days are over! You're just jealous of her. No one understands better than me how she can have that effect on — '

'He's still in love with her! In the name of Christ what are you playing at? Get that woman out of your house now before it's too late. Please listen to me.' Mary made to reach for Connie's shoulders but her hands were angrily slapped away.

'I want you to leave,' Connie said coldly.

'You don't mean that.'

'I mean it.'

'I saw them kissing. Out on the street. For anyone to see.'

'I don't believe you.'

'Why would I make it up?'

'How should I know? I'm not sure I know you at all, come to think of it.'

'You knew her, what — a handful of years when you were both pretty much just children. How long have we been friends, Connie? Nearly twenty years? Plenty of marriages don't last that long. Don't do this.'

'Mary, I really don't want to have this conversation.'

'I'm trying to help, can't you see?'

Connie's head whipped back, her eyes were blazing.

'Help? Really? Exactly how does that work? You give me information that I refuse to believe and even if I did, what am I supposed to do with it? Hmm?'

'They were kissing,' Mary said forlornly. 'How can I not tell you that?'

'It wasn't a kiss. You misunderstood.'

'What then? Mouth-to-mouth resuscitation?'

Connie turned away. She was holding her head.

'If you think you're helping you're just making things worse,' her muffled voice drifted across. 'I have to handle things my own way. I've faced this down before, I can do it again. Now, please, go home. Leave me be.'

'Connie I — '

'Go home.'

It was a wail curling out of Mary's mouth against her will.

'But this *is* my home!'

Connie swivelled around on one heel. Her eyes flashed dangerously and Mary wanted to put up her hand as a barrier, as if she could fend off the words she understood were coming. *Don't don't please don't.*

'It is *not* your home. Don't make me cruel but I'm tired, Mary. I'm tired of you feeding off my life.'

It was worse, far worse than Mary had anticipated. A kick in the gut that nearly made her knees buckle. She felt like retching. She waited for what seemed an age for Connie to retract but that wasn't going to happen. Her friend was closing her out, shutting her down, sealing the family ranks around Greta instead. For telling the truth, the simple unpalatable truth that Matt loved another woman, that this other woman loved him. And yes, standing there weary with regret, having just lost everything that was dear to her heart, Mary caught a glimpse of where Connie was coming from. Knowing the information didn't necessarily mean that you could act in a decisive, fate-altering way upon it. You couldn't just choose to stop loving somebody with a click of wounded fingers, no more than you could stop them loving someone else. There was a lifetime's investment to consider. Children. The future.

'I'm sorry,' Mary said.

'I know.' Connie gave her a rueful smile. 'So am I. So am I.'

'Don't choose her over me. Please,' Mary

whispered. Her head was down and Connie came to touch her cheek.

'If only it were that simple. Nothing to do with choosing. At least not for me. Mary, all I'm asking is for you to stay away for a little while. Don't make it the end of the world. I'm picking my way through a minefield here. I just can't have you blundering in on things you don't understand.'

'I do understand — you're deliberately not seeing.'

'What's the alternative? Deliberately see? What good is that to any of us? Far better if I can get them to see me.'

'Please I — '

But there wasn't time to finish the sentence. The living-room door had been flung open decisively, the look on Connie's face brooking no further argument.

'Another time, we'll talk this through. Right now, you have to go.'

'Can I come over tomorrow?'

'Wait for me to call you.'

'But you will call?' She was standing outside.

Connie had turned her head distractedly towards the kitchen. She was there already even as she closed the front door on Mary's anxious face. As she stepped further into the by now freezing night air, licking cooling fizzles of sleet from her lower lip, Mary wondered when, or if, she would step over this threshold again. She was, the thought pierced with close to surgical precision, extravagantly alone — an outsider, while deep in the womb of the house, a pale-faced, fragile bird flexed her wings revelling in her power. She could do anything it seemed, this Greta.

Surely an old exaggerated scalp scar like that — one good strike and it would crack open like an egg. Amazing that it hadn't cracked open already. Mary felt a desperate need for the dim-lit church, for candles, for absolution of thoughts which should not pass through any good Christian mind.

The church was closed. Strange thoughts lingered all the way home. Seductive images that made her groan with longing. Not so much the cracking of Greta, though that was satisfying in its way, more, Connie turning, a beam of delight sending out sparks from her face. Freshly washed white sheets stretched out on a line behind her, flapping in a gentle breeze. She was a woman in a soap powder advertisement. 'All clean. All clean again, Mary,' she was mouthing. 'Thanks to you.'

16

At the bedroom door, Matt turned to say something but couldn't bring himself in the end. He looked thin and stooped like a shaving of crescent moon. There was an air of vulnerability about his person she hadn't seen since his youth but which made him boyishly handsome again. She longed to touch that face always so dear to her but the invisible barrier between them had magnified beyond anything they could get past. It occurred to Connie that what she had done in effect was to place the medicine in his line of vision while making it impossible for him to reach. In a funny way, if she had consciously planned anything at all, and she hadn't, she had forced decisions upon all of them which might very well have been evaded indefinitely through time and distance. Years could have gone by, eventually fading the cult of Greta. Though in her heart she didn't really believe that for one second.

Equally, if she had planned or speculated, she might have thought that placing Greta in mundane surroundings, in the everyday routine of family life, that she herself might absorb some of their ordinariness. What she could never have anticipated was the potency of the woman's grief, filling any room she entered, slipping around corners like mist in her wake. She was a changed person, there was little doubt about that. But if anything, Matt cleaved more to the altered version than, perhaps, if she had remained the same.

Connie saw, quite clearly, as she studied Matt by the door, that she had simply been trying to do something she had tried all her life — handle them, compress their story into something small and malleable when in truth, they couldn't handle it themselves.

'Are the boys all right, d'you think?' he managed at last. 'They went to bed very quietly.'

'They haven't said anything to me if that's what you're wondering.' She didn't have to add that their silent glances back and forth between their father and Greta were more eloquent by far than any words or questions they might voice. The cat was well and truly out of the bag.

'You had an idea, didn't you? When we went to Rome,' Connie said.

'Aye.' He didn't hesitate. 'Someone I met thought they'd seen her.'

'I see.'

'Connie — '

'Don't. Just don't.'

'She wants to leave today. I think it's best. We'll — All of us — It'll be okay.'

'Mary says you're still in love with her. That she loves you, too.'

He opened his mouth then clamped it shut again. She could see that his eyes had welled up. Even now, he couldn't force himself to be dishonest and a hot spear of hatred shot up through her but didn't last long enough to give her the rage needed to carry this through. He was going to stay with his family and yet she felt defeated. He was going to stay with his family though she had lost him.

'We'll talk when I get home.' He twisted the door-knob. 'I'm not going to say goodbye to her,' he added in a rush before she could say anything. The door clicked shut behind him.

So, there was not going to be a waving-Greta-off scene after all. No finite clang to the front door. No false, tinny promises of visits in the future. Connie and Matt arm in arm bidding their visitor goodbye. It had all been for nothing. Now the boys knew, too, and would know that although Greta had physically left, in spirit, she would always remain. And they would never look at either father or mother in quite the same way again.

Connie buried her head under a pillow to muffle the sound of her sobs.

★ ★ ★

Outside in her car, Mary switched the engine on again to release a blast of heat. She watched Matt leave for work, flexing her cold, numb fingers trying to force blood to circulate. All through the early hours of the morning she'd prayed for forgiveness until around six she drove through the dark, silent streets to take up her usual space for monitoring the house. She'd brought a rosary but her fingers had grown too stiff to thread the mother-of-pearl beads.

When she thought of the damage she'd wreaked on her family by such wanton shredding of Connie's delicate menage, a line of sweat broke out along the creases of her neck despite the frosty morning air. How could she have been so reckless? How could she have missed the obvious — that Connie was perfectly aware of their feelings for one another, had always been aware, would always be. Like them, she had simply been trying to find a way to deal with it. Big crab Mary, pincers at the ready, on the attack for her friend when there was never a time when humongous degrees of tact and discretion were more called for.

Could she do this thing to make amends? Could she? It didn't seem possible one minute when the seams of sweat broke out as she tried to visualize this ultimate sin. The next minute, a dozen justifications scythed through the twisting jungle of her brain. She was hot and cold alternately. Dithering and decisive all at once. Lack of sleep and grieving for Connie, the prospect of life without her, had turned her eyes into puffed-up profiteroles, slitting her vision of the world.

It could be done and should be. Who would know — aside from St Anthony and St Jude and all the saints leading to the ultimate pinnacle of the triangle, the man himself. Perhaps in heaven as on earth there would be a chance to defend herself courtroom style, maybe that was how the twelve apostles spent their time now, on jury service. She knew that she was being fanciful. Deliberately facile in the light of this monumental act she was considering. Perhaps she was even talking, no goading, herself into a form of madness. I saw red, your honour, a red mist descended. Before I knew what I was doing — It was as if I was standing outside myself, watching — Couldn't think straight — Every expository final scene in every cop show she'd ever watched came to mind.

No, no, what no one would ever understand was the ultimate sacrifice she was willing (then again, perhaps not) to make for Connie — her own immortal soul. How exquisitely over the top that phrase rang to her own mind! Look Connie, look — my immortal soul — for you!

She felt watery-veined from tiredness and weeping. If only she'd made her life a bit bigger, a bit more rounded. Thought to add the things that other people appeared to acquire with such consummate ease. But she had thought, had wanted most desperately, a baby of her own, perhaps a husband, just they hadn't come along no matter how hard she'd prayed. Only Connie had, the one true fixture in a life that, yes, she was willing to admit, had pretty much gone adrift. She was back to being a big, tall, ignorable, dispensable crustacean. Just like it had been all those years in boarding school when every oversized bone in her body ached for Mama and the soothing power of a night-time kiss on the forehead. At least she loves me, at least she does. And so it had been with Connie. Nothing carnal or sexual, nothing beyond the deep abiding love of one friend for another, becoming in time, as family.

It was all very well debating this high crime

of passion but how could she explain the rather premeditated business of the hammer, wrapped in an old wool jumper, lying by her feet at this very moment? That would be a tough one for the apostles to swallow entirely. She blew her nose and began to laugh.

★ ★ ★

Connie was on her way downstairs when she saw Greta through a crack in the living-room door. She was standing by the Christmas tree gazing down at the mounds of wrapped presents. There was something in the rounded shoulders and limp, defeated stance that mirrored her own state so piercingly, she had to sit on a step to draw a breath. She watched as the strangest thing occurred — Benny was passing through from the kitchen, he hadn't seen his mother on the stairs, when for some inexplicable reason his attention was drawn to the living room. He stepped inside, opening the door wider, giving Connie a better view. He moved towards Greta in a series of halting, hesitant steps. She didn't signal in any way that she was aware of his presence. Benny stood right by her side until his head had to tip back so that he could look up at her face. They remained still and silent together for perhaps as long as five minutes. Not a movement nor one sound. Until Benny unravelled one arm with the slow elegance of a hypnotic snake to weave his hand around Greta's limp fingers. Her shoulders began to heave up and down in silence.

Connie must have emitted a cry or a sob because Benny turned and looked directly into his mother's eyes. She had never seen that glow of understanding in his gaze before. Sympathy, compassion and, yes, accusation, too, pulsed in the distance between them. Connie's hand flew to cover her mouth. *He knows. How can it be, but he knows.*

'Benny,' she whispered. The sound of her voice broke the spell and Benny turned from Greta to leave the room. He walked up the stairs past his mother but would not meet her eyes again. She heard him enter her bedroom as he did so often when confused or troubled.

Greta appeared to come to with a start. Her head swivelled.

'Connie, if you could call me a taxi? My train leaves Twickenham in about thirty minutes. I've packed already.'

'I'll take you to the train myself, Greta.'

'Thank you. Thank you for everything. You've been too kind.'

'You'll spend Christmas then with Rita?'

'Yes. Yes. That'll be it.'

'And then?'

They shared a slow, lingering smile as separate lifetimes passed between them, closing a circle, bringing them to this moment in time. What had been, what had not, an understanding that they would not see one another again.

'Back to Rome,' Greta said. 'I have no business here.'

Connie uncurled her legs and returned to her bedroom. Benny froze when she opened the door. He had just finished draping something along the bed. It took her a couple of seconds to fully realize what she was looking at. Then she noticed that one of her photo albums lay open on the floor by his feet. He was showing her that he understood what lay across her bed did not now, nor had ever, belonged to her.

'Oh Benny.'

She reached for him as he flew past but he was too quick. He ran to his room, slamming the door. Connie moved to the bed. Her hand reached out, touching. When had he found this? Or had he only made the connection through overheard conversations? What did it matter anyway, she knew in her soul that he would never speak of it even if she pressed with all her might. It would be a shared, unspoken knowledge between them for the rest of their lives. A hand lightly grazed her shoulder, making her jump. Greta stood there, setting down her suitcase. Her eyes were darting from the open album showing the young slender figure of herself in a light embrace with Matt, wearing the slashed American jeans that were now draped across Connie's bed.

'It wasn't Rita. You stole these,' she said quietly, bending to pick up the album. A crooked smile curved her lips as she flipped through her own perfectly preserved past.

'I would have given them to you,' Greta was saying. 'Then again, maybe not. Not particularly pleasant back in those days, was I? Can I say I'm sorry?'

Connie gulped several deep breaths. Her vision was growing blurred, she was certain that in a second she would faint. Greta's nostalgic smile was fading. She flicked the album pages back to look at something again. Then forward to check something else that had caught her eye.

'I see,' she said after a while.

'Do you?'

'And the hair? That was you, too?'

Connie nodded. She wanted to say that she too, was sorry. More sorry by far than Greta but not a word could escape her blocked throat. Clearly, Greta was also grappling for words as the full implication of the sordid little chain of events unravelled in the photographs. She looked at Connie then down again at the captured image of Matt holding her limp body after the bicycle accident. There was no need to ask the question, the guilty answer was written all over Connie's face.

'Oh no,' Greta said after a while. 'Please no.' Connie could only offer a limp nod in response. 'You could have killed me,' Greta continued in a strangely detached voice. There didn't appear to be any accusation in her tone, more a sense of dawning realization. Of things fitting together that had puzzled her in the past. 'I always did think it strange that the bike was perfectly fine that morning and then in the afternoon . . . ' Her voice trailed off until she could bring herself to speak again.

'Poor Constance. How you must have hated me.'

'I didn't hate you. I loved you. It was complicated.'

'Still is,' Greta said, quietly. 'I suppose I should be angry.'

'Aren't you?'

Greta considered for a while.

'Maybe. A little. Like you say, it's complicated. If I hadn't left — it would have

389

been a different life. Or maybe I'd have left anyway. But — one way or another — you did change how everything turned out — for each one of us.'

She placed the album in Connie's hands.

'Strange isn't it? We're all capable of pretty much anything.' Greta lifted her suitcase. 'I'll walk to the train station.'

In that instant, Connie saw the life she had so carefully manufactured at Greta's expense come tumbling down to lie as collapsed rubble by her feet. She saw Matt's face, expression grave as stone while Greta reached up on tiptoe to whisper in his ear. Her sons turning collectively to stare at their mother in mute accusation. In time, perhaps even the police and prison. Greta stepping in to fill the void, slipping inside Connie's life as Connie had once slipped into hers. A cry escaped her lips.

Later, when she would relive the next few moments over and over again, there would be no clear recollection of those few steps taken to join Greta at the top of the stairs. It would always replay as though the reed-like body was already falling away even as the palm of Connie's hand connected with the base of her back. As if, Greta sensing what was about to happen, released a sigh and acquiesced with her own fate. There was no scream or sound of protest. Just that gusty sigh, an exhalation.

The fall itself, the flailing hand beating back air and the rolling cartwheels of the suitcase, would come back with perfect clarity. As would the crystal instant when she realized the small figure of Benny was already poised halfway down the stairs. He must have sensed movement above him because he had craned his head around. His startled eyes searching for hers before Greta connected and the two tumbled in one blur of tangled arms and legs.

17

As Matt approached with two plastic tumblers of tea, Connie's eyes fixed on the trail of dot-to-dot splashes along the hospital linoleum in his wake. Clearly, he wasn't even aware that tea was slopping over the sides. Probably unaware, too, of wet, scalded fingers, though he warned her it was very hot when he handed over the cup. She let it sit on the flat wooden arm of the chair in the waiting room. There was only one other person present, a thin elderly woman who was giving the ceiling her full concentration. Her lips appeared to be moving, possibly praying or simply talking to herself. Like them, she seemed to be expecting news.

'Did you look?' Connie asked.

'Aye. They're still in with him. He just — just looks like he's sleeping.'

'He is, Matt,' Connie said fiercely. She grabbed his hand. 'That's all it is. He's sleeping.' She released his hand and bent forward to hold her head instead. There was so much going on in there she wanted to plunge her fingers in to extract one lucid, rounded thought. One second she could quite clearly see her spread hand against Greta's back, the next Greta was falling even as Connie reached the top stair on the landing. Could she really have done such a thing? It didn't seem possible. But then again, she had been capable of a considerably more premeditated act of destruction once upon a time.

For all those years she couldn't sleep when the darkness pressed down in judgement, at least she could tell herself that it was the reckless act of a lovestruck young girl. She hadn't meant to see it through. She'd meant to undo the damage to the bicycle before Greta mounted. Greta who a day previous had told Connie to piss off and stop hanging around them like a bloody dog. Greta who could dance backwards and wreathe her own head in smoke rings — who had Matt. Connie had left the farm that day with her heart pounding in her throat. It had felt as though it had moved up from her chest to lodge somewhere by her windpipe. She was terrified, stricken and exhilarated all at once. There was every possibility that Greta would not feel the urge to freewheel down the field later that day. In which case, Connie could quickly fix the brakes in the morning. There was the possibility that she might ride the bike but come to no harm. What would happen, what could happen, what might happen, the endless scenarios had played out in Connie's head as she'd paced up and down her floral wallpapered bedroom. She'd seen Greta in great pain in the local hospital, noble, brave and starkly beautiful against a white pillow while Connie fetched for her and carried as the wounded one lavished her with praise and gratitude. She'd seen the pale face surrounded by a halo of auburn hair in a heart-breakingly simple blonde wood coffin, Connie leading the procession of mourners filing past. She'd seen Greta cry out with horror once the bandages were unfurled from her once exquisite face, Connie, with tears flowing down her cheeks, holding out her mother's silver-plated mirror with the handle, for her poor friend to see. *What could happen?* Connie had wanted desperately to know. And at once she had wanted to save Greta, become her, be free of her, teach her a lesson, love, damage and betray her — but most of all, force her to relinquish the farmboy Connie had loved instantly from the moment he'd bent down to pick up a fallen bag of shopping, the shy smile for her while his shiny brown eyes looked over her shoulders for a last glimpse of another girl.

When she couldn't bear the tension another moment longer, Connie had mounted her own bike and raced back to the farm to stop the accident that had afforded her so much delicious and scary pleasure in imagining. All the way, she told herself that she hadn't really meant to harm Greta. It was just a manner of daydreaming mixed with wishful thinking mixed with a practical joke.

'He'll be fine,' Matt cut across her thoughts in a hollow voice. As if there was little connection between what he thought and what he felt compelled to say.

'I know he will.'

All through the day and into the night they had uttered those same words. Benny had a broken wrist but it was the slow drift into concussion, even as they watched, which was the most frightening thing. He had slipped in and out of consciousness until it looked as if he couldn't battle any longer and allowed himself to subside into a deep sleep. All the doctors could do was to monitor his vital signs for the time being. Wait for him to come around in his own good time. It was a nasty tumble, his body was temporarily shutting down to cope with the shock. They weren't to worry overmuch, the brain scan didn't give cause for concern, no internal bleeding. It was then that Connie completely lost it and had to be led from the room by Matt and a nurse.

She tried to explain that there was every cause for worry. That this was Benny, this was Benny they were talking about. You just couldn't tell with him. He could very well choose to remain in a twilight world safe from harm, from things he couldn't understand but absorbed nevertheless in his feral way. Benny who soaked up other people's emotions like blotting paper, who perhaps had reached saturation point. She had tried to convey this to the nurse, to Matt, but the words were garbled and she'd sounded insane. Matt's words of comfort had set her off again so he'd lapsed into silence after a while. She'd insisted that he return home to check on Fred and Joe and to fill them in on what was happening with their younger brother. And now he was back with tea to wait in the waiting room alongside a wife who looked like an escapee from a mental institution.

'Connie?'

'This is all my fault.'

'Why do you keep saying that? Stop blaming — '

'I invited Greta and — '

'Connie, stop now. You're making yourself ill. It was just horribly bad luck that Benny was on the stairs when she tripped.'

His hands were drawing down the sides of

his face. He was ashen with a fretwork of tiny crisscrossing lines standing out under each eye. He took a sip of tea, murmuring 'ah' to himself distractedly, the sort of sound a person makes when a thought overwhelms. How could he understand her guilt when he was drowning in his own?

'Matt — ,' she began, warming her hands which were icy of a sudden, on the silly plastic tumbler. 'It is my fault. All of this would never have happened if I hadn't — '

A hand lightly grazing her shoulder cut her off in mid-flow. It was a gentle-voiced nurse who'd dealt with them earlier in the day. Connie's heart lurched when she took in the wide smile she was presenting to both of them.

'Mr and Mrs Wilson? You said come and get you if — '

But Connie couldn't hear another thing because she was on her feet and racing through corridors and flying up stairs before the nurse could finish her sentence. A doctor who didn't look much older than Benny himself muttered something unintelligible as he left the four-bedded room, though his voice had the lilt of encouragement. Benny's head looked like a small cox's pippin apple in a sea of white. He was blinking rapidly, taking in the unfamiliar surroundings. His mother's worried face.

'Bunny boy,' Connie managed to whisper before Matt stood by her side.

A solitary high-pitched sound erupted from her mouth making Matt look at her sharply, thinking the moment had come when she had well and truly lost it. But she managed to tamp down the rising wave. Her son would be all right, for the moment nothing else really mattered. Her fingers lightly grazed the apple cheek until she felt his involuntary flinch and her hand drifted into the air above his head instead. Soon enough she would have to explain to Matt the bitter irony of Benny breaking Greta's fall and most probably saving her life as a result.

'What happened?' Benny asked in a voice surprisingly crisp.

'You fell.' Matt pressed close to Connie. 'Well, Greta did — on the stairs — taking you with her. How d'you feel?'

Benny's eyes swivelled to take in the cast on his arm.

'Okay,' he said. Another swivel and he stared right into the heart of his mother. 'I don't remember anything,' he added.

'Do you want to remember, pet?' She bent low.

'Why? I fell is all.' As ever he would deal with things in his own Benny way. She wondered at his strength. I fell is all. Maybe he was right, maybe Greta had tripped on the top step in her anxiety to get out of there and her son was simply in the wrong place at the wrong time. Though she had little doubt that he had been presenting to her an acknowledgement of something he couldn't quite understand when he draped Greta's old jeans along her bed. All the years she had worried and fretted herself into sleepless nights because she hadn't understood that her youngest was better equipped to deal with the murky, shadowy complexities of life than most. He simply accepted that this was so. That there were things that could not be explained. As a silent glance passed between them, she further understood that he would remain the keeper of her conscience. And the price she would have to pay for that. If it took the rest of her days which she didn't for a moment doubt that it would, she'd win back his confidence. Unlike Greta with her boy, Connie had been given a second chance.

She stepped back to give Matt a moment with his son. She was dry-eyed leaving the room to go to Greta's ward. There were injuries sustained to her head but Benny had taken the force of the fall. A large tumour had shown up in the X-rays which was inoperable according to the neurologist. Or at least the risk would be greater than learning to live with it. The tumour was almost 100 per cent a result of a previous injury, the fall from a bike with defective brakes. In short, they'd explained, the woman was a walking time bomb. Then again, if she minded herself, took the proper medication — who knew? Years perhaps, years and years.

Greta looked across, grey eyes full of anxiety as Connie approached.

'Is he all right? Is he going to be — ?' She let out a long sigh when Connie nodded. She sat by the bed, taking Greta's hand in hers. There was a swathe of white bandage around the top of her head which, coupled with a ghostly pallour, made her eyes appear like two deep, unfathomable bruises. She looked as vulnerable and child-like as Benny and equally enigmatic.

'I must have twisted my ankle or something,' Greta said. 'How stupid.'

'Greta — ' Connie began but Greta hurriedly cut across.

'Does Benny remember anything?' she asked.

'Not really. It was so sudden, a bit of a blur for all of us. I've been trying to go over what happened exactly in my own head.'

'The main thing is Benny's okay.'

'I'm glad you're okay, too, Greta.' As

Connie said the words she felt a spasm of surprise that she sincerely meant them. More than surprise, there was a sense of shock that she actually cared for this fragile woman at all, and yet she did. There was something between them, a bond that wasn't necessarily about Matt. In their green youth, Greta had engendered such strong emotions in Connie. Envy, hate, admiration and, in the measuring up alongside her, a sense of inadequacy that had taken over and allowed her to perpetrate what might well have been a fatal crime. Nothing could excuse her own actions yet there was the strangest sense of relief that Greta knew now and without a word being spoken, she was equally certain that it would remain between themselves, linking them together for evermore. She squeezed the limp fingers between her own and felt a reciprocal tightening in response. Connie realized in that instant that it wasn't as straightforwardly simple as hate she'd felt for Greta but a tortured, inexplicable love, too.

'I am truly sorry for what I did to you. It's not much of an excuse to say I was a kid. But it's all I can come up with,' Connie said.

'Funny, I never once saw that you wanted him. Matt, I mean.'

'Don't think you saw me at all, if we're absolutely honest,' Connie responded with a rueful smile to show that she wasn't meaning to justify her own behaviour.

'Probably didn't much.' Greta smiled too. 'Wrapped up in myself. My own glorious future.' Her tongue made a little self-derisive click. 'Most likely I'd have headed off in any case. Still lived the life I've lived, not seeing anyone but myself.' She stopped abruptly to stare out of the ward window, lost in her thoughts. An orange haze glowed from streetlights under a canopy of impenetrable black. Greta closed her eyes before continuing: 'When you lose somebody, after a while, after the fog, you see everything in a new, *keen* sort of way. You actually want it to stop. This looking at people, looking at them mess up their lives, mess up a moment that you know they'll never get to have back again. You run up to mothers shouting at their kids in the street. Crazy stuff. Everything — hurts. You'd think that you'd want everyone to be as miserable as yourself but you don't.'

'Of course you don't.' Connie couldn't help but wonder if there was a subterranean agenda under their conversation that they were both lightly skating across, each fearful of being the first to make a fissure. Greta was looking at her very intently.

'The horrible thing about happiness, about

402

reaching out for the possibility,' Greta stopped to lick her dry lips, 'is that, well, sometimes — ', she broke off, unable to complete her train of thought in words, though they both knew perfectly well that she meant that one person's happiness was often predicated on another person's deep despair. Connie slowly released her grip on Greta's hand. Her fingers tingled with pins and needles as they fluttered impotently in the air between them. Abdominal muscles contracted so hard, it felt like a wall of brick in her stomach.

'Greta, what are you saying to me?'

There was a long pause. Greta expelled air rapidly, she seemed genuinely as confused as Connie and yet there was a steeliness about her which was disturbing. She exuded the air of someone who had made a momentous decision but yet was still mulling over the consequences. A 'what might happen' decision such as Connie had herself made so long ago, it seemed to have occurred in another life. Now that she was clearer in her mind that she had not, in fact, tried to seriously harm Greta another time, she felt that she could ask the question about the long ago incident.

'Are you — d'you intend to tell Matt?' she asked.

Greta looked at her, surprised. 'Of course not.'

'Because I will. If you want me to.'

'What would that do for anybody?'

'I don't know. You'd be entitled to — revenge, maybe?'

'Revenge? Connie?' Greta's lips curled. 'We're long past that.'

'I'd really like to think so.' Connie sighed. 'So exactly where are we now?'

'I'm going back to Rome tomorrow. I'll try to make contact with my daughter. Maybe she's ready to see me, maybe not.'

'Greta — '

'I want to try to have a life again. To not let other moments pass. Do you understand?'

A minute went by before Connie could bring herself to respond.

'Are you saying — ?'

But Matt had stepped into the ward, moving directly to the other side of Greta's bed. Connie moved to position herself on a nearby chair. His eyes were devouring Greta's face, flickering from her chin to the bandage on her head and back again. Checking and rechecking that she was really going to be all right. That he had not lost her a second time. Relief gave him back his honesty, painful as it was for Connie to watch. Even in her presence, he could no longer even begin to mask his true feelings or in any way dissemble for the sake of his wife. To an extent, she might not have been there at all, just as it was when they were fledglings on the farm. She had to suppress a cry, hastily clamping one hand to her mouth. The way Matt was looking at Greta, nakedly unambiguous, purely loving, he had never in all the years they'd been together looked at Connie in that way. Unconsciously, he was trailing fingers along Greta's cheek. Connie sat for a while watching them, choking back her sobs. They were completely oblivious to her presence. She stood and moved away, glancing over her shoulder from the ward entrance. Matt was seated sideways on the bed, his long legs curled into a hoop along the ground. He was whispering softly to Greta, holding one of her hands within both of his. Connie watched for a second longer then turned away and left them to their privacy.

★　★　★

Connie stared at the flames licking over logs, dancing and pirouetting up the chimney. She sat with her elbows resting on her knees, chin on the steepled bridge of her fingers. Once she'd returned from the hospital, she'd made a light supper for her other two very subdued sons, doing her best to ignore the silent questions their pinched faces asked so eloquently. Unable to face food herself, she'd retired to the living room to try to make some sense of the thoughts teeming through her brain.

Try as she might, nothing could expunge that look in Matt's eyes as he'd stared at Greta. She tried to imagine what their future would be like together as a married couple, as parents, in time, perhaps, as grandparents — with the memory of that look for evermore imprinted indelibly in one shadowy corner of her mind. Could she face that? Would she want to?

She thought of Carmel, looking for a way to say goodbye to a man she still loved despite the knowledge that he had betrayed her in such a heinous fashion with her own best friend. All the other people who had at various times stepped over the threshold of The Alternative Card Company, bereft, outraged, lonely, vengeful. Love caused so much sadness in the world. Was it really so much better to have loved and lost? At the point of losing, it didn't appear to Connie as if the question had any true relevance. For the moment, at least. That might come in time, as it had for Carmel incessantly replaying each moment when she might have been losing her husband and simply didn't know.

In her own case, Connie knew that Matt had done everything he possibly could to fight his feelings for Greta. It wasn't as though she had entered their lives again at a weak moment. A catalyst in a restless, fractious marriage. They had been happy and committed and settled, particularly in the last few years. In the main, Connie could honestly say that they had been as contented together as any couple should have the right to be. There hadn't been any affairs. No prolonged unspoken grudges. They had been together for so long that they could finish one another's sentences without so much as a thought. She didn't doubt for an instant that he would stay with his family because that was the right thing to do. He wouldn't moan or use his fidelity as a stick to beat her over the head with in years to come. They would make love. Worry over household trivia: should the drains be cleared or should they upgrade the computer? They would enjoy Sunday afternoon walks by the river and they would laugh, if a little too feverishly, at Benny's antics feeding the ducks. He would remain a true and faithful husband, a strong and gentle father to his sons. He would say goodbye to Greta tomorrow and he would make good on his promise to himself to never see her again. And he would remain in love with her until the end of his days.

Connie uncurled the steeple of her fingers, sinking her face into the open book of her palms. She loved him with all her heart, always had. Could she in all conscience wish on him the nebulous, twilight existence that now stretched ahead for all of them? She startled, hastily lowering her hands as Fred stepped in the room. He sat at the other end of the sofa, gingerly, glancing at her from the corners of his furiously pulsing eyes.

'Mum?'

'Fred, pet.'

'It's her, isn't it? Greta.'

When there was no response, he clenched one fist and pounded his other hand.

'I'll kill him!'

'You're upset, pet. Very understandable. But it's not as simple — '

'What's not?' He was practically spitting. 'How dare he do that to you? To all of us? If he was here, I'd — I'd — ' He broke off close to tears. She reached a hand across to squeeze his shoulder. He manfully swallowed a deep gulping sob.

'He's a good man, your dad . . . '

'How can you even — '

'Because you know it's true. And I know it.

He's not a shit. It's not some midlife searching for lost youth crisis. That way, maybe we could hate him, for a while. He'll stay with us, of course he will. If that's what we want. He'll stay and be a good husband and a good father to you lads. Fred — '? She turned to make him look at her. It clutched at her heart to see the tears glistening in the wet brown eyes. His jaw was so tightly clenched she could no longer make out his lips. 'The thing of it is, Fred, he's never stopped loving Greta. I'm not saying that it was something that either of us understood fully, not a thought that crossed our minds every day. Never interfered with the way he feels about you lads. You must never doubt that. Never. But the fact remains — '

'If he hurts you, don't think I'll forgive him. I won't. He'll just have to pull himself together. She'll be gone and he'll change. Things'll be the way they were. You have to get angry. Stop being so — Mum, if you fight back, you can *make* him . . . '

She reached across for his hand. He looked completely lost, dazed and a little punch drunk, the way he had when he turned looking for her that first day at school when she'd released her plump cherub to the heaving mob of jostling boys.

'Fred, nothing's changed the way I feel

about your dad. I suppose what I'm trying to say is — I probably understand better than anyone, that nothing will ever — well, the way he feels about her. I did try to change things once. Tried very hard. So, maybe it's me that has to do the changing.'

She couldn't quite understand why but the minute she'd uttered that last phrase it was as though something entirely unexpected had suddenly clicked into place in her head. Perhaps, after all, there was the possibility that she might yet take control of her own destiny, separate and independent of Matt. Ultimately, the balance of the rest of their lives rested in her hands. He would stay if that's what she chose, and equally, he would go, if she opened those hands, to release him. An eerie calmness descended upon her. For the first time since that day they'd 'happened' upon Greta in Rome, she experienced a sense of composure. A sense of all the jangled nerve-endings subsiding into a background silence. Now she fully understood what Carmel had been trying to express. She didn't *have* to hate her husband in order to not love him. She simply had to choose her own level of acceptance for this new journey in the map of their marriage and if, in her heart of hearts, she could find no credible level of acceptance, then she had to find some alternative that would in time become acceptable. Even if that meant splitting up. This was something only she could decide for herself. The solitary aspect she had any power over at all. Her own response — keep on at any cost, or, for the sake of what was left of her dignity — let it go.

A couple of sparks crackled up the chimney. Connie realized to her surprise that she was smiling and that Fred was looking at her strangely.

'Just remembering things.' She responded to his unasked question. 'Good things.'

They sat in silence for a long while, staring into what looked like a picture story unfolding in the fire. Fred hesitated — young, inarticulate in the light of things that confounded him, innocent, and anxious to comfort an adult when there was nothing that he could possibly do to make himself feel more uncomfortable. She wondered at his newfound adulthood as he drew her closer to place her head against his shoulder. He smelled of quaintly cheap cologne. Okay, there's this, she thought. I made this.

Joe stepped into the room but not with his usual door-wrenching arrogance, he slipped inside, an anxious, hovering spectre, all angles and unrealized potential, sitting quietly at some distance when Fred placed a finger to his lips for hush. This too, she thought. Within minutes, lulled by the gentle hiss of the fire, all three were snoring softly.

* * *

Matt met Connie at the door to Benny's room. She'd come to say goodnight but her son was sleeping. He stepped back inside again.

'I'll sit with him for a while anyway. In case he wakes.' She brushed past Matt, unable to meet his eyes though she knew he was gazing at her intently. Even now, she couldn't trust herself not to cleave to where he stood. A touch, a reassuring graze against the tall leanness of him. It had always been like that. She couldn't be in a room without some part of her body finding a way to stroke or bump against some part of his.

'Connie — ?'

'What, Matt?' She kept her eyes glued to her shoes. 'What's to say? I saw the way you looked at her. You couldn't even help yourself. Am I hurt? Angry? No, let's start with — absolutely gutted? What do you think?'

She saw him, from the periphery of her vision, draw both hands down the sides of his face. She forced her head up and met his gaze

412

head on. Her feet took a couple of stumbling backward steps until the back of her knees met with a chair and she sank down. He made a move as if to go to her but she stopped him with a tight shake of her head.

'Not now,' she said.

Matt slapped his pockets for car keys while his shoulders moved up and down in a fluttering motion. He took a step, hesitated, then turned to address her with his head down and angled to the side.

'Greta's asked me to book a flight for her. Tomorrow afternoon. She's insisting whether the hospital goes for it or not. I'll arrange for a ticket collection at the airport.'

'Tomorrow afternoon?'

'Aye.'

'Well then.'

'Connie. I wouldn't hurt you for the world.'

She couldn't help a bitter little smile breaking on her lips.

'Oh, I think I know that, Matt. The worst hurts are the ones when somebody wouldn't hurt you for the world.'

He winced and it was little satisfaction.

'Are you going to say goodbye to her?' He cleared his throat, adding: 'I have.'

'I'll see,' Connie responded after a while. 'I don't know.'

'See you at home later, then.'

'Yeah. 'Bye.'

Matt left and Connie sat watching Benny's chest undulate up and down in deep, pain-free slumber. Perhaps they'd given him something. He was usually such a light sleeper. He looked so innocent yet worldly-wise in his own complex way, she had to resist an urge to bundle him into her arms to run off into the night to find shelter where they might all be safe from harm for evermore. But no such place existed and, for Benny, who took his every cue from her in a life that constantly confused him, the only safe place he knew, was her. And now she had proven to be not all that safe either.

'Sorry, Bunny Boy,' she whispered, smiling when he responded to her voice in his sleep with a twitch of his nose. 'Sorry.'

An hour later when he hadn't woken, even once, unusually for him, Connie crept out into the corridor and made her way along to Greta's ward. The women either side of her were lightly snoring but Greta was still awake. Her grey eyes were clearly puffed out from crying. She had been staring at the ceiling, deep in her thoughts, then she blinked rapidly at Connie's approach. She had been taken unawares, and there was a moment that made Connie's heart lurch, made her pause in

414

mid-step. For one brief, blistering second, an unmistakeable rictus of fear froze on the other woman's face which she quickly melded into a sketchy smile. There could only be one reason for such a look, Connie surmised, and even if she wanted to know the truth, she understood instinctively that Greta would never say. This, then, was to be their conspiracy of silence. In that instant, she felt certain beyond any doubt whatsoever, that she had, in some fashion, however unintentional, been party to Greta's fall earlier in the day. It might be true that it was an accidental consequence of wanting to pull the woman back to speak further with her. It could well be that she'd lost her own footing in her haste and panic, one shoulder bumping against another's, sending one of them into freefall. The truth of the entire sequence would always remain a blur to Connie, everything had happened so fast. And yet, here, before her own eyes, for the second time in their lives, lay Greta in a hospital cot with a bandage wrapped around her head.

'I don't know.' The words burst from Connie's lips as she stepped closer. She knew that Greta would understand instantly to what she was referring.

'I don't either.' Greta responded, simply.

'Did I — ?'

'Connie. Like I said — '

'But you knew what I was asking straight away. And for a second there, you looked afraid.'

Greta gazed at the ceiling lost in her own thoughts again. After a while she gave a slight shrug of her shoulders.

'Maybe we're both just thinking — y'know, because you did it once. Look Connie, I'm sure I twisted my ankle. Or you did. I was in a hurry to get out of there. Let's just leave it. Let's just, well, whatever.'

Connie perched delicately on the side of the bed. A weariness pressed down on her as if from a great height. If the thought wasn't so ludicrous she could almost countenance scrabbling into the bed beside Greta. Truly, in bed with the enemy, she half laughed to herself. Only that wasn't the complete truth either. She rubbed her tired eyelids and let out a long sigh. Greta was watching her curiously.

'So, have you really said goodbye to Matt?'

'Yes. I'll go tomorrow.'

'Did you ask him to — to see you again? Did he ask?'

'No. Is the short answer to both questions. Does that help?'

'Not much.'

'Somehow, I didn't think it would.' If

416

Connie suspected sarcasm for a second, there was not a trace of it on Greta's face. Instead, she looked defeated, played out, a woman returning to nothing, which was essentially no more than she'd come to expect of her life. Connie felt a spear of pity for her. It would have been difficult not to.

'Earlier today,' Connie began then had to swallow hard. 'I thought you were going to tell me that you wanted to make him part of this — this new life you're hoping to — ' Connie could feel her voice grow husky, she had to swallow even harder. 'You'd only have to click your fingers, Greta. Just a click,' she motioned. 'D'you have any idea how that makes me feel?'

'Every idea. But I wouldn't do that. And Connie — ' Greta's hand shot out to encircle Connie's wrist. 'You're wrong. All wrong. And somewhere deep inside, you know that. Matt has far too much integrity for — Chrissakes, he's like something out of an old-time Western.' They both couldn't help but smile. And it pierced Connie's heart to see that finally, after years of rejecting all he stood for, Greta had come full circle and had come to appreciate the man in the boy she'd once so casually shrugged off. Grief brought many hard won lessons. Recognizing true goodness was one of them.

Greta was crying softly. She turned her head away, fat, rolling drops bled onto the pillow forming a spreading wet patch by her cheek. Connie stood, she knew that she would never see Greta again and in one small chamber of her heart she felt a sense of sadness about that. She bent down and placed a kiss on one damp cheek.

'G'dbye, Greta.'

'Bye, Connie.'

★ ★ ★

'Remember that time you stamped on that girl's foot? The one who was teasing Benny?' Matt said. He was by the kitchen window, staring out.

'As if I could forget. You could hardly speak you were so angry.'

They looked into their steaming mugs of tea. Connie nursed hers with both hands, needing warmth. The conversation had meandered in similar vein for over two hours already, with Fred and Joe drifting in and out as if they sensed that despite its apparent ordinariness, something extraordinary was taking place. Matt took a swig of tea before clearing his throat.

'I'm giving Martin a free partnership,' he said.

'Worth a lot to him.'

'In return he's making you a silent partner. Salary, profit-sharing all that.'

She looked up and saw that he was crying.

'Matt.'

'I'll be fine in a minute.'

'Let's talk about the boys some more.'

Her mind began to drift as they recalled tiny long forgotten details of their sons' childish years. That they existed at all, she owed to Greta. Of course, there would be anger in the future, rage at Matt's betrayal, at being second-best all over again, long sleepless nights with the dark pressing down. But for now, for this moment, they had to think about their sons and what they would say to them.

'And the day Joe set fire to the waste basket at school,' Matt was saying. 'Will he ever give those damn cigarettes up, d'you think?'

'Eventually.' Connie shrugged. 'We can only hope.'

They spoke of Fred, his A level choices, what options he was opening for himself, career-wise. The day he was born after the longest labour of the three. Twenty-four hours when Connie could only marvel at the lusty bellows of the women delivering in rooms either side. The most she could manage through the pain was a deep growl, you had to have energy left to shout.

There was Benny and the first voiced anxieties of teachers. Trying to point out to Connie what she had sensed from the first moment she'd held the bundle of him in her arms. Of course, a mother knew. Maybe there would never be a name for it, a convenient label they could attach to him to allay future fears. She had failed him, in a brief moment of insanity she had forgotten the charge in her care but she would never, ever forget again.

They spoke of holidays and sunsets. Of past bitter rows and kindnesses they had extended one another over the years. Of dark winter afternoons in Consett when it had seemed as though the entire world had to be shrouded in a mantle of red dust. They recalled sounds so clearly, for moments the blows from chimney stacks rebounded across the kitchen walls. Smells of the farm — high, sweet muck, turned-over earth, vegetables on the turn, unpasteurized milk. The sugary cloying scent from Brenda's blackberry jam cauldron bubbling on her stove top. Arthur's face, his tipped forward head the day they put his wife into a scooped out rectangle, mounds of earth either side already frosted with snow.

They spoke of Mary, what a solid friend the wacky kaftan-wearing artist had turned out to be. Always there when she was needed.

Not least the day of Greta's fall. Connie had dialled 999 and rushed out to the street screaming for help. Almost as if she were constantly watching over them, she appeared, taking control, calming a hysterical Connie. Tending to Benny and Greta sprawled on the hall floor with their arms still tightly wrapped around one another. Who had saved whom would always be a moot point to Connie. Looking down at the silent pair as she waited for the ambulance to arrive, she couldn't get the image out of her head, of a mother holding her newborn — delivering him back to Connie.

She thought of Mary's confession over Christmas to Connie. How they'd laughed, the idea of Mary wielding a hammer over Greta's head, hoping against hope that no one would see her and that everyone would figure that the unfortunate woman was just another victim of the recent spate of motive-less hammer attacks in the area. Of course, she would never have gone through with it. Never in a million years. But for seconds, in her cold car, watching the house, playing out the gruesome fantasy had been comfortingly seductive. Connie had not made a reciprocal confession.

As Matt reached further into the past, drawing long dead mutual acquaintances into kitchen, Connie thought of that first evening when she'd set her sights on a sandy-haired boy, astride a bicycle, kissing another girl. He would come back eventually, deep in her heart she felt certain of this. She would wait, however long it might take, and make her amends by waiting. His quiet, honest patience would absorb the battering ram of his sons' anger in time. Only Benny would understand and not make judgements.

There was no part of Matt she had not touched or probed or licked in all the years together. Blood, sweat, spittle, semen, tears — it was comforting to imagine his DNA twisting in a necklace of carbonized beads around her own skeleton, so that when they would open her up, there would be two spines wrought around one another in a locked embrace. In as much as she was ever herself, she was becoming him. He would come back, he would, he could never really be that far away.

She realized as they spoke on for hours, emptying themselves of every important and inconsequential memory that they were making their own album. Only this time, the photographs were all in their heads. Matt had stopped talking. He was looking at her.

'I love you very much, Connie,' he said.

'I know that.'

She understood the time for talk was over. He held out his arms and she flew inside. She listened to the beat of his heart close to her ear. Thunk thunk it went, the sound of the foundries, the sound of their youth. She reached up with both hands cupping his face, fingers dipping in and out of crevices familiar as her own. They held on fiercely for a long time.

And then she let him go.

* * *

He had never understood how it could be done. To turn from the stuff of life, love, duties, responsibilities, how impossible he would have once believed. To face the cold, dank anger of sons who would for evermore measure him as a father and find him sorely wanting. But there might be so little time left, perhaps one day he could find the words to explain that to them. For now they would rally around their mother and he would divide his time between this place and that, a long shadow stretching between past and present like the flitting ghosts of Antica Ostia.

A pale eggshell light glanced across rooftops. There was a tang of distant rain in the air. That he was being ruthless and selfish there wasn't a doubt in his mind. He wasn't about to put up any excuses. But he did think it paradoxical that it should be love that found a way to that ruthless streak in him. Connie could never be so ruthless, he thought, never in a million years. He had wanted her to scream at him, beat him with accusation, he was a terrible father, a terrible husband, at heart — a terrible man. Instead she seemed so limply accepting it only made him feel more shabby. He could only marvel at her generosity of spirit in letting him go without rancour and wonder why he had not found the same reserves within himself, to stay. It was that quiet acceptance that lent strength to her sons. It was Connie with Matt by her side who had explained to them what was about to happen. Who had offered her forgiveness in their presence so that they might find their own way to also forgive, in time.

Matt thrust his hands deeper into his jeans pockets and turned a corner. She was standing on the balcony, waiting. He saw one arm extend towards him while she brushed a coil of hair behind one ear with the other. Without thinking, he raised his own arm in response and the distance between them contracted so that it seemed as though their fingers were touching. Matt could see that Greta was smiling. He moved on quickly into the life he had never lived.

We do hope that you have enjoyed reading this large print book.

Did you know that all of our titles are available for purchase?

We publish a wide range of high quality large print books including:
Romances, Mysteries, Classics
General Fiction
Non Fiction and Westerns

Special interest titles available in large print are:
The Little Oxford Dictionary
Music Book
Song Book
Hymn Book
Service Book

Also available from us courtesy of Oxford University Press:
Young Readers' Dictionary
(large print edition)
Young Readers' Thesaurus
(large print edition)

For further information or a free brochure, please contact us at:
Ulverscroft Large Print Books Ltd.,
The Green, Bradgate Road, Anstey,
Leicester, LE7 7FU, England.
Tel: (00 44) 0116 236 4325
Fax: (00 44) 0116 234 0205

Other titles published by
The House of Ulverscroft:

THE MEMORY STONES

Kate O'Riordan

Nell Hennessy left rural Ireland at sixteen to have her daughter, Ali. In over thirty years, she has never returned. Now she lives an uncluttered, elegant life in Paris, enjoying her independence, only broken from time to time by her married lover, Henri. Until a phone call shatters the peace of her carefully constructed world . . . Her daughter and granddaughter may be in grave danger and Nell can no longer avoid the inevitable. She must return to her childhood home. But what prevented Nell making that journey before? And how has the unspoken impinged on the lives of four generations of women?

THE INDIA HOUSE

William Palmer

The locals call it 'The India House', but they have little to do with the three women who live there: grandmother, mother and daughter. Upstairs, old Mrs Covington dreams of India and the days of the Raj. Her widowed daughter, Evelyn, watches obsessively over eighteen-year-old Julia. She has decided that the girl is to be kept in a state of 'innocence'. As little as possible of the modern world must intrude . . . But it is 1956. Mrs Covington may try to avoid the modern world, but she cannot prevent the arrival of two men, her son Roland, and her eighteen-year-old grandson, James. The fragile paradise the women have constructed is about to be changed forever.

A HERO'S DAUGHTER

Andrei Makine

During World War II Ivan Demidov is made a Hero of the Soviet Union, the Red Army's highest award for bravery and an honour that secures him both society's respect and some modest privileges. But by the time perestroika dawns in the Eighties, the glory of Soviet victory has faded from the collective memory and Ivan begins to lose his way. In contrast, Ivan's daughter, Olya, an interpreter with the Moscow International Trade Centre, has access to a prosperous, metropolitan lifestyle far beyond her parents' dreams. But Olya's work is not all it seems, and she slowly begins to realise that for her, the price of success may be higher than she is willing to pay.

FOR MATRIMONIAL PURPOSES

Kavita Daswani

'Who needs you to be happy? I want to see you married this year.' This is the view of Anju's mother, in the time-honoured tradition of all mothers, but particularly that of the fond Indian parent. Anju now works in New York, living the sophisticated American lifestyle — almost. But when she returns home to her parents in Bombay — usually for another family wedding — she finds herself reverting to the traditional daughter role. At each visit another prospective suitor is brought forward. But what sort of man does the very modern Anju want? How important are her family, her country, her traditions?

NO WONDER I TAKE A DRINK

Laura Marney

A lack of funds forces Trisha, an unsentimental lonely boozer, to return to her previous profession as a pharmaceutical rep. The only good news is that her increasingly distant teenage son is about to move back in with her. The bad news is that her ex-husband wants the house. Trisha's mind is unexpectedly made up when she inherits a place in the Highlands. Having pictured a rural idyll, she finds rain, sheep and kamikaze midges. Her social life is limited, but then she is invited to a ceilidh. A night of whisky-fuelled high jinks leads to a significant encounter with Spider, the local Lothario, and a dramatic discovery that will change Trisha's future forever.